CONSPIRACY THEORY

VEILED INTENTIONS
BOOK 1

ELLE KEATON

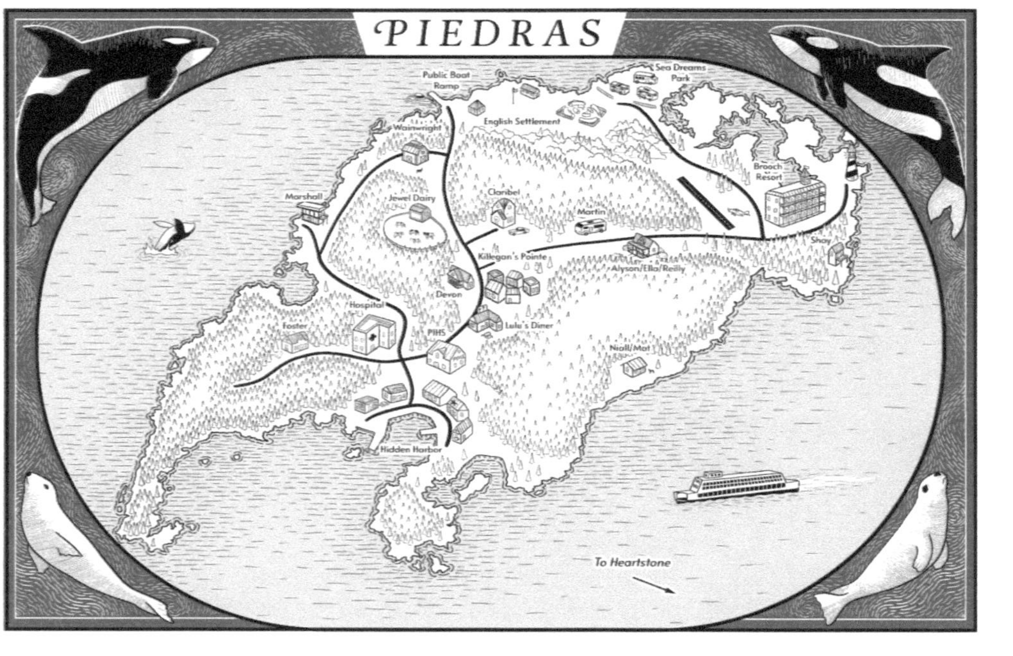
PIEDRAS
Public Boat Ramp
Sea Dreams Park
English Settlement
Wainwright
Brooch Resort
Marshall
Jewel Dairy
Claribel
Martin
Shay
Killegan's Pointe
Alyson/Elba/Reilly
Devon
Hospital
Lulu's Diner
Foster
PIHS
Niall/Mat
Hidden Harbor
To Heartstone

ONE
HAMARSSON

"I'm not in the office today—whatever—you couldn't find me." Chief Meyers tossed the sheaf of paperwork onto her desk. She overshot. The pages slid one by one onto the carpeted office floor. "You can have leave, extended leave, as much vacation and sick time as you need. God and Human Resources know you haven't called in sick in years, much less taken a vacation."

Hamarsson began, "Chief, with all due respect—" He knew better than to use ma'am with Meyers; he liked having both his balls.

"Respect?" Meyers barked out a laugh. "You've never respected me, but you're a damn good detective and I'm not letting you go without a fight."

Hamarsson took a breath, then another, deeper one. "I don't plan on coming back." The words came out mulishly, more like a cranky teenager than a nearly forty-year-old man.

Meyers stood from her perch on the edge of her desk, continuing to ignore Hamarsson's paperwork. "Well, *with all due respect,* Hamarsson, *I'm* giving you time to think about it. Go on a trip, take your boyfriend on a vacation, go somewhere warm. Now, get out of my office. I have a meeting with some yahoo from the city council in an hour."

~

Niall didn't bother stopping by his desk before he left. He *wasn't* coming back; Meyers would have to figure it out herself. He was still wearing his coat because he'd never planned on staying for the day. He'd even driven into downtown to deliver his resignation—which only worsened his mood because the drivers in this city were worse than usual today. And now, after he'd paid twenty goddamned dollars to park for an hour in a spot four blocks away from the Justice Center, Chief Meyers refused to accept his resignation paperwork.

Before he reached the exit, one of the young security guards called out, "Detective Hamarsson, you forgot this!" The guard held out a slip of paper he'd left in the aluminum tray at the security checkpoint on his way in.

Reluctantly Niall accepted the crumpled piece of notepaper. He didn't need it; he already knew what it said.

"Thanks."

Without rereading the note, Niall tossed the paper into the closest trash can and exited through the double doors to Third Avenue and into the deluge. Sheeting rain came from all directions—even up from the pavement, it seemed. Turning left, he pushed his way through the stream of lawyers, paralegals, and other office workers who were arriving at the Justice Center for a day of negotiation and never-ending paperwork. An overly large umbrella came very close to putting out his eye. He threw its carrier a baleful glare.

"Sorry, sorry."

The woman and the umbrella skittered away.

Niall hunched his shoulders, shoving his hands into his coat pockets in an attempt to look unassuming and meek rather than radiating the dragon's fire of bad humor he really felt. In his pocket, the cold plastic case surrounding his smartphone pressed against his palm. The thing had vibrated with a notification while he'd been talking to Meyers, but he'd ignored it and would continue to do so. He'd already heard what Trey had to say—more than once.

He strode by one of the historic pergolas near the Justice Center. Many of the city's downtown homeless were packed underneath it, trying to hide from the weather. One resourceful citizen even had strung up a tarp for shelter. Niall recognized most of them. There were so many homeless these days, the city was at a loss as to how to help those who wanted it. The situation was infinitely depressing.

The rain came down harder. Hamarsson turned left again, striding up the steep sidewalk. A small river ran down the width of the pavement, and his leather shoes took on water, making his feet wet and cold along with the rest of him. By the time he got to his parking spot he was thoroughly soaked. Inside the relative warmth of his car, he fished his cell phone out of his coat pocket, more out of habit than anything else.

Punching in his password, Niall listened to the waiting message. It was Trey. He deleted it—Trey's voice, appealing when they were first together, grated on his nerves these days. Vacation. Personal leave. The words floating around in his brain could have been a foreign language. He was Niall Hamarsson; he didn't rest. He slept and he worked. Trey had a long list of Niall's failings, and his work ethic was at the top of it.

Ironically, Niall didn't know if he could work like that any longer, even if he wanted to. He felt like something inside him had broken, and he didn't know if he could put whatever was broken back together. The effort to keep caring twenty-four hours a day pressed down on him, an impossible burden.

Three hours later, Niall was sitting on a lumpy, orange-tinged vinyl seat on the mostly empty ferry heading to the San Juan Islands, specifically to Piedras Island. Because it was February, as well as midweek, there were no excited mobs of children escaping their parents to run up and down the aisles shrieking for sweets from one of the vending machines. There wasn't much of a view out the window next to him either, the fog and rain still heavy. He hadn't bothered to stop at home for a bag; he'd get what he needed after the ferry docked in Hidden Harbor.

Any roots he claimed were on Piedras. He hadn't been back to the island for nearly a decade—and then only the once, when his grandmother had passed away, to see her properly buried and arrange for a service to stop by the property and mow the grass. As a child, his grandparents' cabin had been his sanctuary. He hadn't returned because of work, he told himself. Work was the best and only excuse, that and he really didn't belong there. Until recently, his workload had kept him from thinking about Piedras, family, and other things he'd rather avoid.

That's what Trey didn't understand. Niall knew they weren't meant to be a long-term couple. Hell, he didn't know if he was able to do what was needed to sustain a partnership. But it was nice to have someone around, and Trey had stuck around longer than most.

The ferry's horn sounded loud and deep, startling Niall from his thoughts. Standing up, he made his way along with the other passengers back down to the car deck and got behind the wheel of his car. The ferry docked with a bump. Niall started the engine and followed the box truck in front of him into Hidden Harbor.

He'd first come to the island nearly thirty years ago, far from everything he'd known back then. Things on Piedras were still the same. Still stuck in time. Still far away from the city. Familiar storefronts, a little more faded than they had been when he was a child. The same gas station at the top of the incline and across from the high school. There was a new hotel where the Dockman Inn had burned to the ground a few years ago. Whoever had rebuilt it had done a great job making it blend in with the existing structures. Niall'd read about the fire; luckily it had been the off-season, and no one had been staying there.

The box truck took a right turn and Niall continued onward, hoping Island Hardware was still in business. It was. He pulled over and parked in front of the doors, staring at them. The past was so close he could almost touch it. When he'd returned to the island for Mormor's funeral, he hadn't stopped in town.

The store was exactly the same. He recognized a yellowed poster pinned to one wall, depicting an eagle flying majestically over a stand of evergreens. In the back corner there were several shelves and a rounder of clothing. Niall picked out two pairs of canvas work pants, some flannel shirts, a package of underwear. Off one of the shelves he grabbed a pair of work boots and some thick socks. As he walked toward the front, he passed a display with a few sleeping bags and low-end tents. On impulse he grabbed one of each, sticking the sleeping bag under his arm and balancing the clothing on top of the tent box.

The checkout counter was deserted and a silver bell with a note reading "Ring for Service" taped to it sat next to the cash register. Niall tapped the bell. It seemed very loud in the empty store. After a short wait a kid, or at least someone younger than him, came out from another room.

"Hi, do you have a question, or are you ready to be rung up?"

"I'm ready." He piled the gear onto the counter.

The kid seemed to understand Niall wasn't interested in

conversation. Quietly and efficiently, he added up the cost and told Niall the amount. Niall fished in his back pocket for his wallet, pulled out his credit card, and handed it to the cashier.

"Hamarsson. I recognize that name." *But not you*, was left unsaid.

"I used to have family here," Niall replied, hoping to forestall any questions from inquiring minds.

"Do you need a bag?"

Niall eyed the stack of gear. "I'll just make two trips. My car is right out front."

Ignoring him, the cashier followed him out to his car with the clothes and boots. "It's shitty weather to be camping," he remarked.

Niall shrugged. It *was* shitty weather, and cold. The San Juans sat in what was called the banana belt of the Pacific Northwest; it was not uncommon for the weather here to be nicer than it was in Seattle, but not this day.

The kid stood under the awning, watching as he pulled away from the curb and drove up the street. He wondered how long before townies learned someone with the last name of Hamarsson was visiting the island—and camping, no less.

Niall's car, a twenty-year-old Subaru wagon, bumped and creaked down the gravel driveway. He had almost missed his turn in the dark that had fallen since he got off the ferry, his headlights barely managing to find the robin's-egg–blue mailbox at the end of the drive. Bushes, shrubs, and tall grasses growing across the drive scraped along the sides of his car as he drove. The service he paid to keep the property up was obviously wasted fucking money. When he sold the place, at least that would be one less thing to worry about, along with less taxes.

And less remembering.

Fridays were always the worst. Mat thought he needed to create a spreadsheet tracking crime for the island, but he was pretty sure Fridays would come up as the day with the most calls—and this one was the worst kind. Deputy Flynn, Birdy to most, had responded to the initial 911 call, and as soon as she'd arrived at the scene she called Mat on his cell phone.

"This is bad." Birdy's voice shook. "I thought it was a prank or someone's imagination, but it's not."

Birdy, while young, was an island girl. She knew the locals and was on good terms with all but the most cantankerous. And there was just one of those. She had a way, too, of managing the wealthy tourists and seasonal population who regularly called the sheriff's office to complain about everything from the Fourth of July fireworks to stray sheep on their property. If she thought it was bad, it was.

Mat parked his patrol car in the marina's fire zone. The car was flashy, and he hated it, but the county had bought the department new vehicles. Personally, Mat thought the money would've been better spent on a youth center or job training or maybe a new evidence kit. But the Island County representative had condescendingly informed Mat it was something about the way the money was earmarked; it had to be spent on transportation.

Birdy waited for him at the marina's open gate. It was set into a chain-link fence flush with the pier so trespassers couldn't climb around it and sneak onto the moored boats. Behind Birdy the currents of San Juan Channel rippled underneath the hibernating boats, which floated up and back down rhythmically with the swells. As marinas went, the Hidden Harbor Marina was small but it was always full. Mat knew the managers had a long waiting list of boat owners wanting convenient moorage in Hidden Harbor.

After yesterday's rain the sunshine was welcome, but it didn't make the discovery of Chastity Reynolds floating in the bay any easier. Face down in the water, her body bumped against a piling toward the end of the pier.

The caller may not have known whose body it was, but any local would recognize Chas by her full back tattoo. Somewhere along the way her top had been torn off, exposing the unfurled angel wings she'd had inked there. The irony of the tattoo was not lost on Mat.

"We need to call marine. Have you questioned anyone yet? Who made the discovery?" Mat asked.

Birdy shivered, looking a little ridiculous underneath the wide-brimmed, plastic-wrapped uniform hat they were required to wear. Mat had conveniently forgotten his, although now he was chilly.

She pointed down the walkway where a man was waiting. Mat didn't recognize him.

"Sebastian Lambert called it in. I asked him to stay and talk with both of us. All he's said so far is that he arrived this morning to check his sailboat after yesterday's storm and found her."

"Has anyone tried to move her?"

"I haven't, and Mr. Lambert said he didn't, that he immediately called us." She paused, then spoke again. "Sheriff Dempsey?"

"I've told you not to call me that. Use Mat or Dempsey and I will respond."

Birdy ignored him. "When was the last time we had a murder on the island?"

"We don't know it's murder. There are a lot of other possible explanations for how she got there. She could have fallen in and drowned."

They both turned again to look at the body. Regardless of what he'd just said, it was hard to imagine anything except murder given the colorful fabric wrapped around her neck. The scarf, or whatever it was, was pulled so tightly her flesh bulged around it.

"No murders since I was instated," Mat answered. "I'd have to look at county records. There was a murder on Orcas, but that was when I was a kid."

"This is going to be bad." Birdy looked at him again, as if she was hoping Mat would contradict her statement. He couldn't.

"Call Duane, he's marine today. Tell him to bring a kit. I'll contact Soper."

Marshal Soper was the county's volunteer medical examiner. He was also Mat's best friend. He'd moved to Piedras after Mat left San Francisco. Between the two of them they had more experience investigating suspicious deaths than the rest of the Piedras County police force.

"You stay here and keep anyone but Soper or Duane on the other side of the gate. Do you need a coffee or anything?" The winter sunshine was bright, but it wasn't warm. Mat needed something to warm his hands.

Birdy shook her head, looking a little green. "Not now."

Mat walked back to his car to call Marshal.

He loved his job serving the citizens of Hidden Harbor and

the islands in general, but he did not need their help. And when news got out the body was Chas Reynolds, rumor and hearsay would fly.

"Hey, Mat, what's up?" Marshal sounded a little out of breath, and Mat wondered if he was out on a run.

"Nothing good, Marshal. This is business."

"Did one of the seniors pass away? I've been worried about Mrs. Herrmann."

Trust Marshal to know the names of all the senior citizens on the island.

"No. Unofficially, it's a local girl. Birdy and I recognize her tattoo, but we didn't touch the body."

"Shit. Where do you need me?"

The residents of Hidden Harbor were beginning to notice the two police cars parked at the marina with their lights flashing. The last thing he needed was a crowd of concerned citizens cluttering the scene.

Mat had Birdy string out the yellow Do Not Cross tape at the entrance to the marina parking lot and at the gate to the private pier. It wouldn't keep people away, but maybe they'd at least stay on the other side where they belonged; once again, he wished the county had bought him a new evidence kit instead of a new cruiser.

The forty-five minutes it took Marshal and Duane to arrive at the scene nearly drove Mat to his wits' end. It was the low season, so the locals didn't have much better to do than gawk. He sure as hell wasn't going to tell them the victim was Chas Reynolds, not until he had to. If he whispered a single word, the information would get back to the Delacombe and Reynolds clans before he could personally notify them, and that would be a nightmare. Chas's relatives were some of the more... volatile on the island. Regardless, they deserved the same professionalism the department offered other families and victims.

He and Birdy questioned Sebastian Lambert together, but he had no useful information for them. He'd arrived at the marina around nine a.m. to check on his sailboat and seen the body floating in the water. Assuming someone had fallen in and drowned, he'd immediately called 911. There was no more information he could share. Lambert was a newer retiree to the island; he had no idea who the victim was. Their first dead end. Lambert wasn't happy to be informed his boat, along with all the others at the marina, was now part of an active crime scene.

Duane Cooper arrived in the department's marine rescue craft, carefully maneuvering the vessel around to where the body was wedged between the pilings, just as Mat spotted Marshal's ancient red Land Cruiser driving too quickly down Fern Street toward the marina.

He pulled aside the tape so Marshal could drive into the parking lot at the same time he endured Mrs. Tenny's high-pitched complaint.

"What is happening? I am going to call my son-in-law. He is on the island council and has connections—"

Mat cut across her strident tone. "Mrs. Tenny, I'll send Birdy over to talk to the crowd as soon as we have something we can share." Which of course would be nothing until Marshal got a look at the body and they had a positive ID, but Mrs. Tenny didn't need to know that.

"What have you got?" Marshal asked after parking and getting out of his car.

"DB. We'll know more after you take a look, but there's fabric of some kind wrapped around her neck. Do you want to look before Duane brings her to shore?"

It was easy to fall into old habits with Marshal; he was laid back and easy to work with. And damn smart.

Marshal pulled on booties and latex gloves before grabbing

his camera and heading out to meet Duane at the end of the pier, and Mat followed him. Why did the first murder in a generation have to happen on his watch?

He immediately felt a deserved pang of guilt. As troubled as Chas had been, she had been a living, breathing human being who deserved much better than a violent death. If that's what this was. If she had been murdered, he'd damn well find out who did it and bring them to justice.

Unfortunately, his tiny department was woefully unprepared for a murder investigation. Drug rings, meth labs, smuggling, environmental crimes—yes. Murder—no. Mat was the only one with any suspicious death experience, and that had been a decade ago in another life.

It didn't take them long, once she was out of the water, to load Chas's expertly shrouded body onto a stretcher and into the back of Marshal's vehicle. He kept the back of his 4x4 ready for this sort of thing, which until today had meant accidental drownings. Thankfully, Duane had been able to untangle her from where she was wedged and bring her into the boat so no spectators on the land side were able to clearly see what was happening.

Mat left Birdy in charge. A murder scene might be new to her, but handling the population of Hidden Harbor was not. He could hear her bossing people away from the gate and the tape as he drove away, following Marshal.

He was perpetually surprised by the sleek, modern medical center, something the county had paid for in the past ten years. Marshal had called ahead to have the staff secure a procedure room off the ER for their use as Piedras didn't have a paid medical examiner; the island was lucky to have him. Marshal was very good at what he did.

"Do you need me to stay?" Mat asked his friend. Watching Marshal examine the body wouldn't bother him, but he felt he needed to get out to the Delacombes' property. The Reynolds place too, he supposed, but Chastity's older brother was nothing if not difficult and uncooperative on the best of days.

"No." Marshal had his back to him while he set up his laptop and voice recorder.

"I'll call you later."

Marshal looked over his shoulder at him. "Be safe out there."

"I always am."

Marshal was already hyper focused on the job ahead. So Mat left, shutting the door behind him,

As was often the case with February weather, it had changed from decent to bad in the blink of an eye. Clouds had rolled in, obscuring the sunlight, and any minute it was going to start raining again. Back at his cruiser, Mat popped the trunk and exchanged his Piedras County Sheriff's Office fleece jacket for his rain parka. As an afterthought, he also changed from his regular walking shoes to hiking boots and grabbed his baton, clipping it onto his belt.

The island was roughly diamond-shaped, with Hidden Harbor built on the sloping western side and nestled around a protected cove. Some of the Delacombes, relatives of one of the first settler families—Native Americans had been on the island far longer—lived on the next jutting tip near one of the original White settlements.

Their property was densely wooded and private, with No Trespassing signs posted at every possible visible location. His cruiser bumped roughly across the cattle guard, and Mat honked his horn, letting them know he was coming.

Once the two-story house had been grand and stately, befitting the wealthy scion who'd built it. However, the family since had fallen on hard times and never recovered. Mat only knew of one Delacombe who'd made it off the island in recent generations. Shay Delacombe was a lawyer in Seattle, and Mat could do without Shay.

He was forced to pull over and park at the tail end of a long line of defunct automobiles. The vehicles spanned decades, and it was possible some had been purchased or salvaged with the intent to restore them. Ambition had faded away, and it looked like they'd most recently been used for target practice. The windshields were blown out, the side panels riddled with bullet holes. The older cars were rusted out, the newer ones covered in moss, mildew, and blackberries. On the plus side, Mat didn't hear any dogs barking.

As he moved closer, slowly and deliberately, the snap of a dead bolt being pulled back reached his ears. Through the now slightly open door, Mat recognized the diminutive figure of Claribel Delacombe. The old woman was the matriarch of the Delacombe clan and Chastity Reynolds' great-grandmother. Mat sometimes worried she suffered from mild dementia. She was in her mideighties, but it was impossible to tell, as she'd been a character on the island as long as he'd been alive—maybe he was imagining she was declining. More likely she would out live him.

"Claribel, Ms. Delacombe, I need to speak to you."

Claribel had been born a Delacombe, but had married young and become a Reynolds—much to the disgust of both families. Nearly ten years ago, just after Mat moved back to the island, she had caused quite a scandal, even for her, by throwing her husband out of the house and then divorcing him. There'd never been any question that Frank Reynolds was a horse's ass, and no one in town had any sympathy for him. It was the much-younger man who'd taken Frank's place that caused gossip. It had carried the locals through an unusually cold winter. Then she'd tossed him out too, announcing she was done with men.

"What do you want, Sheriff Dempsey?" Claribel's voice was clear. She didn't sound at all like a little old lady.

Mat took her question as invitation and moved closer to the porch. "I need to speak to you in private."

"There's nobody home but me. You can talk to me here."

Mat sighed. Not that he'd expected anything else, but he'd hoped one of the younger Delacombes would be available—although none of them were particularly reasonable either. Maybe it was best he spoke with Claribel. He took the three stairs up to the porch, coming to a halt in front of the door. The decking creaked ominously under his weight. He hoped it didn't choose this day to collapse.

"Ms. Delacombe, I need to ask some questions about Chastity. When was the last time you saw her?"

"My fool great-granddaughter?"

"Chastity Reynolds, yes."

"Why?"

"Ms. Rey—Delacombe, I have some unsettling news, and I really think it would be better if you would let me in so you can sit down."

"Just tell me, goddammit. Quit beating around the bush. Policemen have been knocking at my door since before you were born. I was only twenty-one when they came and told me my daddy was dead. The next one who came told me Frank Junior was gone. What are you here to tell me?"

Taking a breath and mentally preparing for the worst, Mat said, "Would you be willing to come to the medical center and identify a body we believe is Chastity? She was found this morning off the marina."

Mat had to hand it to Claribel. She flinched, and an emotion he thought was sorrow quickly passed across her face, but she didn't falter.

"There's no one home to drive me." She threw him a baleful glare.

Yes, because Mat had managed to have her license suspended after she backed into a coffee stand. She probably drove anyway.

"I'll drive you there and bring you home."

Claribel nodded. "Let me find my purse."

Minutes later Mat turned out from the Delacombe property and back onto the road, Claribel his silent passenger. A car passed them going the other direction, a single driver at the wheel. Mat didn't recognize it as an island vehicle. As they traveled by the Hamarsson property, he noted that the overgrown sticker bushes and shrubs looked bent and out of place as if someone had recently been there, but he didn't have time to think about somebody trespassing on land that, as far as he knew, was all but abandoned.

When they arrived at the hospital, Mat parked next to the emergency entrance, then got out of the car and went around to the passenger side to help Claribel. She was tiny and had shrunk further with age. Mat suddenly felt protective of her—no one deserved news like this. With care, he escorted her through the double doors of the emergency room, making quick eye contact with the single security guard before they made their way down the short hallway to where Chastity Reynolds waited. He was surprised none of the community rubberneckers were lying in wait for him.

Once they were safe in the tiny room, Claribel did crack,. He'd texted ahead, so Marshal was waiting for them. Chastity's body was covered with a sheet, and Marshal'd done a quick job of cleaning her up. It wasn't pretty; there was bruising around her neck where the scarf had been and deep scrapes along the right side of her face. Soon enough Marshal would be able to tell them if the injuries were pre- or postmortem.

Mat helped the old woman to sit in one of the plastic patient chairs.

"Damn that child, what did she get herself into?" She stared at Chastity, taking in the injuries she could see, then focused her steel-grey gaze on Mat.

"You'll find who did this." It was a statement—a demand.

Mat nodded. "Yes, ma'am, I'll do my best to bring Chastity justice."

"I know you were a good cop before you came back here. Your daddy used to brag up and down about you all the time. You'll find whoever did this."

He and Marshal exchanged glances, both aware that all too often they weren't able to bring justice. All too often there wasn't enough evidence or the perpetrator somehow managed to slip out of their grasp. Mat missed San Francisco, he missed the vibrant gay community he'd been a part of, but he did not miss cases like Chastity's.

THREE
HAMARSSON

Ever so slowly, Niall returned to earth, his sluggish body painfully reminding him he was closer to forty than thirty. His hip throbbed, his right arm had fallen asleep wedged under his body, and his head ached. With great care, he opened his eyes. The inside of the tent was bright—at least to his aching brain. Niall shook his head to try and get rid of his mental cobwebs. This bright meant it must be full daylight outside, late morning, possibly close to noon.

With difficulty he raised himself up onto one elbow, tipping over the mostly empty bottle of Jack sitting next to him. The remaining liquid dribbled out onto the floor of the tent. And that would be why his head hurt: Jack with a side of potato chips and a granola bar he'd found in the center console of his Subaru. It dated from sometime in the past when he took a little better care of himself. The Jack Daniel's and chips he'd picked up at the gas station yesterday afternoon.

Groaning, Niall rolled over so he could wriggle out of the sleeping bag. Today he would assess the damage his neglect had caused the cabin and make a list of things he needed to order to make repairs. The roof would be first on the list—he'd noticed that a number of the tiles were missing or damaged in the glow of his headlights last night.

The cabin was minute, but it had always felt like home to him, just a little over five hundred square feet of living space. A tiny kitchen and living room, two postage-stamp-sized bedrooms and a bathroom only big enough for a shower and toilet. Last night, it had been too easy for Niall to imagine his grandparents moving around inside, making coffee or sitting together to read the newspaper. Morfar had tempted the frightened child Niall had been with the comics, or as he'd called them, "the funny papers."

The inside of the cabin was a disaster and he had no one to blame but himself. He was pretty sure a family of raccoons had moved in and back out at some point. There were holes in the flooring, and the small couch was torn up, the stuffing strewn around where something had been looking for a nest. The electricity had been turned off after Mormor passed, so Niall didn't bother opening the fridge. He'd just bring a dumpster out and have it taken away.

For a boy fresh from hell, the cabin had been paradise. Now, not so much.

Niall struggled to his feet, the top of his head pressing against the roof of the tent even as he bent over. He'd inherited both his height and his craggy looks from his Norwegian grandparents. He probably inherited something from his father's side as well, but he'd never met the man, so who knew. He shoved his feet into the new boots before unzipping the tent.

Outside the tent, the cold of the day made him shiver, forcing him back inside to grab his parka. He'd slept in his clothes, so at least he didn't have to find where they'd ended up after he'd put himself to sleep with alcohol. Something he probably did far too often.

His head always ached from the drink, but it kept him from dreaming. Closing the tent flap behind him and zipping up his thick coat, Niall walked out to the shoreline, ignoring the protest from his bladder. He may not have dreamt last night, but being at the cabin was as good as. If he hadn't been excruciatingly aware of his head pounding, the fabric of his clothing scraping against his skin, and each individual hair on his scalp, he could have believed he was ten again and seeing the view for the first time.

He'd slept in a tent then too. Funny how that fact had slipped his mind until now.

It wasn't raining today, but everything was covered with a layer of dew and the air was damp. The small beach was rocky. He'd never been able to build sandcastles here; instead he and Morfar built their castles of stone.

"Much better for withstanding a sacking," his grandfather would say, his thick Norwegian accent blurring the words.

Niall'd refused to join him at first—he was too old to build castles on a beach—and neither Mormor nor Morfar pressured him. Slowly, though, the island had seeped into him, winning him over with its quiet and lack of demand. A full belly hadn't hurt. Neither had the impromptu history lessons he received as he watched Od Hamarsson build outrageous stone structures on their little beach.

Far out in the cold waters bobbed a seal, its silky gray-black body sparkling against the waves. Niall turned away and back toward the cabin.

Morning wasn't his friend. The cabin looked even worse in the light. Window screens hung askew, there were more missing shingles, insulation was exposed to the elements, and what looked to be an actual hole was in the roof. It saddened him to note the big picture window facing the water was cracked and fogged. Niall's bladder protested, he had to relieve himself. Instead of going inside, he walked over to where industrious blackberries were steadily taking over the yard.

The missing ingredient to Niall achieving something more

than a stumbling shamble was coffee. After sleeping on the ground, he needed caffeine and Advil.

Why the hell had he returned to Piedras? The question, unwanted flotsam and jetsam, drifted upward and into his waking brain. He didn't have an answer for himself.

After leaving Chief Meyers's office yesterday, Niall hadn't had a destination in mind. He could only blame some long-buried instinct for the decision to board the island-bound ferry. His apartment was nothing. The life he lived was at the station, on his computer, in his cubicle. They were filled with the ghosts of victims for whom he hadn't found justice.

Trey was right about that anyway—or he had been. Niall'd lived and breathed his job. But that wasn't an issue anymore, because this time when Trey had stormed out of the apartment, he'd stopped to grab most of the clothes he kept there for when he slept over at Niall's. Thing was, Niall knew if Trey came back, he'd take him. Trey was easy, at least until he started bitching about Niall's hours. He'd be back, he always came back.

This time, a few of Trey's angry words had struck an unfortunate chord deep inside Niall.

"It's like you're a mannequin—a robot. God, I tell you things, I could be telling you I'd cut my arm off and your expression wouldn't change. You treat me like a child sometimes. You never want to go out, you don't like my friends."

"Funny, you never complain when I'm fucking you."

"See? That!" Trey'd jabbed his index finger hard against Niall's chest. "You're not hearing a word I'm saying!" He'd slammed the apartment door behind him, and Niall'd felt a stab of relief he'd never given in to the pleas that they really live together.

After Trey left, Niall had been angry and irritable all weekend, and it'd bled into his work week. He couldn't focus on his cases, didn't have the energy to work on them. A vague sense of futility had been dogging his heels for a while, and it metamorphosed into something much more real and difficult to ignore. If he couldn't do it anymore—bring justice for those who'd lost the ultimate battle—what use was he?

It scared him.

On Wednesday, word had come down that the DA refused to try one of Niall's cases—a horrible kidnapping and murder he'd been working on for more than a year, one where they all knew the perp was guilty—because of lack of evidence. He'd felt something snap. It wasn't the first time by any means a case of his had been filed away as cold, but this one…

He kicked at a rock, sending it skittering into the bushes where it thumped against a trunk or log. Then Niall walked back over to the cabin. After fishing his cell phone out of his coat pocket, he turned it back on and took several pictures of the cabin's exterior. Clearly, he would need to start there and then work toward the inside.

There were two towns on the island. Hidden Harbor was bigger, but on the west side—the side closer to the cabin—was a town called Killegen's Point. Way back when, a large number of Irish immigrants had found their way to the San Juans and claimed it. Or stolen it from the Delacombes—it depended on which version of history you believed—and they'd both stolen it from the Native Americans who'd been on the island for hundreds of years.

Niall took a right out of his driveway toward Killegen's Point. Last he knew there was a small grocery and bakery there. He'd get coffee and groceries and a better cell signal to check what kind of building supplies he could get on the island and which he would have to order. Easy.

It was never easy.

.   .   .

A cop car passed him going the other direction, and Niall couldn't help himself; the cop in him had to check who was driving. Seeing Mat Dempsey behind the wheel was a shock. And the woman sitting in front next to him had to have been Claribel Delacombe. She may have had a few birthdays since he last saw her, but she hadn't changed a bit.

The quick glimpse he had of Dempsey looked like he'd changed, though Niall didn't want to think about him. Ahead was the turn for Killegen's. He took it too fast and had to steady the car. His hangover was worse than he'd thought.

It had nothing to do with seeing Mat Dempsey.

Chester's Grocery-Mart was still there, but the cement brick building had been repainted in his absence. The joke around the island was that Chester wouldn't pay full price for paint. When Niall was a teen, the store had been repainted from a Pepto-Bismol pink to a horrible neon orange. The pink bled through, so the building looked like a Creamsicle. Now it was several shades of gray. Niall wondered if maybe old Chester did have a sense of humor after all. He pulled in and parked across from a beat-up motor home in the nearly vacant parking lot.

Inside was the same as it had been when he was a child. To one side was a small bakery and coffee shop while on the other was groceries and sundries. It even smelled the same, reminding him of trips to the store with his grandparents. Sitting on the bakery counter was a call-bell and a small sign reading "Ring for Service," same as at Island Hardware. It was definitely the low season on the island.

He tapped the bell.

"I'll be right there!" a voice from behind him called out.

He turned to see the single cashier waving at him from one of the check stands. He was relieved not to recognize her. Seeing Dempsey had unsettled him. He didn't want to make small talk or explain why he was on the island, he wanted to remain anonymous for as long as possible.

She finished up with her customer—Niall assumed it was the driver of the motor home—before scurrying over to where Niall waited.

"Sorry! Two people is a rush this time of year!"

Niall shrugged. "Didn't hurt me to wait."

"What can I get you, hon?"

Niall ordered an extra-large coffee and a cinnamon roll nearly as big as his head. He figured his brain needed the carbs.

"Are you visiting?" The checker's name tag read "Sage." She was probably his age or thereabouts.

"Sort of." The words came out gruffer than he intended as he handed her his debit card.

"Okay, well, have a nice day."

He tried a smile. "It's been a long week," he said as a sort of apology.

"I understand long weeks! You get a free refill if you want. I'll make sure the pressure pot is full."

Niall nodded. There were two sets of café tables for customers. He claimed one and devoured his cinnamon roll while his coffee cooled. Then he grabbed a cart and began to push it around the store. For some reason he couldn't stop thinking about Mat Dempsey.

When had Dempsey returned to the island? Niall knew he'd left for California at some point, hadn't known he'd come back. The car he'd been driving was marked Sheriff. Was he the sheriff, or did he just work for the department? A quick phone search would most likely answer all these questions, but there was no service inside the concrete building.

What would it matter if Dempsey was sheriff? Niall had no claim to the position. Niall remembered Mat, though. He threw a bag of apples into the cart, and some navel oranges. Why had Claribel been in the car with him? Pretzels went into the cart, followed by a half-dozen bagels and a container of cream cheese. Those he would need to eat quickly.

He paid for his groceries and another bottle of whiskey, then refilled his coffee. Out in the parking lot, his car sat alone. Niall looked down the street, where the motor home was just disappearing around a corner. After stowing his purchases, he sat behind the wheel for a minute. Instead of starting the engine, he dragged out his phone and despite the fact that he'd told himself he was checking for building supplies, the first thing he did was search the Piedras County Sheriff's Office.

FOUR

DEMPSEY

"I got nothing to tell you."

Martin Reynolds stood on the other side of the counter, his thick arms folded across his chest, a mulish expression on his face. Chastity's much-older half-brother had been a thorn in Mat's side since he'd taken the job of sheriff. Mat had been disinclined to bring him in, and after discussing it with Birdy, they agreed talking to him at work would be better than asking him to come to the station. Since he was a line cook at the Hook, a greasy spoon that changed hands about every nine months, he'd been easy to locate. After leaving Claribel in the care of Marshal and one of her great-grandsons, Mat had returned to the marina and he and Birdy surveyed the business owners and residents along Spring Street. No one had seen or heard anything the night before. Not entirely surprising, since it was February and the town rolled up the carpets by eight.

"Martin, we're just asking if you knew anything about Chastity's whereabouts in the past few days. Did you talk to her, see her? Claribel hadn't seen her in a few weeks. Was she staying with someone?" Matt was trying to appeal to a side of Martin he wasn't certain existed.

Once Birdy had dispersed the crowd and left Deputy Paul Holstrom guarding the scene, she returned to the station to try to find out more about Chastity's recent life. She'd turned up nothing. Chastity had moved off the Reynolds family property a few months ago, but no one seemed to have her new address. That wasn't a red flag in itself—many people rented rooms or shared homes to try to keep living in Piedras County affordable. There would be no reason for her to report a change of address since, like so many, she also had a post office box. Mat would have to see what was in it too, but that *would* take an act of God.

The biggest difficulty with their investigation was going to be scope, unless they got lucky and someone confessed. There were over four hundred islands in the San Juans. Most didn't have anyone living on them, and only the big five had ferry service, but that still meant there was little chance of catching the perp if they were an off-islander. They would have already disappeared into the throngs on the mainland.

For the time being, Mat was working on the assumption that the perp was a local. When and if he had evidence the murder had been committed by a stranger, he would investigate appropriately. He didn't *want* the perp to be a local—it would do irreparable damage to the fabric of their community—but if they were, he'd bring them to justice.

"Chas don't talk to me. I haven't seen her in months. Happy now?"

"When was the last time you saw her?"

Martin looked thoughtful. "I dunno. Before Christmas, maybe around Thanksgiving. She was giving me shit about QAnon." He leaned forward, his gaze intense. "You gotta take them seriously. The stuff they know is amazing. Chas told me it was ruining my life. Looks like she should have worried about herself instead."

The man shot him a knowing look. This was his baby sister they were talking about, whose remains would be interred in the island cemetery sometime next weekend. Mat had an almost irresistible urge to punch him in the face.

Instead he asked Martin, "Why would a group like that, or any of their followers, want to murder Chastity?"

Mat was unfortunately aware of the popular conspiracy group—Martin Reynolds wasn't the only local who had an unhealthy obsession with them or any of the other random conspiracy groups that popped up. It seemed like each time a new conspiracy group sprouted, a significant number of his citizens bought into it. Mat himself did not understand the mentality, but he had to acknowledge the strength of their beliefs. He'd heard anecdotally of people spending hours searching online for "clues" left by the shadowy leaders of the group, to the point that their relationships and jobs were in danger. The whole thing may have started as some kind of sick joke, but the group had evolved into what could only be called a cult. One that had apparently even reached Hidden Harbor.

"I dunno."

And apparently that was all Martin was going to say.

Mat walked to the front door, but Birdy stayed back. He watched while she said something else to Reynolds, who stomped out of Mat's view back into the kitchen, clearly angry. This time it was Birdy who shrugged before turning and coming back to where Mat waited in the doorway.

"What was that about?" Mat asked.

"I told him I was ashamed of him. If things were reversed and it was him lying in a coffin, he could be damn sure Chas would've been asking questions and demanding answers. She may have been a bit flighty and unpredictable, but she was loyal to her family."

∿

His desk at the station was supposed to be in a tiny corner office, but Mat'd dragged it out so he would be with his deputies, not set apart. Mat's landline blinked with a missed call and he recognized Marshal's cell phone number on the screen. Without listening to the message, he hit redial.

"Mat."

"Marshal, what's the news? I didn't listen to your message."

"She was dead before she went into the water. Cause of death was strangulation."

"I hate it when we're right."

They desperately needed to trace Chastity's last movements. They still hadn't found anyone who'd spoken to her or seen her recently. As soon as Marshal disconnected, Mat put a request in for her bank and phone records, but they probably wouldn't hear anything until next week. The wheels of justice often creaked.

She'd been strangled before she went into the harbor. Marshal said there was no water in her lungs—meaning she hadn't merely been unconscious, she hadn't been breathing. The fabric around her neck was a scarf that Marshal'd had to cut off her neck. He was bagging it for investigators. If she'd been able to fight back against her attacker, the marine water had washed any DNA evidence out from under her fingernails. In a long shot, Mat had asked Marshal to swab the body with a rape kit, but he doubted they'd find anything—and it would be months before they heard anyway. This was the part of his job he hated the most.

They were going to have to talk to Claribel again. There was no reason to suspect the Delacombe matriarch had anything to do with Chas's death, but she had a great deal of knowledge and power over her family. Claribel might be able to help them with Martin and anyone else in the family they needed to interview.

"Where was she?" Birdy asked, plucking the same thought from his brain. She'd stopped beside his desk without him hearing her approach.

Mat sighed. "I don't know, Bird." He looked up at her. "Have Theo or Patrick had any luck on the ferries or at the landings?"

Their search for witnesses was complicated by the fact that whoever had done this could've left not only by ferry but also by private vessel.

Theo Jones and Patrick Radden were two of his five deputies. Both were part-time and neither held a candle to Birdy, but they were dedicated and maybe, in another few years, Mat could groom them into something worthwhile. Neither was a bad person, but neither had any imagination; they never looked at a problem and wondered if there was a different way to solve it. Which was great when the solution was obvious, like speeding or drunken driving. Plumbing the mind of a killer would not likely be one of their strong points.

Birdy shook her head. "So far, no. The deck crew on the *Bainbridge* doesn't remember seeing her. But not all of them work full time, so it will be a few days before they get to everybody. We haven't caught up with the *Snoqualmie*'s crew."

"Martin Reynolds is an asshole." Mat couldn't get the conversation with Martin out of his head. If that had been his sister floating in the marina, Mat would've been setting the island on fire to find out who the perp was. He'd be at the dock every day trying to find answers, witnesses, whatever was needed. He supposed that's why he was a cop and Martin was... a loser.

"Yeah... Dempsey?"

"What?"

"Do you think it's *possible* someone from that conspiracy group he's into could've had something to do with Chas's murder?"

"I guess at this point we don't know. But in my experience, most crimes like this are committed by someone the victim knows. Until we've exhausted every avenue, we need to focus on family, romantic involvements, coworkers. Someone has to know something."

"Okay." She started to walk away but turned back. "FYI, we got another weird call from Harry Harrison. He says a wolf came onto his property. Claims it killed five of his chickens."

"A wolf? For crying out loud. Did someone explain to Harry we've never had wolves on the island? Any wolf or bear or other wildlife would have to swim from the mainland."

"Patrick took the call." Which meant no.

"I'll stop out there on my way home, and at the Delacombes' too."

"Do you want me to go with you?"

Mat considered her offer. "I'll go on my own this time. If I can't get Claribel to talk to me, I'll give you a turn."

Claribel had refused Mat's offer to drive her back home after identifying her great-granddaughter's body, which meant Mat hadn't been able to talk to her much after she ID'd Chastity. It was late in the day now; the morning and the discovery of the body seemed a distant memory. Mat would stop by the Delacombes' on his way home and see if Claribel would talk to him and if she had remembered anything; nothing ventured, nothing gained. Maybe the reality of Chastity's death had settled in since morning and Claribel would be willing to answer questions about her family.

Maybe. Mat wasn't counting on it, though.

. . .

The road back out toward Killegen's Point and home was dark now. The sun set around five p.m. this time of year. Mat wondered, if the county could build a medical center, why couldn't they pay for more highway lighting? During the fall and winter months, there was always at least one major car accident caused by low visibility.

As he drew closer to the turnoff for the Delacombe property, he had second thoughts about bothering anyone this time of night. It would be better politics to stop by in the morning on his way to the station. He wondered about the supposed wolf Harry Harrison had seen. Harry was the last of his family and had lived alone for decades. Maybe his mind was failing, or maybe there really was a wolf—after all, a bear had once somehow found its way to the shores of Piedras. He'd have to check with Fish and Wildlife. Maybe one of his deputies stationed on Orcas or Shaw could take care of that call.

On the other side of the road, through the dense underbrush and old-growth evergreens that had never felt the bite of an ax or chainsaw, Mat thought he spotted an unfamiliar glow. Automatically he slowed the cruiser. There was nothing out there, just the old Hamarsson place falling to ruin. The light was likely a boat offshore passing through the straits.

As far as he knew, unlike Harry, the last of the Hamarsson line refused to step foot on the island. Niall Hamarsson had returned for his grandmother's funeral and left without acknowledging any of the other attendees. The only people out there now, in chilly dark February, would be trespassers or possibly squatters. He considered flipping on his red-and-whites and going to see who might be down there, but his radio crackled to life.

"Dempsey?" Patrick's voice came over the line.

"Dempsey here."

"Stan Elberman reported a dead goat on his property. He claims it's a suspicious death and says if somebody doesn't respond right now, he's taking a shotgun over to the Reynolds place."

Mat flicked on his blues and sped up, hoping to head off a border war between two of the more volatile seniors on the island. Just what he needed on top of Chastity's death.

FIVE

HAMARSSON

Across the street from Chester's stood the Killegen's Point General Store. Niall slunk inside to check out the available building supplies; it seemed ridiculous to move his car. Apparently, February was not the time to be in the market for anything more than tools or bags of cement though. Niall did find a few things—a hammer, a selection of nails—and ignored the flash of anger originating from his past and the feral cruelty of children.

"Can I help you find something?" a gruff voice asked from behind him.

Niall started and turned to find a wizened old man standing there. At least a foot shorter than Niall, he had a shock of white hair standing up in tufts across his head, making it look like he'd been electrocuted. His worn sweatshirt was emblazoned with "Killegen's General Store," and his name tag read "Fred." He shuffled closer to Niall, who stumbled for an answer.

"Um, I need cedar shingles and maybe some other lumber."

"Cold time of year to be up on a roof, son."

"True, but there are holes that need fixing." It had been a

long time since anyone called Niall "son." He wasn't sure how he felt about it.

The man motioned for Niall to follow and led him to the front of the store. He pointed to a small stack of shingles.

"This is all we got until end of March."

Niall bought all the shingles the store had, as well as roofing paper and roof tacks, and Fred insisted on loading them onto a cart and taking them to Niall's car. The old man was stronger than he looked. He kept glancing sideways at Niall too, as if trying to place him.

"What are you fixing up?" Fred finally asked, unable to control his curiosity.

Niall'd known the question was coming, yet he still didn't have an evasive response ready. He'd hoped to stay under the radar for as long as possible, but this time of year, before the spring and summer tourists began flocking to the island, news of his arrival would spread like a wild fire.

"The Hamarsson place."

Fred perked up. "Od and Josephine's place? You must be their grandson."

Niall nodded as he lifted a bale of shingles into the back of his car. "I am."

"It will be good to see it put back together. Put a call in." He handed Niall a business card. "I can likely order anything else you need. Takes a few days, but it's easier than taking the ferry back to the mainland."

Niall nodded. "Thanks," he ground out. The need to escape from Fred's questioning gaze was overwhelming. He wanted to be at the cabin, alone and anonymous, although he figured by bedtime the entire island would know he'd returned, maybe even before then.

Fred patted him on the arm and began slowly making his way back toward the store entrance.

.   .   .

At the cabin Niall hefted the shingles and roofing paper out of his car, tucking them next to the porch where they were sort of protected—although they were going on the roof anyway, right?

He was hungry again. The cinnamon roll had only been enough to keep him going a little while. He dug around in the grocery bag for a bagel and cream cheese, which he ate while sitting on the back bumper and watching the waves come in. That was good, right? That he was hungry? He brushed the crumbs off his lap and stood, walking over to look at the cabin again.

No matter how many times he looked at the tiny building, he still could see the ghosts of his grandparents going about their daily business. Watering flower baskets (also ghosts), reading the paper, knitting, weeding the raised vegetable beds. They'd been old already when they brought him home, in their sixties or maybe seventies. Morfar had passed when Niall was eighteen and Mormor had been nearly ninety when she joined him, but still Niall hadn't been ready. In the short time he'd been with them, they had carved out a space in his heart that was now forever empty. Maybe that's what was wrong with him. He'd always thought he'd have more time. Time to properly thank them both for taking him in, for loving and trying to civilize a feral, unlovable boy.

Now man. Niall wore the disguise of domesticity well. The façade worked for him as a detective—maybe that was *why* he was a good detective. He was still feral and wounded on the inside, and the veneer of society wore thin these days.

The little tent shuddered in the breeze that had picked up in the last hour and brought colder air along with it. The irony of sleeping in a tent was not lost on Niall. He'd slept in a tent when he'd arrived on the island too, refusing to go inside the cabin at first and then, for a while, only to use the toilet. In his young mind the tent was safer. No one could lock the door.

One particularly miserable April—the juncture between Niall's past life and his current one—Od and Josephine Hamarsson took the ferry from Piedras, then drove all the way from Anacortes to Seattle to pick up their grandson, Niall, from the Children's Society (a nice way of saying foster home). The CS was for the impossible-to-place kids, older kids, kids with serious issues. Kids who'd lived in hell and didn't know how to be human. Kids like him. Kids no one wanted, who had no relatives. Except Niall had had relatives, and they'd come for him when the state located them.

"We're here for you."

The first words Od ever uttered to Niall, in the shabby waiting room of the society. Niall'd been angry and scared. He supposed it hadn't really changed over the years—he was still angry. Even though his life had been hell, the younger Niall knew how to navigate it. It was familiar. He'd known when to hide, when to run, and when there wasn't going to be a meal at the end of the day. Kindness was not doled out like candy. His mother had been the worst kind of parent, a meth addict who sold herself and tried to sell her son for drugs, food, a place to sleep.

Od and Josephine were the unknown. The social worker explained to Niall they were his only living relatives and had agreed to take him. In fact, they *wanted* him to come home with them. This comment Niall chose to ignore. His mother constantly told him he was useless, in the way, nothing but a burden. What about him could possibly have changed?

These days Niall didn't remember why the tent had been put up in the first place—if it had been for him or if it had been up already—but he'd claimed it. His grandparents hadn't tried to win him over—not overtly, anyway. At the time, he wasn't aware of their efforts. He only knew they had let him sleep in the tent until he was ready to come inside.

The breeze turned into a stiff wind. Niall walked around the tent inspecting the ties to make sure it wouldn't blow away. Tomorrow he'd see about getting a better sleeping bag and more clothes. Tonight, he'd spend some more time with his friend Jack.

Out of the corner of his eye, Niall caught a glimpse of blue lights flashing on the other side of the dense brush and trees between the cabin and the road. They could've been his imagination, they disappeared so quickly into the night. He wondered if the cruiser was Dempsey's or if another officer was on duty.

Because sure enough, when he'd brought up the Piedras County Sheriff's Office on his phone, there was Sheriff Mat Dempsey at the top of the page. Dempsey looked the same to Niall: black Irish, all dark hair and dark eyes, skin that tanned easily. Easy on the eyes, hard on his teenaged heart. Niall pushed aside the memories threatening to surface—he didn't want to think about his past. That seemed to be all he was doing these days, shoving memories aside. And yet, here he was, in the place most likely to make him remember... and he'd come here of his own volition.

DEMPSEY

"You're home late tonight," Mat's mom said as Mat came through the doorway.

"Long day. I'm sure you heard about Chastity Reynolds. Just now I had to stop at Stan Elberman's. He's threatening vigilante justice, claiming Martin Reynolds is killing off his livestock."

"Martin Reynolds? If he's not glued to that laptop of his, he's flipping burgers at the Hook."

"I know." Mat shook his head. Martin Reynolds was a lot of things, but energetic enough to kill off livestock wasn't one of them. He took off his coat and hat and hung them up in the front closet, leaving his shoes by the front door.

"What a tragedy about Chastity. She was a sweet girl," Alyson replied, moving back into the kitchen. Mat caught up to her next to the butcher block and gave her a big hug.

"What was that for?" she asked.

He shrugged. His mother was the reason he'd moved back from SF. Of his siblings, he was the only one who had no attachments and loved the island enough to live here. When his father died, his sisters and brother had tried to get Alyson to move to the mainland. In their minds, she would be better off there—better medical facilities, for one thing. But Mat knew his mother would never survive long away from the land and home where she'd spent most of her life. It hadn't been a difficult choice for him to return to Piedras.

"Something smells good. I could eat."

His mother smiled. "You can always eat, Mat. I made paella —that way we'll have leftovers for a few days—and salad. It'll be ready in a few minutes. Go change."

It had been an adjustment, moving back in with his newly widowed mother when he returned to the island. There were days when his time in San Francisco seemed like a dream. He knew his mom worried he didn't have anyone, a partner or husband. Yes, things had changed on the island since he was a kid, but he wasn't convinced they were ready for an out gay sheriff. Or ever would be.

In his room on the second floor, Mat changed out of his uniform and into a worn pair of jeans and a flannel shirt over a t-shirt. His uniform he hung in the closet next to his others. Then he padded back downstairs to where his mother waited for him in the dining room.

She insisted on setting the dining room table for dinner every night: "It's important, Mat. And this way I get your full attention."

"So, what can you tell me about the case?" she asked after they'd sat down across from each other. Mat needed to take apart the chairs and reglue them; his creaked as he lowered his full weight onto it. Either that or he needed to get back to his daily runs.

"Not much, Mom, you know that. And, to be honest, we don't know anything more than what the *Island Times* reported. Sebastian Lambert—he's new to the island—found the body this morning when he went to check his boat."

The *Island Times* was only online nowadays, but it used to be the Piedras County newspaper. It was fool's luck the single reporter had been on the mainland when the news broke about Chas Reynolds. It had taken him several hours to get back to the island, and by then the crime scene had been cleared and Chastity's body taken safely away from prying eyes.

Mat had made sure the marina security video was collected. They'd checked the boats along the pier, and none had been broken into; all had their protective winter tarps securely fastened. Birdy had taken pictures of all the boats, the surrounding areas, and the parking lot. Anything that could be useful. The lot still had yellow tape at the entrance, although Mat had little hope of keeping people out. With only five deputies covering the five islands 24-7, there wasn't enough manpower to have someone guard it through the night.

Instinct and experience told Mat the marina wasn't the crime scene, that Chas had been killed somewhere else. But, even in February, the likelihood of having an altercation along the main part of Hidden Harbor without someone noticing was low. The tattoo was the most recognizable thing about her; she had definitely been in the water for a few days. Her body had likely been carried to the marina by the current and helped along by the recent windstorm.

His stomach growled again. Mat blinked, realizing he'd been sitting there thinking about the case instead of eating, and his stomach wasn't happy about it. Picking up his fork, he shoveled a big bite of paella into his mouth.

"I heard something interesting today," Alyson said.

Something about his mom's tone had Mat immediately wary.

"Mmmph?" Mat asked, his mouth full of rice and spicy sausage.

"Fred saw Niall Hamarsson at the general store."

His body went hot and cold at the same time—an impossibility, to be sure, but that was what it felt like. It was everything Mat could do to swallow his bite of paella instead of choking on it. If Hamarsson was back that explained the lights he'd seen coming home.

"Oh?" he asked once he could speak.

Alyson continued as if she hadn't turned Mat's world upside down. "He came into the store looking for some kind of supplies. Fred sold him roofing shingles and a few tools. He might be ordering more supplies later, Fred wasn't sure."

"Did he say why he's here?"

"Fred said he wasn't very talkative."

That sounded like Niall.

Why would he be on the island? As far as Mat knew, Niall hadn't been here since before Mat moved back. It had still been scandalous gossip when he arrived that the Hamarssons' grandson had come home for Josephine Hamarsson's funeral and left again on the next ferry without speaking to anyone.

"Huh."

Niall Hamarsson.

Mat wasn't sure how he felt about Niall being back on the island. He'd known Niall was a detective with the Seattle Police Department because Mat had paid attention to his mom's gossip over the years. And then done a little checking himself too.

"The boy had a hard life." Trust his mom to think of Niall Hamarsson as a boy. Mat thought Niall was a few years older than him but didn't know for sure.

"I don't think he's a boy any longer, Mom."

What Mat knew about the man in question was what other kids his age had known. Hamarsson had appeared out of the blue when Mat was seven or so. None of the island kids knew what to do with him. He didn't talk to anyone, including the teachers at school. The island school was small—which meant when a few kids figured out Niall could barely read, the whole school found out.

"What do you know about Niall?" he asked.

His mom's expression turned serious. "It's not my story to tell, Mat. I was good friends with Jo and Od. I know they would've brought Niall home a lot sooner if they'd known he existed." She sighed. "Drugs have taken so many of our young people from us. Ana Hamarsson was one of them."

He cocked his head, trying to place an Ana. "I don't remember her."

"She was gone before you were born, Mat. Ana was in trouble before high school, and Jo and Od didn't know what to do. Then she disappeared. Left without graduating and only contacted them when she needed money. Those calls eventually stopped too, and she never told them she'd had a son. They found out when CPS called them."

Mat pushed his plate away. The paella sat heavy in his stomach. How had he not known Hamarsson's history? It was still true about the drug problem in Piedras County—and now it was not just pot and meth but also opiates and mystery mixes that were wreaking havoc on the population.

He took his plate into the kitchen. A stack of dishes sat waiting in the sink. He turned on the hot water and squeezed some dish soap over them.

"I'll do those in a bit," his mom said from behind him.

"I'll do them now and then you won't have to."

That night Mat had a hard time sleeping. The events of the day rolled around in his head, not making any sense: the wolf Harrison had reported, the dead livestock, Chas Reynolds. A shadowy figure Mat thought was Niall Hamarsson watched over them all.

When he dragged himself out from under the covers at five a.m. to the sound of his phone beeping, Mat was resigned to the fact that he would likely be stopping by the Hamarsson place before the day ended.

"Dempsey," he growled into the receiver.

It was Paul Holstrom, and he sounded panicked. "Sheriff, we need you out at Harry's place."

Mat tucked his phone between his chin and shoulder while he listened to Holstrom and tried to get dressed at the same time. He never had mastered putting on socks one-handed.

"What's the situation?" Damn, maybe he should've stopped by Harry's last night.

"He claims he saw a wolf again, and he's been rounding up folks to go hunting for it."

"How'd you find out?" Surely Harry wouldn't call the police for an illegal wolf hunt.

Holstrom huffed out a laugh. "Harry called me at home, forgot I work for the county now."

Mat tucked his shirt in and finished buckling his belt. "I'll be there in ten."

He didn't have time to leave a note, but his mom would probably know the details before Mat got done at Harry's. Jesus Christ, sometimes his people confounded him. Did Harry think they wouldn't get wind of some sort of wolf posse? If nothing else, there would be a slew of trespassing calls as the men tramped across acres of Piedras Island.

The old man tried to stare Mat down. Six of them were packed onto Harry's front porch: Mat, Deputy Holstrom, Harry Harrison, Stan Elberman, Brian Delacombe—who had a domestic violence conviction, and Mat knew Brian was just clueless enough to have forgotten he had a record and couldn't own or be around firearms—and Stu Dennis, Piedras's self-appointed historian. Why Stu was there, Mat had no idea.

"Harry," Mat began, "you can't go traipsing around with

shotguns taking aim at anything you think is a wolf. It's illegal. Very, very illegal. I'll have one of my deputies call Fish and Wildlife and see if they know anything about a wolf. Maybe it's a coyote." It was still dark too; the sun wouldn't be up for another couple of hours. The last thing Mat needed right now was a crowd of septuagenarians wandering around in the woods with firearms.

"What about Stan's goat?" Harry demanded. "Something killed it."

"Yes, something, or someone, did kill Stan's goat, but please let the proper authorities look into the matter. If you don't calm down, I'm going to have to do more than give you a lecture. Don't make me ask for your permits. Because, Harry, there is no such thing as a permit to hunt wolves in this area."

Something in his tone must have finally broken through to Harry, whose shoulders slumped in defeat.

Mat turned. "Brian, I don't know what you're doing here, but if I catch you with a firearm, you're going back to jail." Brian was Mat's age, but he looked older, the result of a lot of bad choices over the past twenty-five years or so.

Brian paled before flushing red. Without saying goodbye, he jumped off the porch and trotted to his pickup. He was gone in seconds.

Mat felt a twinge of something close to pity for Brian. Though he'd been far from innocent in the situation, his girlfriend at the time had had her own run-ins with law enforcement. Brian had claimed he was defending himself, his girlfriend had said he hit her and pushed her into a wall, and Brian had been sent to jail. While he served his time, the girlfriend had moved on to another guy and ended up in a similar situation, only that time there were witnesses who testified she'd started the assault, and she'd ended up incarcerated too. Still, Brian didn't need to be running around with a weapon in his hand.

That left Stu Dennis. "Stu, is there a reason you're here this morning? I didn't take you for a hunter."

"I'm not. Harry called me to witness the hunt, and I figured it would be pretty incredible if there was a wolf on Piedras, so why not?" Stu had a mischievous glint in his eye.

Mat squashed his groan. He looked at Deputy Holstrom and saw the younger man was trying to keep himself from smiling. Stu needed another hobby, and Harry—Jesus, Harry was going to give Mat more gray hairs.

He glared at the three men left on the porch. "It's too early for these kinds of shenanigans." Sternly, he said, "Harry?"

"What?"

"I need some caffeine. Holstrom here got me out of bed worried because you old men were going Rambo. You got coffee in there? I could use a cup."

Harry grumbled but opened his front door. "You all can stay on the porch. I haven't had time to clean up in here."

Personally, Mat thought Harry never cleaned, and he had no intention of entering Harry's abode unless he had to. Mat was a firm believer that what he didn't know (yet) wouldn't hurt him. And he really wanted a cup of coffee.

Before he and Holstrom departed, Mat reminded the three older men not to go after anything they thought was a wolf.

"Call the station, call Fish and Wildlife. Do not go after the animal with a shotgun—or any other kind of weapon," Mat clarified.

By the time they left Harrison's, it was nearly eight and past time to get to the station. He and Birdy had a long list of people they needed to talk to, and he needed to check in with Marshal to see if anything else had been discovered.

Running a murder investigation with his inexperienced skeleton crew of a staff was problematic. Mat missed the resources he'd had at his fingertips in San Fran. He was going to petition the county for new evidence kits, and it would be nice if the powers that be included a decent print kit. Maybe he should try to get a training grant? Thirty hours a year for a reminder of basic training was not enough.

The overgrown driveway to the Hamarsson place caught his eye as he drove past and he added another item on his list.

Niall Hamarsson.

SEVEN

HAMARSSON

Niall shivered in the cold air. The outside temperature had not warmed up overnight. He clutched his coat tight around himself, wishing he'd thought to pick up a little camp stove so he could at least make his own coffee instead of driving into Killegen's Point for a caffeine fix.

Sleep last night had been elusive, though he'd made significant progress on the whiskey he'd bought at Chester's. But not even alcohol was quieting his brain. Even now, in the light of day, the last dream remained unfortunately clear in his mind.

His eight-year-old self, eyes wide, watching terrified as the closet door closed and everything went dark. His mother's voice on the other side telling him he needed to be quiet, assuring him it wouldn't be long this time. The adult part of himself wanted to fling the door open, knowing—remembering—that it *had* been a long time before anyone opened the door again. So long he'd peed himself and the closet smelled like urine, and when the door finally opened, it hadn't been his mother who stood there.

Thankfully, he'd woken himself up. And damn if he hadn't wanted to reach for the Jack again to try to drown out the dream-memory. Instead he pulled on his rumpled clothing and crawled out of the tent.

His car keys were icy against his fingertips, reminding him he had a way to get to the coffee he desperately wanted. He pissed in the blackberries again before getting behind the wheel and heading to town.

The cashier was the same as the day before; not surprising, really. Today she seemed to understand Niall had no interest in making small talk beyond "Hello" and "Thank you." On the way out, he caught a glimpse of someone in the glass door. He almost didn't recognize himself. Gone was the well-manicured police detective; in his place had emerged a Viking marauder.

It had been years since Niall allowed his beard to grow, and now he had three days of growth on his face and his hair stuck out in all directions. For a scant second, he'd thought it was his grandfather standing there. He was seeing a ghost and the ghost was he. Niall almost turned around to go back and search out a disposable razor but shrugged, deciding it wasn't worth the effort. He had no one to impress; he'd wait until it was so itchy he couldn't stand it any longer.

Leaving his car in Chester's lot, Niall crossed the street to the general store, the coffee cup warm in his hands. Before he entered, he gulped down the hot liquid, feeling its heat all the way to his stomach. Once inside, he quickly located a cheap camp stove and a couple bottles of propane. Then remembered he hadn't bought any ground coffee and didn't have a coffeepot. Luckily the store carried small camping carafes. He grabbed one off the shelf, but he was going to have to go back to Chester's for coffee.

At the front of the general store was a different, less curious cashier, a sullen younger man who didn't look any happier about being out in public than Niall. Niall swiped his debit card before carrying his purchases back to his car and stashing them behind the passenger seat. Then he took a deep breath, ready to brave

Sage and her questioning looks again. Anything for more caffeine.

The day before, he'd mapped out a plan in his head of how he was going to attack the cabin remodel. Since he already had shingles and paper, he'd start there. Once the roof was patched, he'd bring out a dumpster, if he could, and gut the inside. It gave him a twinge of guilt. Morfar had hand-built and installed all the cabinets himself, but rodents and exposure to the elements had ruined them.

Fixing up the cabin was something he could think about. What he was going to do after, both with the cabin and his life, could wait until he was finished.

Behind the cabin was an even smaller storage shed where Morfar had kept his tools. Niall pulled the weathered door open, surprised to see the contents of the shed had fared much better than the cabin. His grandfather's handmade tools were still neatly tucked away in their cubbyholes, covered with dust and cobwebs, but—Niall pulled out Morfar's hand planer and brushed it off—it looked like all they needed was to be cleaned and oiled.

The custom ladder was still tucked in between the cubbies and the shed wall. Niall pulled it out and took it outside. After inspecting it for damage, cracks, and loose rungs, Niall leaned it against the cabin. The hand tools he stowed in the back of his car. Next run into town, he'd see what oil was needed to fix them up.

Hours later, Niall eyed his slow progress. It was taking him a lot longer to get the old shingles off than he'd expected. He still had about a quarter of the roof to go, and his back and shoulder muscles were protesting. He wasn't used to this sort of physical labor. Od Hamarsson had been a true craftsman and carpenter—

the cabin was made to last and was only in disrepair because of Niall's negligence.

He'd long ago stripped off his coat and left it in the car, but even in the cool weather he'd sweated through his long-sleeved t-shirt and taken it off too. Now that he'd stopped working, he shivered. It was damn cold.

A noise coming from the direction of the road and getting louder caught Niall's attention. As he peered toward the driveway—which was a little easier to use since he'd driven up and down it the past few days—a police cruiser appeared out of the brush. Niall blinked.

It was Sheriff Mat Dempsey in a tricked-out cruiser bristling with antennae and painted an intimidating shade of blue-black. What the fuck was he doing here? Niall did not have the band-width to deal with a small-town cop. Especially small-town cop Mat Dempsey.

Bumping slowly down the driveway, the cruiser drew closer to the cabin and came to a stop directly behind Niall's car. Niall belatedly realized he was holding his own breath in anticipation of his first in-person glimpse of the man Mat had grown into. Fuck that. Niall stayed up on the roof, wanting Dempsey to have to look up at him.

The cruiser door opened, and Dempsey got out. He looked good, far too good. He was a man now, with a man's muscles and a man's stance—sure of himself and his environment. Because Niall was an asshole, he was going to force Dempsey to speak first.

Dempsey tramped through the overgrown weeds between the drive and the cabin. "Niall Hamarsson, is that you? Someone told me you were out here, but I didn't believe them. Had to come see for myself."

"Now you've seen me, you can back that cruiser right off my property."

Mat crossed his arms over his chest. If he'd been shirtless,

Niall would have been treated to heavily muscled pecs and beefy biceps. Goddamn him.

"Is that any way to greet an old friend?"

Niall felt his nostrils flare. Dempsey winced.

"As I said, you've seen, you can leave. Unless you're here to serve me with a warrant, there is no reason for you to be on my property."

Dempsey frowned and nodded. "Nope, not here to serve you, just making sure my citizens aren't imagining things. We've got a few things keeping us busy right now, last thing I needed was to find a squatter out here."

"Not a squatter," Niall ground out.

"No, but it's close to ten years, maybe more, since you've been around. Far as I know, you haven't set foot on the island since I've been back, and in the past couple of years you stopped even having someone take care of this place."

Niall ignored that last part, although it reminded him he needed to get to the bottom of what he *had* been paying for.

A gust of wind came up and Niall shivered again. In his anger, he'd forgotten *he* was shirtless. Without answering Dempsey's inferred question about why he was back, Niall grabbed his sweaty t-shirt and pulled it over his head. The damp shirt didn't warm him, but he felt better anyway, no longer exposed to Dempsey's searching gaze.

"You're going to get sick not wearing proper clothing..." Dempsey's focus moved away from Niall to where the tent was set up. "Are you sleeping in that?"

"I've had enough of your questions, and I don't have to answer any of them. Feel free to leave anytime. I have work to do," Niall snarled.

Turning his back to Dempsey, Niall picked up the hammer again and went back to prying the old shingles off the roof. He was cold, his muscles hurt, and he had blisters on his hands from not wearing gloves, but he wasn't admitting any of that to this man.

Not soon enough, he heard Dempsey start his engine, followed by the sound of rocks and gravel popping from underneath the cruiser's tires. Niall did not stop hammering. Only when he was sure the man was gone did he put the hammer down with a groan. He knee-crawled over to the ladder, and between his stiff hands, aching back, and blisters, he was barely able to make it to the ground.

EIGHT

DEMPSEY

Mat turned out of Hamarsson's driveway and pulled to the side of the road. He needed oxygen. He hadn't known what to expect when he decided to confirm the rumor flying around Piedras that the "Hamarsson boy" was back. Even the younger people were calling Niall the Hamarsson boy, and they'd never met him.

Hamarsson was not a boy. Not by any stretch of the imagination. The sight of him on the roof shirtless had rendered Mat speechless for a moment, and then he'd said the stupidest thing —because Niall was right, they'd never been friends.

With Niall's shirt off, Mat had seen the dark ink of several tattoos across the other man's chest and along one arm, with the hint of one continuing onto his back. Until today Mat hadn't considered himself a tattoo man, but Niall's ink sparked something in him. Something he was going to need to extinguish because Niall clearly hated him.

And Mat wasn't looking for a relationship.

The errant thought spooked him more than the immediate lust he'd felt seeing Hamarsson for the first time since high school. Where had *relationship* come from? Why would he even be thinking it? He was happy as he was, a "confirmed bachelor." His priorities were his family and his job. Everything else was secondary. Niall Hamarsson didn't fit into Mat's well-ordered life.

Reminding himself of his priorities calmed him down. Mat took another deep breath before pulling out onto the road heading toward Hidden Harbor. He would spend the day focusing on the Reynolds case. The longer it went unsolved, the less likely they would be to catch the perpetrator, and Mat wasn't the only one who wanted justice for Chastity.

Justice for Chastity was going to have to wait another day. As soon as Mat arrived at the station, Birdy informed him they'd had a credible report of a meth house on the north end of the island. A long-abandoned property—ironically, much like Hamarsson's. The land was too rocky for farming and the only spot where a structure could be built—where the condemned home lingered in its death throes—was within one hundred feet of the shoreline, so the county had refused to issue new building permits. The dilapidated house on Preacher Road had sat empty for years, and every once in a while Dempsey and his deputies had to go chase trespassers off the property. Mat had considered sending his deputies to follow up on the call, but even with Birdy taking the lead Mat wanted to be there too.

He and Birdy drove out together with Deputies Radden and Jones following them. The last thing Mat wanted was to surprise some jumpy meth-heads. It saddened him that meth had reached the furthest boundary of his little island.

"Did you bring a kit?" Mat asked Birdy as they sped along.

She nodded. "Yes, sir."

When they arrived, the first words out of his mouth were, "Wear your masks and gloves, everyone. We don't have the time or manpower for meth-related illnesses."

Someone must have warned the drug makers since the house was empty of humans but ripe with the distinct odor of meth cooking. He didn't want to waste a kit—the damn things weren't free—but he had Birdy test anyway. The freaking stove was still warm, for crying out loud.

After confirming that no one was inside the house, the four of them fanned out, checking each room for obvious evidence amongst the trash and human effluvia.

"Sir?" Birdy asked from behind him while Mat was pulling disgusting cushions off a ramshackle couch.

He turned to look at her. Birdy held a woman's wallet in one hand.

"It's Chastity's. Or, at least, her driver's license is inside."

Well, crap.

Drug rings were never small—they should be called drug vortexes or, well, cartels, but that was already taken. Mat monitored several state info sites where law enforcement noted drug activity. The lists were searchable by keyword. Hours after leaving the scene, Mat was still sitting behind his desk and logged into the network, typing in Chastity's name to see if she'd been picked up somewhere else or if any of her known associates had, trying to find some sort of connection that would make sense. It would help if he knew who her known associates were, of course. Mat typed in *Martin Reynolds*, Chastity's brother, and got no hits related to Chastity.

After another several minutes of fruitless inquiry, he took the search a little broader. A case from a few years earlier popped up. One of the local high school students had been busted selling meth and was linked to a drug ring on the mainland. Mat's agency hadn't been a part of that bust, but he was on good terms with the man in charge.

Another, different search, and Mat had a tenuous connection. Chastity had been in high school when the dealer was arrested. They hadn't been in the same class—Chastity was younger by two years—but that was something, at least, a solid place for Mat to start. He sat back in his chair, which made its usual protesting sounds, and ran his hands through his hair, hoping this would be the break they needed.

All day he'd managed not to think about Niall Hamarsson, but now that he'd stopped concentrating on the Reynolds case, his thoughts slipped right back to the image burned in his brain: Hamarsson, bare chested and tattooed, illuminated by the teasing February sunlight. He'd looked magnificent and nothing like Mat remembered. Nothing like the skinny boy who'd been the unfortunate target of teasing and unkind jokes.

It's called bullying, he told himself. Bullying. And he had taken part. He was just as guilty as if he'd initiated the taunts himself. Guilty by lack of action.

"That's a mighty big sigh, boss. What'd you find out?" Birdy asked.

Mat started guiltily out of his childhood memories, sitting forward in his chair with a thump.

He pointed at the computer screen. "Looks like there's a possibility Chastity was involved with those kids who were selling meth at the high school a few years ago—or at least knew them."

Birdy frowned. "I'm sure she knew them, we all know each other. Heck, *I* knew them. I just don't see it. We weren't friends or anything, but the Chastity I knew was into sunrise yoga and natural medicine—and, yeah, she was kind of an airhead. I don't see her being into meth." She raised a hand before he could respond. "I know, we found her wallet out there, but... what if it had been stolen or lost, and one of those losers found it?"

"I'm gonna call the guy who was the lead on this regardless, just to rule it out." The high school arrests had been led by a detective out of Whatcom County since one of the perps had traveled there to buy meth.

Birdy nodded.

"You touch base with her friends in the yoga community—there's got to be a local website, or if not, I want you to stop at all the bulletin boards in town and see if you can find something posted there. Someone knows something, and they may not be aware of it."

"Also…"

Mat raised his eyebrows, waiting.

"It's started to snow, sir."

"What?"

"Just a few flakes, but the weather service says we may be in for a late storm. They're not sure when, maybe tomorrow or tomorrow night."

Mat groaned. How had he missed that the weather was going to take a turn for the worse? Snow in his community was a nightmare. Very few of the locals' vehicles were prepared for icy conditions, and many were retirees who *shouldn't* be out driving in it. The weather was conspiring against him and his deputies.

"Send out a bulletin reminding people to use their heads and stay safe—and send the same thing out again in the morning. Make sure the rest of the deputies are notified as well. If it happens, it's going to mean required overtime. We don't need another Snowpocalypse."

A few years ago, a mere six inches of the stuff had paralyzed the entirety of Piedras County. Mat and his deputies had spent a long, cold forty-eight hours pulling people out of ditches—most alive, thank god—checking on the housebound elderly and keeping the reckless from using the steeper hills on the island as sled runs. He'd never been so tired or wished more he had someone else he could rely on; Birdy had been too new and inexperienced at the time to be much help.

On the way to his cruiser, Mat called his mom, letting her know that he was headed home and about the possible bad weather. It seemed fine, for now anyway. The flurries had stopped, so he sent a little thank you to the weather gods. He didn't need snow on top of everything else going on.

NINE

HAMARSSON

"God damn fuck!"

Niall grabbed his right hand with his left to stop the flow of blood from the deep gash he'd just inflicted on himself. It hadn't started to hurt yet, but that was coming. He could practically sense his pain receptors gearing up for the hit.

He flung the awl aside. It clattered and rolled to the edge of the roof, then thumped to the ground. Niall swung around and felt for the ladder with his toes. Trying not to think about falling and injuring himself worse, he climbed down, leaning against the ladder and using his elbows to steady himself.

Safely on the ground, he took a look at the wound again. There was no way he didn't need stitches; it gaped open slightly. Hopefully stitches were all he was going to need. He flexed his fingers. They seemed to work. With luck there wouldn't be any serious damage.

He wrapped his flannel shirt around his hand as tight as he could and then couldn't figure out how to get into his coat.

Fuck it. He tossed his coat and wallet into the passenger seat. Moving as quickly as he could, he got into his car, started the engine, and backed it around while holding his hand up close to his chest. Once he made it out onto the main road, he automatically headed toward Hidden Harbor. If things hadn't changed too much, there was still a small medical center located there.

It took him thirty minutes. Driving with his left hand and trying to keep the other above his heart and not bleed all over the fucking place was a challenge. Signs directed him to the small hospital and, he was pleased to note, it at least had been remodeled sometime recently.

He was starting to feel a little light-headed, which was probably shock and not blood loss—he hoped. Instead of parking in the lot, he left his Subaru in the loading zone with the keys in it. If they needed to move the thing, they could.

The emergency room receptionist took one look at Niall and raced from behind the counter to lead him back to a small examination room.

"Lay down, and I'll notify the doctor you're here. I'll need your information, though. Do you have any allergies he needs to know of? Any medical history?"

Niall shook his head. "No allergies, no history, and not taking any medication."

She left but quickly returned, a concerned man in a white lab coat following her.

"My name's Marissa, this is Dr. Soper."

Dr. Soper moved around Marissa. The doctor was around Niall's age, and underneath his white lab coat he wore blue jeans and a black t-shirt. He wasn't as tall as Niall, but not many people were.

"Do you mind if I take a look?"

"Go ahead. It isn't pretty, but I think it's clean."

"Sir—"

"Hamarsson. Niall Hamarsson."

"I'm going to have Marissa take the wrap off, and we'll see

what we can do to get you fixed up. Can you tell me what happened?"

Marissa carefully unwrapped his hand while Niall looked the other direction. He'd seen it already.

"The damn awl slipped and gouged my hand."

"Better than a power tool. Those can do a lot of damage."

Niall watched Dr. Soper. His blond hair was short but was managing to stick up in several directions, giving him a boyish look—the opposite of Niall's too-long hair and weather-beaten appearance, like somebody'd left him outside in the elements. The doc muttered something under his breath about being used to taking people apart, not putting them back together.

"Dr. Soper!" Marissa scolded.

"Excuse me?" Niall said, wondering if he'd heard correctly.

"Doctor, I need to get back out front. The phone is ringing off the hook today. Would you like me to call another MA down to assist?"

Soper shook his head. "I'll let you know if I need anything else, Marissa. Thank you."

Once she left, Dr. Soper shot him a grin. "Don't worry, I'm licensed. Filling in for the regular ER doc who's enjoying a much-needed vacation in the Bahamas. I'm actually the volunteer medical examiner, but I take hours here to keep my skills up."

"Does Piedras use an ME a lot?" Niall asked.

As the words passed his lips, Niall realized most civilians might not refer to Soper as an ME.

"In the field, are you?" Soper asked.

"I suppose you could say I'm more used to bringing work to an ME than most."

"Police, are you? Homicide, I'd guess. Lie back."

"Recently retired. Very recently."

All the time they were talking, Soper was gently working on Niall's hand. He'd injected a local anesthetic so Niall couldn't feel anything much, but he still flinched when Soper cleaned the wound. He looked everywhere except at his hand the doctor was beginning to stitch up.

"You have some magnificent blisters." Without waiting for an explanation for the blisters, Soper continued, "You're young to have retired."

Niall nodded, the back of his head rustling against the paper-covered pillow.

"Been on the force"—he rolled his eyes up, thinking—"sixteen years."

"How long in homicide?"

"Ten." Ten long years.

"I'm sure you heard about our recent case, the first on the island in years."

He hadn't. After researching the sheriff's office, Niall'd let the battery in his phone die on purpose. He didn't want to know anything, didn't want to talk to anyone. The best way for that was to make it impossible for anyone to reach him. The last time he checked, when the battery power was at something like 1 percent, Trey had called five times and left messages Niall chose not to listen to. Chief Meyers had called too. Niall hoped his silence would convince her he was serious about resigning.

Still, his curiosity was piqued.

"What happened?"

"A local's body was discovered at the marina a couple of days ago. It's causing a lot of ruckus."

"No suspects?"

"Open scene, reasonably certain she was strangled somewhere else and dumped. Those are the facts I can share. Not that we have much more than that yet."

"Keep my mind off what you're doing to my hand. Tell me about the victim. What was her name, who was she? Did she live here on the island?"

Soper kept his attention on Niall's hand, stitching carefully.

"She was a born and bred Piedras girl. Seems she'd moved recently, but no one knows where to. The town is shocked that there was a murder at all and that Chastity Reynolds was the victim. I've been here less than ten years, and we have our share of domestic violence, stupid accidents, drownings and the like, the occasional feud between families—but they don't lead to murder."

"Drugs?" Niall remembered the Reynolds family. One in particular had made it his mission to make Niall's life as miserable as possible. He'd been impossible to avoid around school, and Niall had known better than to tell any of the teaching staff. Most of them already thought his grandparents were making a bad bet on him.

"We've got those too, but there doesn't seem to be a connection—at least, one I've been informed of. Okay, this part may hurt a bit."

Niall gritted his teeth. It hurt a fucking lot.

"Okay, that's it." Soper straightened up on his roller stool, putting the instruments and gauze onto a tray while he talked. "I'm going to prescribe a painkiller, take it for the next forty-eight hours until the worst pain passes. Then, if you need it, use ibuprofen or another over-the-counter pain reliever. No driving or alcohol."

Great. Niall thought about his car and his cabin and having no one to ask for help.

"Keep it clean. No midwinter gardening. Come back in a week so I can see how it's healing."

"The other doc's taking a long vacation, I guess."

Soper flashed another bright smile. "Pretty much."

His hand was expertly wrapped now so that only his four fingers poked out the top of the bandage. Soper wrapped a sling over his shoulder and underneath his forearm. "Keep it immobile for forty-eight hours. You need to let it heal."

"Forty-eight hours?"

"You have an appointment, something you need two hands for?" Soper asked.

"Not even for jerking off, the left one will do fine."

Soper narrowed his eyes. "I'm not kidding. You came close to severing a tendon. Let your hand heal, and you won't have to have surgery. Otherwise…"

"How am I supposed to get back to my place?" Niall wasn't going to be able to bluff the good doctor, especially since his car was sitting in the no-parking zone without a driver in it.

"You're alone?"

Niall nodded.

"Seattle PD?"

Niall nodded again.

Soper dragged a cell phone out from underneath his coat. He punched in a number and waited until someone answered.

"Richard? Marshal. Yeah, hi. Quick one, I know you've got stuff. Niall Hamarsson. You know him?"

There was a great deal of nodding and hmm-ing from Soper's side of the conversation. Niall only knew one Richard, and he was the chief medical examiner for Seattle.

Soper said goodbye and shoved the phone away.

"How about you stay at my place, for tonight at least? I've got a big house on the other side of the island."

"Why would you offer a stranger a place to stay?" Even though Soper had verified Niall's identity, it was a generous thing to do.

"Hamarsson? Is it okay to call you Niall? Hamarsson is quite a mouthful."

Niall nodded, wondering if maybe the pain meds were having an odd effect on him.

"This *is* Piedras Island. We may be a little quirky, but we take care of our own. You aren't the first resident I've offered to give a hand to—ha ha, little joke there. But no, seriously, I had Harry Harrison for a week when he had the flu. I told the old codger to get a flu shot, but he didn't and ended up not quite sick enough to be admitted but not so healthy I wanted him on his own."

"Harry's still around?"

"Alive and kicking. How about it?"

"Fine." He didn't have a choice.

"Tell you what, as an added bonus I'll wrap that hand so well you'll be able to take a shower. I'm done with my shift in an hour. I'll escort you to the waiting area."

A shower. A shower, especially now that he had dried blood caked on himself, sounded incredible.

As promised, Soper wrapped his hand, and Niall was able to take his first shower in days. The pain medication made everything a little blurry, but the feeling of being clean was heavenly. When he stepped out of Soper's bathroom, his clothes had disappeared, replaced with a clean t-shirt and a pair of gray sweatpants.

"I put your clothes in the wash. Those should fit—they're baggy on me," Soper called through the door. "When you're ready, there's some soup on the stove."

Sleep won out over hunger. That and the fact that he didn't think he could talk to Soper any more today, regardless of his kindness. He was worn out. Careful of his hand, Niall lay back on the spare bed in Soper's—*Marshal's*—guest bedroom. Tomorrow he'd rethink his plan for the cabin. Tomorrow he'd deal with recharging his phone—no doubt Soper's call set off some sort of internal warning system back in Seattle, and *people* would figure out where he was. Richard Hansen and Chief Meyers were at least friendly.

Niall hadn't talked much about Piedras or his grandparents with the people he'd met in Seattle. Trey knew he'd lived here as a teen, but he didn't like any of Niall's work friends and they didn't like him back. Trey wouldn't be telling anyone where

Niall might be. But the fact that Soper lived on Piedras would be a clue as to where he was. Not that he believed a horde of people would come looking for him.

His last thought before falling into a dreamless sleep was that hospitality like this was something his grandparents would have done too. Soper was right: the island took care of its own. Except it seemed to have failed Chastity Reynolds. What had happened there? Niall tried to recall if he remembered her as a child. He'd known Martin Reynolds, and there was no love lost between them. The Reynolds-Delacombe clan were generally bullies who believed the world owed them something—at least, they had when Niall lived on the island, and he couldn't imagine they'd changed. Still, Chastity didn't deserve her fate. No one deserved to have their life cut short.

TEN

DEMPSEY

"Oh, who's that?"

Birdy's question floated over the partition between the station's reception area and the deputies' desks just as the doorbell buzzed, letting them know someone had come through the entrance. Whoever it was, Birdy could handle them.

"Is Mat Dempsey here?" Niall Hamarsson's gruff words followed Birdy's.

Mat froze halfway to standing. What the hell was Hamarsson doing at the station?

Birdy answered stiffly, "*Sheriff* Dempsey is a very busy man, especially right now. Do you have an appointment?"

Mat snickered. Something in Hamarsson's attitude had turned Birdy against him. Mat made his way toward reception. He might as well see why Hamarsson was here.

"I'm sure he is a very busy man, Deputy Flynn. Would you let Sheriff Dempsey know Hamarsson is here to see him." Hamarsson forgot to add the lilt at the end to make his statement a question.

"I—Hamarsson?"

Mat waited a beat, wanting to know how Hamarsson would respond.

"Yes."

Mat rolled his eyes. Typical wordy Norwegian.

Mat came around the partition and stopped behind Birdy, taking in the man waiting in the lobby. Hamarsson's right arm was in a sling, and his hand was thickly bandaged. On the other hand, he'd taken a shower recently and looked somewhat civilized—as close as Hamarsson ever got, anyway. Even his clothes were clean, which was a change from when Mat had seen him a few days ago.

"Hamarsson," Mat said by way of greeting.

They stared at each other. Mat had no idea what Hamarsson was thinking, but Mat was recalling Hamarsson up on his cabin roof, shirtless and irritatingly sexy. Close up, Mat was able to see his pale green eyes, at odds with his darker features and permanently tanned skin.

Birdy's head swiveled as she looked between the two men, her eyes narrowing when her gaze landed on Hamarsson again.

"Dempsey."

"Why does it feel like there is about to be a WWF smackdown here? Sheriff, do I need to call Holstrom or Jones?"

Mat returned Birdy's concerned look. "It's fine, Birdy, and I told you to call me Dempsey. See how easy it was for Hamarsson here?" Mat gestured toward the man in question.

"Do you have time?" Hamarsson asked.

Time? Time for what? Time to wind the clock back and change everything? Time for a quickie in the men's room? Mat battled back the heat threatening to rise to his face.

"Sure, I have a minute. Come on back."

"Sir!" Birdy burst out.

"Birdy?"

"Protocol!"

"By all means, Deputy Flynn. Please bring him back to my desk when you are finished."

Mat walked back to his desk, happy for the short reprieve while Birdy collected Hamarsson's ID and made him sign a waiver.

Soon enough it was over, and Birdy was leading Niall Hamarsson back to Mat's desk.

"Have a seat." Mat indicated the chair sort of by his desk. "What happened to your arm? Hand?"

Hamarsson lowered himself into the plastic chair. He made it look like something from an elementary school room. When Hamarsson had been up on his roof the other day, Mat hadn't been able to appreciate the true breadth of his shoulders, his slim waist, and the fact that somewhere along the way he had shot up close to six foot four. Mat himself was over six feet, but Hamarsson was taller. His beard had grown out farther, and in Mat's opinion it needed a trim before it started looking like an overgrown hedge. Hamarsson touched his face with his good hand as if he could read Mat's thoughts.

"I can't shave and keep my hand out of the shower water at the same time. The damn bandage is a pain in the ass."

"What happened?"

Niall frowned. "You care?"

"I care about all the citizens of Piedras."

Some bleak emotion darkened Hamarsson's eyes, but it passed before Mat could categorize it.

"Of course you do. I cut myself working on the cabin. Now I have stitches and time on my hands."

Mat leaned back in his chair. It squeaked. "Why are you here, Hamarsson? When I stopped at the cabin, you told me to get off your property."

"I'm not here to see *you*, Dempsey. I'm here to see the Piedras County Sheriff."

"And here I am," Mat said slowly and clearly, knowing Hamarsson hadn't missed that Mat was sheriff these days.

"I'm not here to start a pissing war with you. I'm here to offer my assistance."

Mat sat up abruptly, his chair rolling a little backward so he had to steady himself.

"What kind of assistance could you possibly offer?"

"Chastity Reynolds." Hamarsson tossed the name out like a piece of candy at a parade; Mat could pick it up, or he could leave it sitting in the road.

"So, one minute you're hiding out on your grandparents' old property trying to lay low, and the next you're here offering assistance? That doesn't strike me as something you would do."

"You know nothing about me, Dempsey, and don't presume to now. I'm offering my assistance as a seasoned fifteen-year-plus SPD detective, the last ten in homicide, and nothing further. You and I both know you'd be a fool not to accept my offer. How well trained are your deputies? How many extra hours of specialty classes can Piedras County afford to send them to? Do they know how to process a crime scene? Interrogate witnesses? Shit, I bet they're related to most of the people on the island, which makes the process that much more difficult."

Only a few steps past bedraggled, and Hamarsson managed to be an arrogant asshole.

Hamarsson was right—of course he was right—but his words and implications pissed Mat off. Who did he think he was, coming to the island and interfering where he didn't belong? A very quiet voice whispered, *He does belong here, and you'd be a fool not to accept his offer.* Mat ignored it. Maybe if Hamarsson weren't such an arrogant asshole, he would—what? Mat would let him take the case over? Mat would let him see the skimpy file they'd put together on Chas Reynolds? He had some pride.

"I have faith in my deputies and staff. We'll bring Chastity's killer to justice."

Hamarsson looked up at the ceiling. Mat followed his gaze. The ceiling tiles were different shades of white, and several were yellowed and stained where the roof had leaked a few years ago. There was no money in the budget to replace them. Hamarsson looked back down, catching Mat's stare. He stood up, looming over Mat where he sat in his desk chair. Mat was reasonably sure the looming was on purpose; he didn't imagine Niall Hamarsson did anything without purpose.

After staring at Mat for a long moment, gauging, passing judgment on both Mat and his department, Niall said, "Whatever," dismissing Mat and the entire department as he turned and left.

Mat ground his molars together. He had the urge to tackle Hamarsson to the ground and pound some sense, or at least manners, into him. Instead, he waited until he heard the reception door open and then close again before he released the lungful of air he was holding.

"That went well!" Birdy commented.

"I suppose you heard everything?"

She had the grace to blush but, in fact, the reason the work area was open was because he wanted his deputies to be able to hear and know what was happening. How many times had they solved something because one deputy overheard something another deputy was talking about and put two and two together? It was a high percentage.

"He's not very nice."

"Birdy, your family's been here on the island for a while, right?"

She nodded. "Forever."

"Longer than Hamarsson's, for sure."

"Yeah, why?"

Mat didn't know why he'd asked. It was just one of those

things he wondered. A lot of people came and went, but a core of his citizens were serious longtimers. In the past few years more newcomers had been moving to Piedras and the other islands, thinking it was cheaper than the mainland. It was, in a sense, but jobs were hard to find and most were low paying, and traveling back and forth on the ferry system was not easy on the wallet.

"I'm just thinking."

"Wondering why Niall Hamarsson would be back after all these years?"

Mat nodded, looking out the door where Hamarsson had disappeared from view.

Birdy shrugged. "Maybe he's going to sell?"

One thing Mat could not imagine was Niall Hamarsson selling the piece of paradise his grandparents had left him.

ELEVEN

HAMARSSON

Niall stalked out of the station wondering why the fuck he'd stopped there in the first place. Dempsey was never going to admit he could use help. He viewed Niall as something nasty stuck to the bottom of his shoe, much as the rest of the residents did. Most of the islanders thought his grandparents had made a big mistake believing they could bring home a traumatized orphan who'd lived on the streets most of his life and settle him in on Piedras. The fuckers had worked hard to prove it to them too.

An odd loose piece inside himself had shifted into place that long-ago day when he stepped out of Morfar's beat-up Datsun station wagon and saw the beach beyond the cabin for the first time. He'd been at the home for a few months by the time Josephine and Od claimed him, but the horror of the dark closet hadn't faded. There were no closets outside, only the wide-open strait and rocky beach.

Time on his hands was going to be an issue. He didn't need or want time to think. He needed to keep busy and moving, and now that the pain meds were gone, his brain was turning back on. He'd stayed at Soper's place for two nights, deciding when he woke that morning that he'd infringed on the good doctor's hospitality enough; it was time to get back out to the cabin. So when Soper went in to work that afternoon, he'd had Soper drop him off at the lot where they'd moved his car on Sunday—ticket-free, thanks to Soper pulling some strings. He hated that he owed the man a favor. Stopping in at the sheriff's office had been an impulse, one he wouldn't be giving in to again.

Fucking Mat Dempsey. The man was a fool not to accept his offer of help.

Niall snapped out of his brooding when something cold hit his cheek. He looked up and realized it was snowing—at least, one single snowflake had made its way down from the clouds to brush against his face. An unfamiliar kid-like emotion sparked in his gut, and his anger faded away. He couldn't help but break into a grin. He hoped it would snow hard enough that he could build a snowman—well, if his hand wasn't too fucked up, anyway. He couldn't remember it snowing on the island more than a few times while he'd lived here.

Driving with a fucked-up right hand was difficult (and technically illegal with his arm in a sling), but Niall managed it. Being left-handed, he'd had to deal with this kind of shit all his life. He gave himself a pat on the back for not buying the stick shift he'd wanted at the time. Pointing the car in the direction of the cabin, he drove, slowly and carefully. The snow began coming down a little harder. It would be cold at night and he'd miss Soper's cushy mattress, but he'd slept out in colder weather.

Darkness fell while he drove, the Subaru's headlights illuminating scant white flakes drifting down to the road. The clock on the dashboard told him it was just after six in the evening. During the long summer days, it was easy to forget how dark it got in the winter. A lot of people couldn't handle it. The dark, the gray, and the rain made it seem like living underwater—or maybe in a cave.

Niall loved the dark winter days. He loved the rain and the clouds, always had. Maybe it was because they made him feel somehow hidden, protected from others' critical stares and prying eyes. If people couldn't see him, they couldn't judge him.

He'd taken one of those personality tests once. Trey had hounded him about it until Niall caved; he smiled bitterly, remembering Trey's demand.

"It'll be fun!" Trey said.

Niall'd doubted it. How would an online personality test be fun? But he did it, because Trey was nothing if not persistent.

The test hadn't told him anything Niall didn't know about himself already. He was extremely introverted. Big surprise. Being social exhausted him. Big surprise. Also, he held himself and others to impossibly high expectations. He'd laughed at that —shouldn't everyone hold themselves to high expectations? Wasn't that how people improved themselves?

Trey used the results to badger him about their relationship, and for whatever reason, Niall had sort of let him. With Trey, it had often been easier for Niall to go along than to resist. Arguing with Trey exhausted him, and, he admitted to himself in the dark of his car, Trey had been simple. Until the end, anyway. Niall worked, he'd text Trey and let him know he was home, and Trey would come over—or they'd go out to eat, since Niall didn't cook and Trey didn't like to. They'd end up in bed together, and the sex was fine. Maybe that's why they lasted as long as they did.

Trey was nothing like Mat Dempsey. Trey was well coiffured and searched out the latest fashion. Trey was slender and came up just past Niall's shoulder. Compared to Mat Dempsey—they were almost polar opposites. Niall had a hard time imagining Mat browsing in a high-end clothing store or paying for an expensive haircut every three or four weeks. Dempsey was first and foremost a cop. And Niall hated that he found himself attracted to him. Still attracted to him. Dempsey wasn't *how* Niall realized he was gay; he'd kind of always known. But once he'd turned sixteen, Mat had starred in a lot of his fantasies. Juvenile fantasies, the kind where a kid like Niall could have a boyfriend and belong on Piedras Island. Impossible dreams.

He flicked the turn signal on, even though no one was on the road behind him, and bumped down his driveway. *His grandparents' driveway.* Thinking about Dempsey pissed him off. Piedras County could use his help, as a consultant if nothing else. He didn't *need* to investigate Chastity Reynolds's murder, but it wasn't unusual for cases like hers to be cracked because two cops were sitting around brainstorming and they came up with a connection or idea that they wouldn't have considered alone. His injured hand protested, and Niall realized he'd been unconsciously trying to clench his fingers into a fist.

The headlights landed on the cabin and the pitiful tent. In the past two days it had sagged significantly without Niall there to make sure the stakes were firmly in the ground each night. He hadn't exactly told Soper he was sleeping in a tent. The man hadn't been home until late in the evening last night, and unlike the night before, Soper hadn't seemed like he felt like making small talk.

Soper was a nice guy, and Niall was sure the man was gay. He was good-looking in a kind of midwestern boy-next-door way, but Niall wasn't attracted to him. Maybe he was broken inside. That would explain why he was only attracted to assholes, not nice, safe men like Soper. Instead he gravitated to men like Trey—who was a user—and ones like Dempsey, who he couldn't trust.

"Christ."

If he didn't trust Dempsey, why the hell had he offered to help with the Reynolds case? Niall rubbed his face with his good hand. He hadn't shaved at Soper's, too afraid he'd fall or do something else stupid in the shower. His face itched like anything, and he wasn't fond of the grizzly bear look. Maybe tomorrow he'd see if there was a barber in Hidden Harbor.

He extricated himself from his car, shivering when the cold burrowed through his clothing and reached his skin. He should probably invest in heavier clothing. Maybe once his hand healed he'd head to Seattle and pack a more practical bag.

Inside the tent, the half-empty bottle of Jack Daniel's tempted him, a treacherous siren. Niall heeded Soper's warning about drinking. Instead, he swallowed down a few ibuprofen tablets followed by the last stale bagel. After he wolfed it down, it sat in his stomach like a rock. More groceries would be a good idea.

It was a long time before Niall was able to fall asleep. When he woke, the tent was brighter than it had been previous mornings—and warmer. He crawled out of his sleeping bag and unzipped the tent to poke his head outside, discovering the world was now covered with a glittering, thin layer of snow. Ignoring the chill, Niall fumbled his boots on—he couldn't tie them with his stiff fingers—and stood up so he could see more than just what was directly in front of the tent.

Everything around him was white, with just the hint of dark green at the tops of the evergreens. Even the rocky beach had a fine coat of snow, making it look like a very lumpy blanket. It took Niall a minute before he realized he was smiling. As quickly as he could with his injury, he got his clothes straightened. Closing up the tent behind himself, he stepped out into the snowy wonderland. He knew the snow wouldn't last, but it felt like a gift from the gods and he was going to do his best to enjoy it.

As he was leaving the office Tuesday night, Mat heard a familiar voice call to him.

"Dempsey! Where're you headed this late in the day?"

Mat twisted around to see Marshal striding toward him in the small Piedras County Sheriff's Office parking lot.

"Finally home. I'm hoping" —Mat crossed his fingers like a kid would—"to get some sleep tonight before this predicted winter storm rolls in and the entire island acts like they've never seen a snowflake before."

Marshal grinned. "Mat... they mostly *haven't* seen snow before, or at least not very often."

"Exactly," Mat grumbled.

"If it does snow, I expect I'll have a few overnight guests at my house."

Mat shook his head. "Marshal, you don't have to offer a bed to everyone. Call us, we can get people home."

"I already had a guest the past couple of nights. And not my normal ailing senior."

"Oh?" Mat's memory flashed back to Hamarsson, his hand

wrapped and arm in a sling yet looking less rough then he had when Mat had stopped by a few days ago.

"Niall Hamarsson. Do you know him?"

Trust Marshal to take home the one man on the island Mat wanted. Couldn't have. Wanted.

"Mat?"

"What?" His face heated, and he hoped Marshal wouldn't notice. "Yes, I know Hamarsson. His family—well, his grandparents—moved to Piedras in the late 1930s or early 1940s, I believe."

"So they weren't what you call an 'old family'?" Marshal teased.

"No, the Delacombes and Reynoldses were the first White families. I think Birdy's family has been here for a couple hundred years."

When Marshal moved onto the island, Mat had made sure he was aware of the island's complicated history when it came to the residents. There was a kind of slow-boil feud that had been on hold during the years Claribel had been married to Frank Reynolds. When she tossed him out, tensions between the families rose once again. Of course, Mat hadn't been born when the two families had taken to settling arguments with weapons and intimidation, but he'd listened to his dad tell stories about livestock theft, moonshine, even attempted murder.

"No, the Hamarssons weren't an old family, but they were good people, well-liked on the island. Why was he at your place?"

Marshal raised his eyebrows. "He isn't particularly talkative, but from what I gathered, he's doing some work on his property and gashed himself pretty well. He was lucky he didn't need surgery, only ended up with the Soper special—eight stitches, four on the inside and four on the surface. He'll be fine if he gives it a rest, which I suspect he won't."

A stab of worry shot through Mat's gut. Hamarsson certainly was elusive, and Mat needed to learn how to read the man, but he agreed with Marshal—Niall Hamarsson wouldn't take it easy. It wasn't in his blood.

Snow began falling more seriously on Mat's drive home, but he still thought it likely wouldn't stick. His mom would be waiting for him with dinner ready. She spoiled him.

To be fair, after his father died in a freak boating accident and Mat moved home, things had been very different. Mat had never known two people more devoted to each other than his parents. Her husband's death devastated her, and the first few months he was home it was Mat who did the cooking and cleaning, making sure his mother ate, ventured outside, exercised.

It was only when the sheriff's position came up for election that his mom snapped out of it, insisting Mat run "so one of those Delacombes or even more worthless Reynoldses" wasn't elected. Mat had won by a landslide—likely because of his father's reputation, but he felt he'd proved over the years he was worthy.

The house was lit up, and warm air rushed out when Mat opened the front door.

"Hi, sweetie!" his mom called from the kitchen.

"Hey, Mom, what smells so good?" Mat answered, shaking his head that she thought he was sweet.

"Lasagna, from scratch."

Mat's mouth started to water. His mom's lasagna was famous. People begged her to bring it to potlucks and other island functions. When he asked her for the recipe, she always laughed and shook her head at him.

"Nope, this is my secret."

He peeled off his winter layers, coat and sweater, and then

his shoes before making his way upstairs to change out of his uniform. When he came back down, his mom was waiting for him in the dining room.

"I heard the Hamarsson boy was in the emergency room," she said as he sat down.

Mat blinked away that damn image of Hamarsson towering above him, no shirt, the tattoos Mat hadn't quite been able to make out gracing his chest and arm. His mother's grapevine was impressive, seeing as Mat had heard less than an hour ago.

"Did you hear me? Is there something wrong?"

"No, nothing's wrong, sorry. And yes, I heard from Marshal that he cut himself and had to get stitches."

"I wonder what he's going to do with the cabin?"

"I don't know, Mom, why don't you ask him?" he snapped.

Mat immediately felt guilty for his sharp words. There was no reason to take his irritation and frustration out on his mother.

"What did you do today?" he asked, trying to change the course of the conversation.

Alyson smiled. "I facetimed with your sisters. They both pestered me about moving in with them again, which I only put up with so I could see the grandbabies."

Mat's sister Fiona had twin boys. They were close to two years old and just starting to really cause trouble. Ella had a girl. Riley was six and, in Mat's biased opinion, was the cutest, smartest human ever to be born. Both sisters lived in Texas, a long way for visits.

"Would you want to live with them? Or near them?" Mat asked. He'd asked before, but maybe the grandkids had changed his mom's mind.

"As much as I love both your sisters and the grandbabies, I don't see moving away from Piedras. This is my home—my roots are here. When they're older, I'll have them come for the summers. Riley is ready now, in my opinion, but Ella doesn't think so. Why wouldn't Riley be ready for Camp Grandma?"

Mat chuckled. Camp Grandma would involve a great deal of spoiling but also hikes and crafting and swimming in the waters off the island. He'd get to teach Riley how to kayak and sail.

"What about Sean? Have you talked to him lately?"

Mat and his older brother didn't really speak and hadn't since high school.

As if reading his mind, his mom responded, "I wish the two of you would get over whatever it is you fought about. It's been years now. Let bygones be bygones. We can't replace family. You'd think with your father dead it would've brought you closer."

Some family he could do without, including his older brother.

Mat took a deep breath. "Mom, we've talked about this. It's not me, it's Sean. When he pulls his head out and changes his attitude, then maybe we can repair our relationship. I'm willing if he is."

"I wish I could do something. I don't like it when my family argues."

Mat shoved another bite of lasagna in his mouth so he wouldn't say what he was thinking: that he didn't think Sean would be changing his ways. How his parents ended up raising a conservative, repressed son like Sean, Mat had no clue.

"Anyway, I saw Marshal today."

"How is my other son doing?"

"He's fine. You know, helping everyone out."

"Is he seeing anyone?"

"No, Mom, as far as I know Marshal isn't seeing anyone."

As far as Mat knew, he and Marshal were the only two gay men on the island. He'd thought about coming out to his mom. There was no reason for Mat to think his mother would treat him any differently if she knew he liked men, but there was no reason for him to come out either. He and Marshal were never meant to be a couple.

He hadn't recognized his sexuality until high school. Sophomore year physical education had been a nightmare of learning to look at everything but the other boys in the locker room. There'd only been one boy in particular, but Mat didn't need his ass getting kicked by the larger juniors and seniors.

Niall Hamarsson had grown out of being the skinny, awkward child who first came to the island. Then he'd proven to everyone he wasn't stupid by graduating with his class—and cum laude on top of it all—after his rocky start. Mat hadn't been able to keep his eyes off Niall as a teen: broody and mysterious. He'd rarely talked to the other students, his remoteness making him a target for bullies like Mat's brother and the Reynoldses of their generation.

Niall'd never talked in classes or called attention to himself in any way, but from sophomore year forward, Mat knew where he was and was drawn to Niall as if he were a magnet. Every expression, mood, emotion of Niall's Mat wanted to learn. In class Niall often appeared lost in thought or memory, and Mat had always wondered what was going on inside his head. What made him sad and quiet, why he kept himself separated from the rest of the students.

His mom spoke again. "I worry about you being alone. It's not right. You're not the type of person who likes to be by yourself. What will happen to you when I'm gone if you haven't found the right person yet?"

"Mom, what's gotten into you? Is there something I need to know? Did you have a doctor's appointment I didn't know about?"

She laughed. "I'm good—you know, except for the getting old part. I just know you, my son, and you are not the type who chooses to be alone."

"I have you."

"I've made my point."

Mat opened his mouth, the words "I'm gay" ready to spill across his lips. Instead he said, "Great lasagna, Mom."

Alyson gave Mat an odd look, as if she knew he'd been about to say something else, but thankfully she didn't question him.

THIRTEEN
HAMARSSON

The phrase "idle hands" popped into his head, and Niall actually looked at his hands to confirm they were, indeed, idle. He was bored. The snow had melted within a couple of hours, leaving no trace behind except in random shadows where daylight couldn't reach. That was usually how it was with snow in the region; it disappeared even faster than it appeared.

He couldn't work on the cabin with his hand messed up. He didn't feel like reading a book, and even if he had felt like reading, he didn't have a book. It was damn cold. Sitting in his tent was uncomfortable, but the inside of the cabin made him shudder. He was looking forward to getting back to work on it. He wasn't the carpenter his grandfather had been, but he was sure he could learn.

Instead, Niall thought about Chastity Reynolds, rolling what he'd learned from Soper around inside his head. Wondering what kind of headway had been made on her murder, if any. Dempsey had been mighty defensive when Niall offered his help. Niall could relate; Piedras was Dempsey's turf, and someone under his protection had been murdered. Niall'd probably feel the same way. But, in his opinion, there was no reason—other than pride—for Dempsey to refuse his assistance.

What would it hurt for him to stop by the Reynoldses' on his way into Killegen's Point for more groceries? He recognized this was flawed thinking. There were many things wrong about stopping by the Reynoldses', including the fact that Mat had refused his help. Niall probably wouldn't learn anything anyway.

If the Reynoldses asked, he'd tell them he was a private citizen looking into Chastity's death: the truth, just not the whole truth. Niall'd found over the years that if he acted like he was in charge, people followed along—usually. It was always good to interview people where they felt most comfortable. Often they told you more than they intended.

He ignored the shrill voice repeating that this was a bad idea, that if Dempsey found out he was going to be pissed off. Niall shrugged. He'd had plenty of people angry at him throughout his career, and he'd always managed to weather the storm.

From the tidbits Niall'd coerced out of Soper, he had no reason to believe Chastity's family were suspects—except, of course, history had consistently proven more often than not that the perpetrator was someone close to the victim. Regardless, family almost always knew something that could point investigators the right way.

The highway was empty in both directions. Niall turned the Subaru right, toward Killegen's Point and where he recalled the Reynoldses living past the Delacombes, almost on the border of the small town. He doubted any remaining Reynoldses had moved away—after all, it was prime property. After stopping there, he'd go into town for groceries.

He'd forgotten, or maybe he'd never known, what the Reynolds compound was like. The place was a FEMA disaster zone. After ignoring several No Trespassing notices, he parked his car next to a tractor that looked like it hadn't run in decades. The original house had to be well over one hundred years old and had fallen into complete disrepair, one entire side open to the elements and the porch slumped to an impossible angle with the front door permanently ajar. There were at least two mobile homes—no, there was a third, an older one blackberries had laid siege to. He couldn't see the windows through the spiny brush. It appeared the Reynoldses had moved out of the house and into successive mobile homes once each prior residence had become unlivable.

While there was nothing inherently wrong with mobile homes, these were all obviously well on their way to the same fate as the broken house. For the first time, Niall considered if coming here had been a bad idea.

Everything was still, as if the Douglas firs and cedars were holding their breath, waiting to see what was going to happen. A curtain twitched in one of the windows in the newer-looking mobile home.

Mentally shrugging, Niall got out and slammed his car door shut, a sort of announcement of his presence, and purposefully approached the home. Before he raised his fist to knock, its door opened.

A male voice he recognized snarled, "What do you want?" At least that's what Niall though he said, although it sounded more like "Whaddyawant."

Niall assumed what some called his cop face. "I'd like to ask some questions about Chastity Reynolds. I'm Detective Hamarsson."

"Hamarsson." The man opened the door a little wider. "Aren't you a cop in Seattle these days?"

One of his childhood nemeses, Martin Reynolds, stood between the door and its frame, holding it so Niall couldn't see past him to the inside. Despite the cold, Martin wore nothing but a grimy t-shirt with the sleeves cut off and baggy shorts of an indeterminate color. The temperature inside Martin's home must have been set high. The warm air was rank and thick as it flowed outside.

"I am, but I'm not here to arrest anyone, just asking some questions."

This was one of those times when Niall was glad for his late growth spurt. Sometimes, like on airplanes, being six four was a pain, but times like this, when he was faced with a piece of shit like Martin, his size came in handy. Most of the time he didn't intentionally intimidate suspects, or witnesses, but he'd happily intimidate the shit out of Martin Reynolds.

"I recognize you, Hamarsson. Piece of shit," Martin spat.

"And I, unfortunately, recognize you, Martin. Believe me, I feel the same about you as you do about me. But I'm not here about you. I'm here about your sister's death. Is there anything you can tell me about her? Had you talked to Chastity recently? Did she live here with you?"

Martin narrowed his eyes at Niall as if he could somehow read his thoughts, see where his questions might be leading.

Sneering, he said, "I'll tell you what I told our useless sheriff. Chastity didn't understand the power of QAnon. She said I was ruining my life and that QAnon was nothing but a hack. Look who's dead now. Not me." Martin pointed at his chest in case Niall was confused. "Somebody taught the girl a lesson." Martin leaned closer, and unfortunately, Niall was able to get a glimpse of the inside of his trailer. The kitchen was trashed, dishes and old frozen food containers piled precariously high in the tiny sink behind him. Niall recognized a foul odor as rotting food.

"You believe QAnon killed your sister? Seems like quite a leap. Why would she be important to them?"

Martin shrugged. His thin, greasy hair was slick against his skull. "Ears and eyes are everywhere. Maybe she was killed so they could show their powerful reach? She said she was going to show me how wrong I was about them. I bet she stirred up something she shouldn't a' messed with. Now get off my property before I decide to use this shotgun I have here next to the door."

Niall didn't budge. He crossed his arms over his chest before asking another question, mostly to prove to Martin that he wasn't scared of him. He had little doubt there was a shotgun handy. He *wasn't* scared of Martin, but it would be very inconvenient if he got shot and had to go back to the ER. He didn't think Dempsey would have much sympathy.

"You aren't sorry your sister is dead? You don't want her killer caught?"

Martin shrugged again. "If Chastity had to die because the powers that be thought that was the right thing, I'm not going to argue with them. Have you followed him? What he knows, what he can find out—that's where it's at. You need to pull your head out and realize who is really controlling this country, the world! Every single thing, there is a link, a connection—you are the one who's blind to the truth."

Niall didn't like where Martin was heading with his belief in a conspiracy theory known to be started by a bored video gamer. He seemed sincere enough, though. He honestly believed it was possible his sister had met her death at the hands of a shadowy conspiracy group and seemed fine with it.

"If you remember anything, stop by the sheriff's office." Niall turned in the direction of his car.

"You come around here again and I'll use my shotgun." Martin's words floated after him.

Slowly and deliberately, Niall crossed the space between the mobile home and the Subaru. He opened the car door and sat behind the wheel, watching Martin Reynolds watch him, then he carefully backed up the potholed driveway and out onto the empty road, thankful for four-wheel drive. He'd wasted a trip, and if and when Dempsey found out about it, he was going to be pissed.

Minutes later, in Killegen's Point, Niall stopped in at Chester's to pick up a selection of groceries, Martin Reynolds never far from his mind. He wondered if Martin really remembered him; Niall remembered Martin. Lost in thought, Niall paid for the groceries and made his way out to his car, where he stashed them before heading over to the general store.

Martin had been one of those kids who sensed others' weaknesses and exposed them to anyone who would listen. When Niall started high school, Martin was a senior and had nothing better to do than to torment Niall—he certainly hadn't been studying. Niall quickly learned the only place on the school grounds to hide from Martin was the library. By the time he graduated, he'd read just about every book the school had.

In the back corner of the store he found what he was looking for, a small selection of paperbacks for sale. He picked out a couple with interesting-looking covers and took them to the front to pay.

"Nah," Fred waved his money aside. "Just bring 'em back when you're done with them."

Niall nodded. "Okay, thanks."

It had been something of a reprieve for Niall when Martin finally graduated. Niall suspected the teachers all got together and agreed to pass him, no matter what his grades were; he was a bully and general troublemaker. But graduating only meant Martin couldn't torture him at school. All the other places on the island were fair game because Martin never left Piedras.

Seeing Martin today and knowing himself to be the better man hadn't brought Niall any satisfaction. And now he'd purposely stirred up a hornet's nest. How long would it be before Martin worked himself into some sort of righteous anger and came looking for him?

Probably not as long as Niall hoped. Yeah, idle hands had

definitely gotten him in trouble, and he only had himself to blame.

~

Even before he arrived at the section of driveway where the brush opened up and he could see the strait, Niall sensed that something was wrong, very wrong. Maybe he smelled the smoke, even though the wind was blowing the other direction. Maybe there was something else the primitive part of his brain kept an eye on and his conscious mind didn't recognize—but he knew to his core that something was wrong. Not until his car emerged from the cover of the trees and shrubs was he able to see what it was.

Martin had been quick, that was for sure. There was no point in Niall rushing out of the car—even if he could try to save the structure with one good hand, there was no hose or bucket for him to use. All the water he needed only a hundred feet away, and he couldn't carry enough to save Morfar and Mormor's home.

With his mind's eye, he saw their ghosts twisting back and forth, dancing within the flames engulfing the cabin. Whoever it had been—Martin, logically—had to have used gasoline. In this damp weather, there was no other way the old building would have burned so quickly. As he watched, the wind shifted and a lick of flame reached out toward his pathetic tent. The fabric didn't burn so much as melted and shrank until it was an unrecognizable lump of nothing, his cheap sleeping bag gone along with his only shelter.

In a sort of daze, Niall opened the door and got out of his car. There was nothing he could do but watch as his belongings and the only real home he'd ever had turned to dust. The old saying was true: he hadn't known what he had until it was gone.

Gone forever.

How long he stood there next to his car, cold and numb, watching the embers spark and snap, Niall had no idea. The sky darkened quickly as the winter sun headed toward the horizon, and Niall wondered if he should try to clean anything up, if he should see if there was anything to salvage. Darkness would make searching more difficult.

Slowly he forced his cold, stiff body to move toward the remains of the cabin. He felt as if he'd been the only witness to the last gasps of a living thing. The sight of the smoldering wood was killing him inside. He wanted to scream and yell, but no one would hear him, and the effort would be as useless as it had ever been.

Crying had never helped him in the past, so why would it now? Christ, even his phone was destroyed. He'd tossed the thing into one corner of the tent where he didn't have to see it.

With no clear objective, Niall drifted closer to the remains and scuffed his boot through the ash of the porch. Heavy-gauge wire on which a colorful flower basket had likely once hung poked out, a skeleton now. He kicked at it. In the dying light, he spied broken crockery—a cup, maybe, or a casserole dish, he didn't know.

He didn't know.

He'd thought he'd have time, and now that was stolen from him too.

FOURTEEN
DEMPSEY

"Um, Sheriff?"

Mat looked up, about to comment that yes, he was still sher-iff, but Birdy seemed apprehensive. Mat immediately went on high alert.

"What's up, Deputy?"

"Dispatch just took a call from Martin Reynolds. He claims he had a trespasser on his property and wants us to do some-thing about it."

"What fool would venture out there? He's got the damn place booby-trapped with god knows what."

"Um, sir, Sheriff, he said the name of the trespasser was Niall Hamarsson."

Mat threw his pen down. It hit the top of his desk with a satisfying smack, but it wasn't as satisfying as it would be to get his hands around Hamarsson's neck. He stood up too quickly and his chair shot backward, hitting the wall. "What the everloving fuck does he think he's up to?"

"Sir!"

"Excuse me, Deputy. I'll put a dollar in the swear jar later."

Mat grabbed the keys to his cruiser out of his top drawer and his coat off the back of his chair.

"Are you going to talk to him?"

"I'm going to talk to Hamarsson, if that's who you mean."

Birdy nodded. "Would you like me along to assist?"

"No, thank you, Deputy, I'll take this one on my own. But I'll check in with you after I get home if you're worried."

"No, sir, I don't think you have anything to worry about. The man did have his arm in a sling, so I don't think he's that dangerous."

Mat sped through the dark, furious with Hamarsson for getting Martin riled up, for sticking his nose in Mat's jurisdiction. He had no business—Mat had very clearly told the man he didn't want his "assistance." The only reason Mat could think of for Hamarsson to be out talking to Reynolds was Chastity Reynolds's murder. The infuriating man was interfering with an active investigation, god damn him. Mat had half a mind to drag Hamarsson back down to the station and read him the riot act.

What a selfish asshole. Mat specifically told him to butt out, and Hamarsson had immediately butted *in*. The island population was already wound up enough. Mat didn't need an overgrown Neanderthal stomping around making everything worse.

He pounded a fist against the steering wheel, imagining how satisfying it would feel if he punched Niall like he wanted to. He wouldn't, but the desire to was bubbling to the surface, fueled by his anger.

By the time he turned onto the Hamarsson access road, Mat was thoroughly worked up. The drive had not calmed him down; he was furious with Hamarsson and was going to give him a piece of his mind. The cruiser's headlights broke through the brush along the drive, and for just a flash, Mat thought he'd taken the wrong turn in his anger and distraction because the Hamarsson cabin wasn't where it should be. His lights lit up the Subaru he knew belonged to Hamarsson, but the cabin wasn't there. Leaving his lights on, Mat turned off his engine and got out of the cruiser. As soon as he opened the car door, the remnants of acrid smoke assaulted his eyes and nose.

"What the fuck? What the everloving fuck?" Mat asked aloud. He thought distractedly that if Birdy had heard him cussing for the last fifteen minutes, he'd owe at least five dollars to the station swear jar.

Without thinking, Mat stumbled over tall tufts of grass and brambles to the spot where the cabin had stood for so long. Had stood. In its place was a smoking pile of debris.

"Jesus Christ."

Why the fuck hadn't anyone reported a fire? Had no one seen it? Although this time of year, the area was not highly populated. The wind was blowing out toward the strait, which was probably why Mat hadn't smelled it until he got out of his car.

Quelling his panic, Mat carefully circled the still-warm ashes, choking back the thought he might have to identify another body. The anger he'd felt toward Hamarsson was gone. In its place was a desperate hope he'd find the man alive. Surely Mat would be able to tell if there was a body—it took a lot of heat for a human to be cremated. He'd never investigated arson when he was in San Francisco, that hadn't been his unit, but he knew what to look for.

Back at his car, Mat popped the trunk and grabbed his flashlight. Flicking on the bulb, he swept the beam back and forth over the smoking remains. He didn't see anything that looked human to him, but the fact remained that Hamarsson's Subaru was parked in its spot a little away from the burned-out cabin. Niall had to be close though. The man had nowhere else to go.

"Niall! Hamarsson!" Mat shouted, trying to calm his racing

heart, to use his years of training and police work to his advantage. Panicking would do nothing, help no one. If Niall was wandering in shock or, worse, *injured* and in shock, Mat needed to call Dispatch and get a search crew out, stat. An ambulance —Mat would call Marshal, he'd be able to—Mat's thoughts threatened to spiral again. At the very least, he needed to have the volunteer fire crew come out and douse the embers just in case. They did not need another fire started by an ember or spark.

He twisted in place, moving the flashlight back and forth, sweeping the beam through the dark night. The light landed on something out on the beach, something out of place. Mat slowly moved toward the shape, and as he drew closer, it resolved into Hamarsson.

The man sat hunched over his knees on a log amid the rocks and sand. It looked to Mat like he was staring out over the black water of the strait. It couldn't be comfortable. Jesus, he wasn't wearing a coat, only a t-shirt and jeans, his bandaged hand cradled against his chest as if he'd hurt it again. Or as if he was mourning.

"Hamarsson! Niall! Are you all right?" Mat called out while he picked his way from the cabin to the beach. Niall didn't move or answer. When he reached him, Mat grabbed his shoulder— ready to shake him, demand a reply, anything so Mat would know he was okay. Residual anger from earlier threatened to resurface. More likely fear, Mat acknowledged. Before Mat opened his mouth to repeat himself, he shined the flashlight directly toward Niall's face.

Hamarsson's face was perfectly blank. He didn't acknowledge Mat's presence in any way, just stared unseeing out over the black water. Mat looked out in the same direction. All he could see was dark waves and the hint of a moon. Any stars were hidden by cloud cover.

Carefully, Mat moved around to face Niall, kneeling in the

damp sand in front of the log. Mat's knees complained, but he ignored the twinges.

"Niall, look at me." Mat took off one glove and gently stroked Niall's cheek with the backs of his fingers. "Niall. Look at me," he repeated.

Ever so slowly, Niall's eyes, pale pools of unfathomable pain, moved so he was looking at Mat instead of the wide expanse of water.. Mat wanted to make the pain go away, he wanted back the fire and anger he'd seen in their last encounter. Anything but this... blackness.

"Niall, can you hear me? Are you hurt?" Mat spoke loudly enough to be heard over the surf.

Niall shivered. Mat felt the ripples of Niall's body underneath his fingertips, still resting against Niall's cheek. Hastily, he pulled his coat off and draped it around Niall's shoulders. Maybe the warmth from his body would transfer to Niall. He needed to get Niall inside, but there was no inside close by anymore.

"Niall, can you stand?"

Niall continued to stare without answering.

As gently as he was able, Mat urged the other man upward with a hand under Niall's elbow. Niall was unpleasantly compliant and Mat missed the arrogant, defiant man he knew. Niall swayed slightly before Mat put one arm around his shoulders and turned him toward the cruiser, carrying as much of the larger man's weight as he was able. He wasn't giving Niall a choice about where he was taking him. If Niall ended up angry about it, Mat would ask forgiveness later, but the man needed to be cared for now.

Slowly the two of them stumbled together to the car. Several times Mat had to grab Niall to keep him from falling to his knees; it was a long way down and Mat wasn't confident he could lift him back up. By the time they reached the cruiser, Mat was sweating profusely despite the cold winter air. He propped Niall against the car while he opened the passenger door.

"Sit down."

Niall obeyed him, which scared the shit out of Mat. Once Niall was seated, Mat pulled the seat belt around his hips and fastened it. Then he went around the front of the car and got behind the wheel. He didn't have the time to warn his mother he was bringing Niall home, so he chose not to worry about it. She would do the right thing, and together they'd take care of him.

FIFTEEN

HAMARSSON

"Niall? Niall?" Dempsey kept repeating his name, and Niall wanted to tell him to quit talking, but he also wanted to hear his name from the man's lips again. It reminded him he was alive.

"Niall, goddammit, I know you're in there. Say something, you motherfucker."

Niall felt a thread of amusement curl up from the dark depths of his soul. He enjoyed hearing Dempsey all riled up and pissed off. The timbre of Dempsey's voice changed. "Hamarsson, I know we need to talk, to clear the air between us, but believe me when I say I will find out who did this and bring them to justice."

"It doesn't matter."

Dempsey swung his head around at the sound of Niall's voice.

"Eyes on the road, Sheriff."

Niall's throat hurt; his voice sounded raspy to his own ears. Like a heavy smoker. He didn't remember breathing smoke, but he must have.

"Don't speak, you sound awful."

"First you're calling my name, demanding an answer, and now you're telling me to be quiet. You need to make up your mind," Niall rasped.

"Look, asshole—" Dempsey cut off whatever else he'd been about to say.

It was too much effort to turn his head, but out of the corner of his eye he saw Dempsey's fingers flex on the steering wheel.

Dempsey took a long breath before opening his mouth again, his eyes fixed on the road ahead. "Look, I know you're in shock right now, so I'm going to give you a pass." He shook his head. "I thought maybe you were dead, just—" Again he broke off, not finishing his sentence. Niall was too exhausted to pursue it.

"Sorry," Niall whispered, but he didn't think Dempsey heard him.

Sorry was the only thing he had, a tiny word to encompass all the things he was feeling. His brain was fuzzy and untethered. Yes, Niall was aware he was riding in Dempsey's cop car to some unknown destination, but he was also a boy reliving things a child should never have to witness. The door was shutting on him again, and he wished more than anything that he was strong enough to keep it open, to be able to run away. He wished he wasn't always hungry, and he wished his mother would come back and let him out. Niall shook his head, wanting the memories to fall back into the shadows where they belonged.

He must've shut his eyes because the next thing he knew Dempsey was shaking his shoulder. "Hamarsson, I need you to get out of the car. As much as I might want to, I can't carry you into the house."

The house was illuminated by the car's headlights. When Mat shut them off, it took a moment for Niall's eyes to adjust. The house was early twentieth century, two stories with a porch that extended its width, a porch swing on one side of it. That swing would be a nice place to sit on hot summer nights.

"Where are we?" Niall asked as he moved his feet from the car to the ground outside. He forgot about his injured hand, lifting it to pull himself out of the car, but Dempsey grabbed his upper arm before he could hurt himself and helped him stand up.

"My house." Dempsey did a head waggle. "My mother's house, but I live here."

The front door opened. A slice of light cut through the night, and Niall saw an older woman standing on the other side of it, waiting for them. For Mat, anyway.

"Mat?" she called out.

"Hey, Mom, do you mind putting some tea on for Niall?"

Mat's mom nodded and disappeared inside, leaving the door open for them.

"Come with me. My mom makes the best tea on the island."

"I don't like tea."

Mat stopped in his tracks, forcing Niall to stop too. "Are you being an asshole right now? The shock must be wearing off. I'm warning you—you can be an asshole to me, but if you're an ass to my mom, I'll put you back in the cruiser and drive you back to where I found you."

Niall just nodded. He didn't have the strength to explain about black tea hurting his stomach, and the thought of being where there was no cabin anymore frightened him more than anything else in the world right now.

Inside Mat's house, Niall had the impression of comfortable furniture with bright throws and pillows. He wasn't really paying attention. The effort of putting one foot in front of the other was sapping the last of his energy.

"Sit him down on the couch."

Niall wanted to protest. He was filthy, covered with ash, dirt, and sand, and he'd likely dragged in seaweed stuck to the bottom of his boots. Reluctantly, he sat and leaned back against the soft cushion. Someone wrapped a blanket around him.

"What happened?" a concerned female voice asked.

"There was a fire," Dempsey answered. "The Hamarsson place is gone."

The words were the truth, but Niall wished he didn't have to hear them right now.

An older, dark-haired woman came around to stand in Niall's field of vision.

"Sweetie, I'm Alyson Dempsey, Mat's mom. You can call me Alyson, or Mom."

Niall snorted, wondering when or if anyone had ever referred to him as "sweetie" before. A few minutes later a warm mug was pressed into his hand.

"Sip this. It's sweet tea, my own herbal mix."

Niall obediently sipped, studying Alyson over the rim of the mug. He recognized her as one of his grandmother's friends. She'd visited regularly, especially in the summertime when his grandmother was working in her garden. Niall had never talked to her. At first he'd been scared of strangers other than his grandparents, then he'd been too stubborn. But he knew Alyson and his grandmother had been good friends despite their difference in age.

Mat didn't look much like his mother, although they had the same eye shape and wide smile. Niall tried to remember what Mat's dad looked like. He wondered if he was where Dempsey got his height and dark eyes.

"Where's your dad?" Niall asked Mat, who was hovering behind his mother. He didn't miss the flash of pain that shot through his eyes.

"Sean was killed in a boating accident," Alyson answered for her son. "I miss him every day. It was hard at first."

She sat down next to him on the couch, her smaller body a comfort against Niall's own.

"Mat insisted on moving back to the island to take care of me. He's a good son."

Niall didn't think she was implying he was a bad son, or a bad grandson, but the words still hurt, hitting him somewhere he normally kept hidden away but that was unexpectedly exposed by the day's events.

"I'm sorry to invade your home." Niall's throat burned. "Can I borrow a phone? I'll see if I can find a place to stay tonight."

Maybe he could see if Doc Soper might put him up, at least for the night. Tomorrow Niall would see if there were any rooms he could rent or something… he didn't know what. He sipped at the tea again. His throat hurt, but the tea-sugar concoction was doing its work.

Both of his hosts frowned at his words.

"You're not going anywhere tonight," Dempsey stated. "Tomorrow, after you've slept, we'll talk about next steps."

He was tired, so tired. Protesting was impossible.

"Mat, Niall can take the guest bedroom. Why don't you take him up there now?"

Niall opened his eyes. Dempsey stood directly in front of him, his expression far too complicated for Niall to translate.

"Yeah, Mom, I'll help him upstairs."

Mat's mom gently patted Niall's face. He liked the unfamiliar touch.

"You'll feel better in the morning, sweetie. I promise."

Niall doubted that, but there was no point in arguing at the moment.

Dempsey leaned down and, for the third time that night, tugged him almost effortlessly upward. It would be nice to think someone could always do that. Pull him up when he needed it.

"This way."

Niall opened his eyes, momentarily disoriented. Raindrops smacked loudly against an unfamiliar bedroom window. He blinked, and the events of the night before came flooding back. Hungry flames consuming his grandparents' cabin, the dark water he'd wanted to dive into. Dempsey calling his name, then Dempsey standing in front of him, his face full of worry. He was at Dempsey's house.

"Shit."

Niall lay in the bed, staring at the ceiling. His throat was sore and his injured hand ached, but otherwise he felt okay. He turned to roll over, intending to swing his legs out of bed, and was immediately hit with a full body cramp. Everything hurt, even his earlobes. An involuntary groan escaped his lips. He felt like he was about eighty years old. An out-of-shape eighty-year-old.

Slower on the second try, Niall rolled over and sat up, his feet resting against the wood floor. He'd slept in his clothes, but now he wanted nothing more than to get them off his body. Except he didn't have anything to replace them. Then he noticed a stack of clothing sitting on a chair across from the bed. Next to the chair was a simple writing table, and a piece of paper was propped up against a framed snapshot of the Dempsey family. Niall stood and shuffled over to grab the note.

Niall, I think these things will fit, we're close to the same size. Mom is going to insist on washing your clothes. Take a shower, it's down the hall, there's coffee downstairs. Don't leave before I get back or I will make life very difficult for you.

Mat

Dempsey had terrible handwriting. He should've been a doctor, not a cop.

In the bathroom, Niall peeled off his filthy clothes while the shower water heated. He wadded them up, not sure if they were worth washing. The small room quickly steamed up. Niall was glad when he couldn't see his reflection in the mirror anymore.

He moved to step into the spray, then remembered his hand at the last second.

"Fucking hell." Childlike tears threatened. Suddenly, taking a shower was the most important thing in his life, and he couldn't because he still couldn't get his fucking stitches wet. Niall hadn't cried since he was a kid, and a shower was going to set him off?

There was a light tap on the bathroom door followed by, "Hamarsson?"

"What?" Niall replied more gruffly than he intended, gruffer than Dempsey deserved after all he'd done.

"Do you need help covering your hand?"

Niall wrenched the door open. Dempsey waited on the other side, a plastic bag in one hand and masking tape in the other. "I thought you were gone."

Mat's eyes widened. "You might want a towel."

Great, he'd forgotten he was naked. Niall snatched a towel from one of the hooks and clumsily wrapped it around his waist, holding on with his good hand. Dempsey was a big boy, surely he'd seen naked men. "Sorry."

Mat moved closer, the small bathroom shrinking exponentially. The two of them took up all the space and more.

Niall stuck his arm out. Dempsey pulled the plastic bag over his bandage and taped it in place.

"An amateur job, but it should hold."

"Thanks."

"Anytime."

Dempsey stood there.

"I'm gonna get in the shower now," Niall said.

"Yeah, okay."

"I'm gonna need to drop the towel."

Dempsey flushed. "Christ, of course." He backed out of the bathroom, pulling the door shut behind him.

Niall pulled the towel from his waist and draped it across the toilet seat lid before stepping into the shower. The hot water felt incredible against his skin. He stood under the spray as long as he could justify, the dirt and ash washing down the drain at his feet.

What was it he'd read about the stages of grief? Niall had seen a lot of grief as a cop, and the fact that some psychologist thought it could be boiled down to five stages was ridiculous. Regardless, Niall recognized the emotion he was feeling this morning as anger and figured he was done with denial; now he was out for justice. When Niall got his hands on Martin Reynolds he would be sorry he had ever born—by legal means, of course.

Dempsey's jeans proved to be a bit short for Niall but fine in the waist. The long-sleeved shirt with "SFPD" emblazoned on it stretched a little tight across his shoulders, but the garments covered his body and fit better than the ones Doc Soper had loaned him. He really needed to quit finding himself in situations where his clothes got trashed.

Picking up his dirty clothing, Niall left the bathroom and padded down the hallway to the landing. Domestic sounds reached his ears, the clatter of dishware and water running in a sink. Gingerly, because his body still hurt although the shower had made him feel better, he made his way down the stairs.

Dempsey was nowhere in sight, but his mother, Alyson, was rinsing dishes and humming to herself.

He cleared his throat. "Good morning." It came out raspy. He wished his throat didn't hurt; even a polite greeting somehow came out sounding like he was a grumpy fucker. Which, in general, he was.

Alyson turned around to greet him with a big smile on her face, although Niall recognized worry in her eyes.

"Niall! Good morning, I've been waiting for you. Are you hungry? I've got everything for a hearty breakfast. Mat had to leave, but he said he'll try to be home early."

Niall had opened his mouth to tell her he wasn't hungry when he realized he was famished.

"Breakfast would be nice. Thank you."

"Are those your clothes? Let me take them. I'll toss them in the wash."

He hadn't intended to stay, to eat, to let Dempsey's mother take care of him, but somehow that was exactly what happened. It wasn't as if he had anywhere to go.

"Sit at the kitchen table. Do eggs and bacon sound good? Do you eat meat? I can make waffles."

For the second time that morning, tears threatened. Niall nodded because if he opened his mouth, tears would spill out his eyes. It made no sense, but he knew that's what would happen. Alyson offered him eggs and bacon and he had a break-down? Niall didn't cry—not because of an outdated concept of what it meant to be a man, but because if he started crying after all this time, he might never stop.

Alyson must've seen something—something in his expression, Niall supposed. She set the mixing bowl and wooden spoon she'd had in her hands down on the counter.

"Oh, baby. Josephine worried about you."

No one had ever called Niall "baby." He wanted to laugh, but his throat closed around the sound.

"Jo always told me you needed more love than most, but you refuse to accept it." Alyson was standing in front of him now, much like Mat had been earlier. "So I'm not asking your permission, I'm giving my love to you anyway."

Before Niall realized what she was doing or could stop her, Alyson advanced closer to put her arms around his shoulders. Mat's mother wrapped her strong arms around him and held him while he broke wide open. He couldn't stop the flood of emotion. Niall cried for things he'd never cried over before, things he'd pushed aside. For the boy, for the man, for Morfar and Mormor, for the cabin—even for his own mother, who didn't deserve his grief.

The harder he tried to stop, the more heavily the tears fell.

They physically hurt. The tears themselves ached as if he was expelling poison from his body as he sobbed, jagged pieces of liquid glass flushing wounds Niall had neglected for years. Throughout, Alyson made quiet soothing sounds and petted him, a kind hand stroking through Niall's hair as if he were a little boy, as if he were *her* boy. Her chin rested on the top of his head, and she kept repeating, "It's okay, everything will be okay, you'll be okay." Niall wondered how she could believe that. If a person had never been okay, how did they get there?

All his life, except when working a case, Niall had felt like he was barely holding on, as if any minute the façade of humanity protecting him would crumble to dust, and Niall would be revealed as a sham, a fake, an imposter. Being okay seemed an impossible goal, so he'd thrown himself into police work and attempted to bring closure to victims' families. It was the least he could do, the only thing he knew how to do.

After what seemed like hours, Niall was finally able to get a gulp of air and force the remaining tears back behind the wall where they belonged. Alyson stood up and left the kitchen for a moment, returning with a box of tissues.

He took the box from her, tugging a tissue out, blowing his nose, and wiping his eyes. He didn't want to look at her. He was embarrassed for breaking down in her kitchen, for exposing himself.

"Well," Alyson said, her hands on her hips, "aren't you lucky? When I cry, I look just awful."

He appreciated her attempt to lighten the mood. Somehow Niall was sure the last time Alyson Dempsey cried was when her husband died.

"I'm sorry about your husband."

"It was years ago now. I won't lie to you—I miss him like the dickens. But I had him, you know? Sean was all mine while he was alive, and we got to raise a family together, and all the kids were healthy and happy. Sean would've loved the grandkids…"

Her voice trailed off, and she shrugged. "I miss him. It's been wonderful to have Mat back home, but I can't help but worry he's sacrificing his own happiness for mine. Anyway, enough of that. How about some breakfast?"

Niall's stomach rumbled loudly at her words, and she chuckled.

"Mat was jealous I was making breakfast for you this morning. Usually I do this on his days off. He does love his waffles."

Niall attempted to eat the scrambled eggs, bacon, and homemade waffles like a civilized person, but he was so hungry he found it difficult.

"Mat will be home this evening—earlier than usual, he hopes. He was waiting to talk to you this morning, but he got another call and had to leave. I just don't know what is going on around the island these days. Between the poor Reynolds girl, drug houses, Harry spreading rumors of wolves—and it doesn't help that one of Stan's goats died—we're having quite a crime spree."

Niall nodded as he chewed.

"Another waffle?"

Niall nodded again, finishing his bite. "Things are usually pretty quiet?" he asked.

Alyson scooped batter up with a measuring cup and poured it into the waffle maker.

"Yes—well, this time of year anyway. In the summer, Mat and the rest of the sheriff's office work twenty-four hours a day. It was that way when my Sean was sheriff too. Summer would arrive, and the kids and I wouldn't see him until after Labor Day."

"I didn't know your husband was sheriff."

"Pshaw, that's not the sort of thing a young man pays attention to—unless he's up to no good."

"Did Dempsey—Mat—move back to Piedras to be sheriff?"

Alyson hmm-ed before she answered his question. The light

on the waffle maker turned on, and she plucked the golden-brown waffle out with a fork, bringing it over and plopping it on his plate.

"That part is my fault, I'm afraid—not that I'm not happy Mat's sheriff," she added, "but after Sean died, Shay Delacombe started talking about running for the position." She waved the fork menacingly at Niall. "Over my dead body is a Delacombe sheriff on this island."

Niall remembered Shay Delacombe. The man, only a few years older than Niall, was currently a defense lawyer who practiced in Seattle. Niall had rarely come up against him in court. Shay had a reputation for a bad temper and a wicked intelligence.

"After I pestered Mat, he agreed to run and was elected by a landslide. Shay was mad as a hornet, but he doesn't even live here! He claimed he was a resident because his family still lives on the island. We're smarter than that!"

Niall couldn't help but smile a bit. Alyson Dempsey was not to be trifled with.

SIXTEEN

DEMPSEY

Fucking hell. Mat had come close to swallowing his tongue. He'd knocked on the bathroom door, knowing Niall would need help wrapping his hand. He'd heard Niall get out of bed and move from the guest bedroom to the bathroom—it was an old house, and the floorboards squeaked. But he had not expected the man would open the door and be standing stark naked on the other side of it.

Stark naked.

He hadn't been able to stop himself; Mat had stared openly at Niall's incredible body. Niall definitely didn't spend all day behind a desk. Mat greedily drank down the man's form from the top of his head down to his broad shoulders and wide chest with a fine dusting of dark hair, farther to his slack but well-proportioned cock, then on to his thick, muscled thighs also dusted with dark hair, and all the way to his toes—even noting his second toe was longer than the first. All in the seconds it took before Mat found the words to tell Niall he might want to cover himself with a towel.

Fucking hell.

Back downstairs, his cell phone buzzed insistently in his

pocket, and Mat knew he couldn't linger any longer at home. He had to go into the station. A second Piedras resident had reported a suspicious livestock death. The Wainwright sheep farm abutted the Reynolds property to the north, but to get there Mat had to drive to Hidden Harbor and then out toward Preacher Road and around to the northeast tip of the island. It would be quicker and easier to hike through from the Reynolds side, but no way in hell was Mat poking that hornet's nest this morning.

They were going to have to question Martin Reynolds again, this time about the fire, and Mat was certain the conversation was not going to go well. He'd definitely take Birdy with him. But, from the few words he'd gotten out of Niall last night and the call Martin had made to the station about a trespasser, he was first on Mat's list.

And, incredibly, Birdy'd found a witness who thought they'd seen Chastity Reynolds talking to a "handsome" stranger several times on the ferry in the weeks before she was discovered in the marina. The witness was none other than Stu Dennis. So Mat had Stu to question as well, but not until he finished with Wainwright and Reynolds.

While Mat was on his way to Merle Wainwright's sheep farm, one of the island's volunteer firefighters called, confirming the fire at Niall's had been set with gasoline. Mat was relieved he'd called the volunteers last night before taking Niall to his house. When they arrived on the scene, the wind had started to turn and a few embers tried to spark, but the firefighters doused them again until they were completely out.

"Too bad about the Hamarsson place," Devon said, his voice soft. "It was a special place."

"Yeah, it was. I don't suppose you found anything pointing to *who* might have started the fire?" It would have been nice if they found a note to tie things up nicely.

"Nope, sorry."

~

When Mat turned down the sheep farm's driveway, Merle was waiting for him next to his pickup truck.

"Didn't want you to have to drive up to the house."

The Wainwrights raised sheep for wool, and they'd been successful at it. From what Mat understood, there was quite a demand for their yarn or whatever.

"Thanks for coming out, Sheriff."

Merle extended a hand and Mat shook it. "I'm sorry about the circumstances. What can you tell me about what happened?"

Merle walked around to the back of his truck. Mat followed to see a dead sheep lying in the truck bed. It didn't look like it had been mauled by a wolf or anything else.

"How was it killed? You're sure it wasn't natural? It's been cold, could it have died of exposure?"

Merle shook his head. Leaning in he lifted the sheep's head, twisting it so Mat could see a well-defined entry wound caused by a bullet. "Pretty sure it didn't shoot itself."

"Shit."

Merle nodded grimly.

Mat thought back to the posse of old men he'd broken up yesterday—or had it been the day before? Jesus, his days were starting to run together, and sleep had been elusive last night. But Harry had been after a wolf or coyote. There was no way a sheep would look like a coyote, even to an old man.

"A .22, likely," Mat commented. A gun almost every long-timer on the island owned and kept close at hand.

"Yep."

"Where'd you find it?"

Merle motioned with his head. "Back up on the second pasture. This one didn't come back last night, so I went out looking first thing this morning."

"I don't suppose you took pictures?"

Merle smiled grimly. "I did."

"Do you mind taking me back out there so I can look around?"

Mat couldn't help but admire the scenery while Merle drove, the truck bumping along the access road out to the pastures. The Wainwright property was perfectly situated, rolling right down to the waterline, and had an incredible view of the water. Mat thought they'd discussed building a boutique bed and breakfast at one point, but apparently sheep farming kept them busy enough. He was constantly amazed—regardless of how the island's population grew or diminished over the years, through recession or boom, it maintained its intrinsic do-it-yourself character.

Jesus fucking Christ, this was not the time for one of the years-old feuds between certain families on the island to flare up. Between Harry and his wolf, Stan and his dead goat, the Hamarsson fire, Martin Reynolds pissed about trespassers, and Chastity's murder, Mat had enough on his hands. He was damn glad the snow hadn't stuck around to add to his list of complaints.

An hour and a half later, Mat pulled into the sheriff's office parking lot. He and Merle hadn't found any smoking guns—or cartridges—but Mat confirmed his suspicion that the particular pasture where the deceased sheep was discovered backed up along both the Harrison and the Reynolds parcels.

Birdy was waiting for him inside the station.

"Mr. Dennis said to tell you he'd be at the Hook for lunch, if we want to talk to him."

"I'd rather talk to him somewhere where the entire island won't be listening in," Mat grumbled.

"Yes, sir. I think the attention makes him feel important.

Maybe if we meet him there, we can suggest he come back here with us?"

"Great idea, Deputy."

Half of being a good cop was psychology, and Birdy had that down pat.

"Why don't you go collect him while I make a fresh pot of coffee?"

Birdy left, and Mat went into their little break room to make a fresh pot of coffee. The department might not have a big budget, but Mat always made sure they had decent coffee. After living in San Francisco, it was impossible to go back to the weak coffee-flavored water he'd found at the station when he was elected sheriff.

Twenty minutes later, Birdy returned with Stu.

Mat offered Stu the chair next to his desk, noting the older man certainly didn't fill it the way Hamarsson had. He gestured for Birdy to roll her desk chair over. He wanted her to run the show. Stu definitely had an eye for "the ladies," and while Mat would never encourage his deputies to do anything illegal, he felt Birdy's soft touch might help the man recall who and what he'd seen.

"Coffee?" Mat offered.

Stu shook his head sadly. "The doc says no more caffeine for me."

"Bummer." Mat leaned back in his chair. "Why don't you and Birdy go through your conversation for me?"

As it happened, Stu was "romancing an enchanting woman" who lived in Anacortes, so he'd been taking the ferry more than he normally did.

"I didn't pay any mind that Chastity was taking the ferry with me. It must not have been until my third or fourth trip when I realized I'd seen her on the ferry before—you know how the mind sees something, but it doesn't register? She'd been catching the same ferry as I'd been, at least for a few weeks in a row."

Mat and Birdy nodded. "Go on," Birdy said.

"Well, you know how it is when you ride the ferry all the time, you bring a book or your laptop to keep busy. At any rate, I realized I'd seen Chastity several times, and I was going to say hello. You know, one local to another. But she was deep in conversation with a young man, and I didn't want to interrupt."

"What do you recall about the young man?"

"Hmm." Stu looked up at the ceiling, then back at Birdy and Mat. "Well, I didn't get too much of a look at him—I didn't want to stare—but he wasn't an islander. He was young, maybe a little older than Chastity, but not by much. He had a polished look about him, you know? He was definitely from the city. His clothing seemed trendy and new."

"Can you describe him physically?" Birdy asked.

Stu nodded. "He was wearing sunglasses, which was odd for this time of year, but young people these days do odd things. He wasn't much taller than Chastity—I only recall because they stood up at the same time."

"What color hair?"

"Mmmm, I'm not sure. He wore a black knit cap. Possibly lighter colored?"

"So, black beanie, no taller than, say, five eight or nine, trendy clothing and mid to late twenties?"

Stu nodded.

"Anything else pop into your head? A tattoo or something else unusual?" Mat asked.

This time Stu shook his head but added, "I don't think Chastity got off at Anacortes. I think she rode the ferry back."

"What made you think that?"

"I didn't see her afterward. You know how all the foot passengers have to disembark from the middle level of the ferry and use the footbridge to get down to the terminal. I thought I might say hello to her then, but I never saw her."

That was interesting. Birdy and Mat glanced at each other. Mat knew Birdy was thinking the same thing as he was: what had Chastity been doing, and who was the man Stu had seen her talking to?

"One last request, Stu. Can you recall the dates you took the ferry to Anacortes?"

Birdy handed Stu a steno pad. Stu leaned over Mat's desk and jotted down five dates and the times he caught the ferry. Mat read the notes upside down. The last date was only a few days before Chastity's body was discovered.

"Thanks for coming in, Stu. How's the romancing going?"

Stu grinned, his whiskered cheeks bulging with his smile. "Quite lovely, thank you."

While Birdy escorted Stu out of the station, Mat scooted up to his desk and jotted down thoughts from the information Stu shared with them. He wondered if the WSDOT would give the department a copy of their security camera feed or if he'd need a warrant. Had anyone else noticed a city boy who looked out of place or an island girl who, instead of getting off at Anacortes, may have ridden all the way back to Piedras Island.

Mat's stomach rumbled, reminding him he hadn't had lunch yet and the time was edging close to two o'clock, but they still needed to question Martin Reynolds about the fire at Niall's cabin.

"Deputy Flynn?"

She was back by his desk in an instant. "Yes?"

"How about we take ourselves out for a visit to Martin Reynolds. I want you to ask the questions. He's riled up, and I don't want either of us out there by ourselves right now."

Mat didn't normally consider Martin dangerous, but he seemed to be more volatile these days. Mat suspected Chastity had called it when she told him QAnon was ruining his life.

"Should we call Deputy Holstrom? He's on good terms with Martin."

Mat considered it. "No, I think three is too many. Two of us, hopefully he won't feel threatened."

Mat parked his cruiser as close to the line of derelict vehicles as he dared. Birdy angled in next to him, squeezing between Mat and the defunct tractor. They got out and, together, looked over at Martin's trailer. He was definitely home because there was a smoldering pile of leaves no one was tending, and Mat didn't think even Reynolds was reckless enough to leave it entirely alone.

Sure enough, after only a minute the trailer door opened and Martin appeared, wearing what looked to be the same t-shirt and shorts from when Mat talked to him a few days earlier.

"Took you long enough!" Martin yelled across the… *yard* was likely what the patch of land between them and the front door was *supposed* to be.

"Can we talk, Martin?" Birdy stepped forward, and Mat followed as she took the lead.

"If Hamarsson comes out here again, I'm not holding back. A man has a right to protect his property."

"Martin," Birdy said when she and Mat were only a few feet from the door, "we're not here about your trespassing complaint."

Martin cocked his head and narrowed his eyes. "What then?"

"We're here to ask a few more questions about Chastity, to start with."

"What about her? I told you I had nothing to do with it. We didn't even speak. She moved out"—he nodded at the second trailer—"and didn't tell me where. That's all I know. Now I got Claribel breathing down my neck about a funeral when I need to be keeping my eye on the forums for breadcrumbs. Something big is going to happen, I'm sure of it. Did you see that airplane crash? They did that to get *one* target."

They ignored the last of Martin's words. There was no point trying to reason with him about the conspiracy group. "So, Chastity moved out and you don't know where?"

"Isn't that what I just said? Are you hard of hearing, girl?"

Birdy stiffened, and Mat knew Reynolds had crossed her patience line.

"Martin Reynolds, you should be ashamed of yourself. Your sister is dead. Even if you weren't getting along right now, you will never get to talk to her again, do you understand that? Claribel is your great-grandmother, and she shouldn't be burying her great-granddaughter, that's not how it's supposed to work." She sniffed the air and wrinkled her nose. "And for Christ's sake, take a shower and change your clothes. You smell like a horse's ass. Help out your great-grandmother with Chastity's funeral. Do your part for once in your life."

Before Martin could react, Mat asked, "Did you hear about the fire, Martin?"

Martin transferred his scowl from Birdy to Mat. "What fire?"

"The Hamarsson place burned down last night. Whoever did it used gasoline."

Martin's eyes widened, then narrowed again. "Are you accusing me?"

"You claim he trespassed on your property yesterday. It's mighty convenient that his place burned to the ground not long after he left here."

"I had nothing to do with any fire!" Martin's voice rose in protest.

"If we find out you did…"

"I didn't!" His voice rose even higher, and as much as he disliked Martin, Mat believed he was telling the truth. Frankly, the effort of getting gasoline and driving over to Niall's was probably too much for Martin.

"Call Claribel, or else. I'm checking in with her tonight, and if she tells me you're still giving her the runaround…" Birdy let her voice trail off.

Martin honest to god pouted. The man was at least forty, and he was sulking about arranging his baby sister's funeral. Apparently, Birdy's words carried enough weight for him to agree. "Fine," he spat.

Birdy nodded. "Good."

Together she and Mat turned and strode purposefully back to their cars. Mat was well aware of Martin watching them and also aware he probably had a .22 next to his front door. The space between Mat's shoulders twitched.

Out on the road, Mat pulled over to the shoulder and opened his window. Birdy pulled up beside him, and her passenger window rolled down.

"Nice job."

Birdy nodded grimly. "He is a worthless piece of—"

"Swear jar," Mat reminded her.

"Yes, sir. He just makes me so angry."

"Have you been in touch with Claribel?" he asked.

"Yes, sir. The funeral is Sunday. It's going to be small. I helped Claribel arrange it. The remembrance will be at the Spiritual Living Yoga Center, where Chastity was taking yoga classes. Claribel wants to spread her ashes over the bay by the Center."

"Do you think it's too late for us to stop by and ask her if she knew about the young man Stu saw talking to Chastity?"

Birdy looked at her watch. "It's not that late, sir."

They parked next to each other at Claribel's. Her yard was a well-kept English garden compared to her great-grandson's. Birdy tapped on the door, and the two of them waited. Mat heard voices and then the sound of heavy footsteps before the door opened.

Mat was damn glad Birdy had come along because he was momentarily speechless. He had not expected Shay Delacombe to answer the door.

"Mr. Delacombe, Sheriff Dempsey and I are here to ask your grandmother a few questions. Is Claribel available?"

Shay Delacombe was an attractive man, medium height, with the characteristic Delacombe ice-blue eyes and dark hair. The suit he wore didn't hide his lean athletic body, it accentuated it. And Shay knew it. A slight smirk flitted across his lips.

Shay's cool gaze flicked from Birdy to Mat. "Sheriff. Deputy. Come inside and have a seat. I'll check with Claribel."

After a quiet discussion with his great-aunt, Shay returned and led them into the kitchen. Much like Mat's mother's kitchen, it was a spacious room with a large table against one pale yellow wall and a door leading to the backyard. A window above the table looked out over the back of the property, and somewhere a few miles or so out was the Wainwright sheep pasture.

"Do you ever get sheep wandering over this way?" Mat asked.

"Sheep? What kind of fool question is that?" Claribel retorted.

"Just curious."

"Sit down. Ask your ovine questions so you can leave. Shay and I have things to take care of."

"Claribel, did you know if Chastity was seeing anyone?" Birdy asked. "Did she have a boyfriend, or girlfriend?"

Claribel's lips straightened into a thin line. Mat thought she looked more careworn than she had a week earlier. Chastity's death had affected her more than she was willing to admit. As much as Mat disliked and distrusted Shay, he was glad the man had come to be with his great-aunt during this time.

"No, no, I have no idea if Chastity was seeing anyone—man or woman. As far as I know, she spent most of her time at the yoga center. We'd had an argument. She asked for money to start her own studio, and I... well, I said no."

"And now I wish I hadn't" was left unsaid but heard by them all.

Mat squashed down irritation that Claribel hadn't told them this earlier. "When was this? When did she come to you?"

"Before she moved off Martin's property."

Claribel looked over at her great-nephew. Shay hadn't sat down with them; instead he leaned against the kitchen counter and listened to their conversation.

"Did she talk to you, Shay?"

Shay shook his head. "Chastity and I weren't close enough in age."

"So you wouldn't know if she'd been seeing anyone?"

"No, I wouldn't know. Why are you asking, have you found something out?"

"Possibly," Mat replied. "She was seen on the ferry talking to someone. We'd like to find that person."

"So would I." Shay straightened from the counter. "Claribel's worn out. I'll walk you to the door."

Outside, Shay stopped them before they descended the stairs.

"Do you have anything?" he asked.

Mat shrugged. "This unknown person is the best lead so far, but we don't have a great description. We're going to need the security video from the ferry, and even that will be a long shot."

"Let me know if I can help."

Mat quirked an eyebrow. "You have connections that can get us that feed, legally?"

"Consider it done. Thank you."

Without waiting for a response, Shay went back into the

house and shut the door behind him. Mat and Birdy picked their way through the dark to their cars.

"That went well," Birdy said.

"Better than I expected, anyway."

"Shay surprised me."

"Me too, Birdy, me too."

By the time Mat got home, Niall was asleep, but Alyson was waiting for him in the kitchen.

"He's exhausted, Mat. I imagine he'll be close to normal tomorrow."

Mat'd pushed aside his latent worry over Niall all day—he had to concentrate on solving Chastity's murder, figure out who or what was killing livestock, and keep his citizens from dispensing vigilante justice. All in the day of a Piedras Island lawman.

After wolfing down leftover lasagna, Mat headed upstairs. He was exhausted, and the possibility that he might actually be too tired to sleep was at the forefront of his thoughts. On the way to his bedroom he stopped in front of Niall's door. He couldn't help himself; carefully, Mat turned the door handle and pushed the door open just enough so he could see the bed.

An inexplicably elegant bare foot dangled from the side of the mattress, and Niall's bandaged hand poked out from underneath the comforter. In the dim light, Mat could barely make out his dark head against the pillows. Niall made a sound and turned over, his back to Mat now. Quietly, Mat shut the door and continued down the hallway to his bedroom, where he undressed and got into bed.

Despite his own exhaustion, Mat lay awake for a long time wondering what the hell he was going to do about Niall Hamarsson. In the dark of his room, Mat admitted to himself he wanted the man. He wanted Niall in way he'd hadn't felt in years. Likely not since Niall graduated high school and left Mat with no one to fantasize about.

Seeing Shay again had only confirmed Mat's suspicion. Shay paled in comparison to Niall's rugged wildness, his drive for justice, and, Mat knew, a unique kindness hidden inside as well. Niall wasn't the asshole he showed to the world; he couldn't be that and also the dedicated detective Mat had heard about. The untamed Niall spoke to Mat's soul in a way Shay had never come close to.

"I am so fucked," Mat whispered even though no one could hear him. Also making a mental note to drop a twenty in the swear jar the next day.

SEVENTEEN

HAMARSSON

The second morning Niall woke in Mat Dempsey's house, he decided it was time he moved on. Except, he reminded himself with a groan, his phone had been incinerated and his car was still parked at the cabin—or where the cabin had been. Leaving the Dempsey household was going to be problematic.

He avoided thinking about the sinkhole of his life for the moment, how the cabin going up in flames was pretty much a metaphor for everything right now. He didn't need to break down again; the first time had been excruciating. Tears were painful and never did anyone any good.

After finishing breakfast the day before, he'd come upstairs to lie down and ended up sleeping for several hours, waking when Alyson knocked on his door to ask if he was ready for a snack. Her lasagna had filled him, but almost immediately he was ready for bed again. Since he wasn't ready to talk to Mat, he'd hidden in his borrowed bedroom, not expecting to fall back to sleep and stay that way all night. It had been a long time since he'd slept through the night without nightmares or Jack Daniel's.

Today he needed to snap out of his funk and start focusing

on his future. He made a mental list of things he needed to take care of. First, purchase a new phone. Then get to his car and find a hotel room—one of the hotels on the island would have space this time of year. Andersen Lawn and Garden popped into his head—he definitely needed to check in with them and find out why they'd stopped their yard service. He inspected his bandaged hand. He should probably check in with Doc Soper too, although his hand felt fine, just itchy as fuck while it healed.

Niall let out a sigh. Maybe he should hone in on his immediate future, like actually getting out of bed. Slowly he sat up. Yesterday Alyson had washed his clothes, now they were folded and sitting on a nearby chair. Niall slipped into his own jeans and long-sleeved t-shirt and headed downstairs, leaving behind the clothing Mat had lent him folded on the bed.

Alyson was in the kitchen talking on the phone, and after looking outside and not seeing the cruiser, Niall figured Mat was gone for the day.

Good. Niall didn't want to see him.

"Sunday at two? Okay, is anyone putting a note in the paper —or you know, online? Okay." She nodded to the speaker on the other end. "We could host it here if you'd like. Oh, Shay's helping?" Alyson's expression changed, but she kept her tone civil. "That's good of him. I'll spread the word. Goodbye, Claribel." She clicked off, then turned to Niall. "Sorry."

"No worries."

"I'm sure you know about Chastity Reynolds. Her memorial is Sunday." Alyson sighed. "Claribel shouldn't be burying her great-granddaughter. I hope Mat catches whoever did this. I'm not the biggest fan of that family, but no one deserves that."

Pulling a mug out of a cupboard, she said, "Mat asked me to ask you to please call him today. He's hoping to be home early enough tonight to touch base with you, but with everything going on... Anyway, would you like a cup of coffee? It's fresh."

"Ah," Niall started, "I think I'm going to head out. I appreciate your hospitality."

Alyson turned from where she was pouring coffee into the large mug. "Where are you going to go?"

Niall shifted uncomfortably. "I need to replace my cell phone, and I was thinking I would see if the Dockman or another place has a room."

"You're welcome to stay here, you know. There's no reason for you to spend money on a room."

"Money's not an issue. I'd just prefer a room to myself."

Niall hated that he sounded like such as asshole, but he needed to get away. He couldn't allow himself to get used to Alyson's freely given kindness. It was too much. Deep down, Niall recognized her affection as something he craved, but he couldn't let himself have it. Because when she got to know the real Niall Hamarsson, she would turn away.

Alyson handed the mug to him. "If you're sure. But you're always welcome here. Before she passed, I promised Josephine I'd watch over you, and I admit I haven't done a good job at all —especially with Sean passing just after her—but I don't like to break my promises. But she also said you'd be difficult, so I'm not giving up."

"I'm really not worth it," Niall assured her.

"Mmm." Alyson made one of those mom sounds meaning she disagreed but wasn't going to pick a fight about it—for the moment, anyway.

"Do you need a ride somewhere?"

She was good. Very, very good.

Niall glanced out the kitchen window again, wondering if he could get away with walking to his car. It was only a few miles from the Dempseys' to his property. Unfortunately, the weather had not changed from yesterday. It was wet out and threatening to rain more. Even though it was past eight in the morning, the day was dark and gloomy, and the part of the sky he could see through the trees was gray and ominous.

"A ride to my car would be appreciated."

Niall hadn't prepared himself for seeing the ruins of the cabin in the light of day. He'd put it out of his mind and skirted the issue —a land mine to be avoided at all costs. And motherfucking hell, when Alyson's car pulled past the trees, he stepped right on the damn thing. Kaboom. Niall felt like he'd been punched in the stomach, like he might vomit, and he was glad all he'd had was a cup of coffee.

Instead of getting out of the car and letting Alyson get back to whatever she had planned for the day, Niall stayed glued to the passenger seat. He didn't even unbuckle his seat belt. It was so much worse than he'd hoped. Which was stupid, because he'd watched with his own eyes as the cabin burned, felt the heat against his skin, choked on the smoke. Fucking hell. His eyes burned, and it wasn't from smoke.

A sound caught his attention. In the side mirror Niall saw Mat's cruiser pull in behind them.

"I texted Mat." Alyson's voice cut across his thoughts—she didn't bother to sound apologetic. "I don't think you should be out here on your own. Don't blame him if you're angry. Later you and I can have a discussion about it."

Niall's stomach did an uncomfortable little twist, which did nothing for the nausea already stationed there. He watched in the mirror as Mat got out of his vehicle and approached Niall's side of the car. Mat's gaze met Niall's as he tapped Niall's window and gestured for him to get out. Niall got out.

"Thanks, Mom." Dempsey waved to Alyson, who expertly turned her car around. They both watched as she headed back up the driveway and disappeared behind the trees and shrubs. It occurred to Niall that it might have been better to stay at the

Dempsey house all day and bare his soul to Alyson than to be left alone with her son.

Ignoring Dempsey, Niall turned and headed toward his car, wondering where his keys were.

"You have got to be the most stubborn ass in the world," Dempsey called after him.

"Why are you here, Mat?" Niall yelled over his shoulder.

"I'm here because my mother is worried about you and didn't want you to be out here by yourself."

Niall kept walking. "I'm a big boy now, I can handle it."

But he really couldn't. Niall was lying, and he was reasonably certain Dempsey knew he was lying. He stared out over the rubble: the twisted debris that was left of the stove and fridge, bricks from the chimney sprawling across the grass, the inexplicably unburned handle of a broom.

Dempsey ignored his comment and strode toward him. Niall hid a shiver that had everything to do with the cop now standing next to him.

"Here's the thing," Dempsey started. Niall glanced over, but Dempsey was looking at the pile of ashes, not Niall. "You're in my territory now. This is my county, and you are one of the people I've promised to take care of. Not like some sort of weird feudal thing, but that's how I view my job as sheriff. You don't have to rebuild alone—if you are planning on rebuilding. People are going to be lining up to help you out if you let them. Maybe they're doing it because they remember Jo and Od Hamarsson, but that doesn't matter. What matters is you have help, and all you have to do is accept it.

"I'm not going to pretend I know what kind of shit you have going on inside that head of yours, I'm not a mind reader, but... there's no reason for you to do this alone. We islanders stick together, help our own..."

"No offense, but I've never felt invited to the party." Niall couldn't help but recall the taunting and bullying he endured before he left for Seattle. Being shoved in lockers by Martin Reynolds, his backpack stolen and riffled through, the contents strewn over the high school campus. His juvenile sketches taped on walls and lockers with "Niall likes boys" scrawled across each and every one.

The terrifying realization, the first day of third grade, that he was dressed all wrong and would never fit in with the other kids. His grandparents dressed him for practicality during the years they'd homeschooled and had a limited budget, which until that very instant Niall hadn't cared about. Fashion didn't matter when he was safe with Jo and Od. Niall endured each school day, counting the minutes until he was home again and could help his grandfather with his carpentry projects or sit with his grandmother so they could practice reading together. She never mocked Niall for being behind in school; she'd understood it wasn't anything he'd had control over, and between the two of them Niall had been able to catch up by the seventh grade.

Dempsey sighed and shoved his hands in his uniform pockets. "No, you're right. You weren't made to feel welcome here. I apologize for that."

The tone of sorrow in Dempsey's voice had Niall turning to look at him. "It's not like it was your fault, was it?"

He shrugged. "I suppose not entirely, but I knew it was wrong and didn't speak up."

"No offense, Dempsey, but you were even more of a shrimp than I was. You're what, maybe a couple years younger than me? What would you have done?"

"I don't know, but whatever it was, I wish I had done it."

Niall shivered again and this time wasn't able to hide it from Dempsey. The past was the past, and Niall didn't want to think about it.

"You need a coat. You weren't wearing one when I found you."

"I think I remember trying to put out the fire with it,

maybe…" Which would explain where his car keys were. Fucking damn. "Dammit, my car keys were in my jacket pocket."

Dempsey stepped to the back of his cruiser and popped the trunk. Niall watched as he reached inside and pulled out a fleece jacket.

Mat handed it to him. "Courtesy of the Piedras County Sheriff's Office."

Niall took the fleece and pulled it on; a PCS patch was sewn onto the left shoulder. He zipped it up and stuck his hands into the pockets.

"You really don't have to do this alone. I meant every word I said."

Niall sighed, looking out over the devastation again, trying to use the right words. "Dempsey, I'm not used to having help… or accepting it."

"If you plan on sticking around, you're gonna need to get used to it. We're a motley crew out here, but when things get dicey, we help each other out."

That reminded Niall. "I heard your mom on the phone. Chastity Reynolds's funeral is Sunday."

Mat frowned, his dark eyebrows drawing together. "I'm still pissed at you about talking to Reynolds. What the hell were you thinking?"

Niall hoped that was a rhetorical question. He shrugged. Dempsey probably didn't want to hear he'd had too much time on his hands—or that he figured the Piedras County Sheriff's Office was running on a skeleton staff and Niall doubted that any of the deputies had experience investigating a homicide.

Dempsey poked him in the chest with a beefy finger. "Look, keep your nose out of my office's business. I *know* you know better. I'm damn sure if I tromped around one of your cases you'd be pissed as hell."

Niall looked down at Dempsey's hand and his finger still pressing against Niall's chest, then back up to Dempsey's face without saying anything. There wasn't anything to say. Dempsey was right. If Dempsey had tromped around in his territory, Niall would be pissed as hell. But asking a few questions was not interfering with an investigation. Niall could ask all the questions he wanted, and Mat couldn't stop him. Dempsey dropped his hand back down to his side.

"If you could give me a ride to Hidden Harbor, I'd appreciate it."

When Mat pushed through the front doors of the sheriff's office, Stu Dennis was waiting impatiently for him in the reception area. Mat had to shove aside his simmering anger and frustration with Hamarsson, who'd insisted on being let off at the Orca Motel a few blocks away. The old man popped out of his chair as soon as Mat was inside, hurrying toward him.

"Sheriff, I think I saw him again."

At first Mat didn't know who Stu was referring to, but then his brain caught up and he realized Stu must be talking about the man he'd seen with Chastity.

"Come on back." Mat moved around the partition toward his desk, gesturing for Stu to follow him. Birdy wouldn't be happy Mat hadn't signed him in... Oh well.

"Only an hour or so ago," Stu added.

Mat dragged a chair over for Stu to sit down in before pulling out his own and plopping behind his desk. Stu waited while Mat hunted around in the mess in front of him for a notepad and pen.

"Okay, tell me what you saw."

Stu leaned in. "I was out for my morning walk. I have a

regular route. Just about in the middle of it, I pass the high school and come back down the hill toward the ferry terminal. If I want, I can stop for tea or a pastry at the Hook and gossip with the other old-timers. I was stopped in front, trying to decide what I wanted to do, when I saw him."

"Where did you see him?" Mat prompted.

"I think it was him. He was walking from Front Street, over by Marine Safari, toward the ferry dock—or maybe the other side of the ferry dock."

"When was this?" Mat checked his watch; the ferry had just left at 11:30, and there wouldn't be another for three hours this time of year. "How sure are you it was the same man?"

Stu looked Mat straight in the eyes. "I may be old, but I've still got good vision. I'm sure enough that I came here to tell you about him. Something in the way he was holding himself, and I think he was wearing that same knit cap—at least it looked like it from where I was standing. As far as time, it was just after ten or so. I wanted to be sure, so I tried to see where he'd gone, but by the time I got down there, he'd disappeared. I walked up and back down but didn't see him."

"Stu," Mat growled, "the last thing I need is an amateur detective roaming around getting in trouble. If it was the same person, it's possible he's dangerous, and I don't want you—or anyone else—hurt."

Stu had the grace to look a little guilty, a kid caught with his hand in the cookie jar.

"A murder investigation is serious business, not some *Murder, She Wrote* TV script. This stranger is the only lead we have on Chastity's death. Please, please, keep it to yourself for the time being. *Please* don't tell your buddies at the Hook or post about it online."

Now Stu looked offended. "I won't."

"Or tell your girlfriend," Mat added as an afterthought.

· · ·

Once Stu left, Mat sent an email to all the deputies with the description of the person of interest and the location where Stu had seen him. Why would he still be in the area, Mat wondered. If he had choked Chastity to death for some unknown reason, why would he stick around? If he *wasn't* the perp, why hadn't he come forward? He had to know she was dead. What had their meetings on the ferry been about?

Just as he was about to leave for a drive up and down Front Street to see what he could see, Birdy arrived, looking harried.

"What's up, Deputy?"

"Sheriff, I don't know what's going on anymore. Dispatch just reported another dead sheep at Merle Wainwright's, and Stan Elberman found one of his pigs dead and is accusing Reynolds of poisoning it."

"Martin Reynolds is too wrapped up in his conspiracy theory stuff to poison a pig. He barely gets to work on time."

"I know, but all of them are riled up and I'm afraid they'll do something stupid."

Leaning back in his chair, Mat groaned and ran his hands across the top of his head, restraining himself from actually tugging on his hair. This was the last thing they needed right now, some kind of island gang war when they really needed to be concentrating on finding Chastity's killer.

Sitting forward again, he asked, "Did you see my email yet about a person of interest?"

"No—I mean, I saw it. I haven't had time to read it."

"Well, we need to deal with the pig war before it becomes something serious. Once that's taken care of, we'll make sure everyone's looking for this person."

It was one of those days that, by the end of it, had Mat regretting his choice to go into law enforcement—especially on

Piedras Island. He could've done anything when he returned. He could've bought a bed and breakfast or gotten a boat and led tours, but no, instead he'd purposely run for sheriff.

It had taken them several frustrating hours to deal with the accusations flying between Elberman, Wainwright, and Reynolds. Due to geography, the Delacombes were involved too, which was not good because, despite Claribel's marriage to Frank Reynolds, there'd always been bad blood between the two families—it probably made it even worse.

Martin clearly had no affection for his great-grandmother, accusing her of trying to place the blame for the animal deaths on him so she could get her hands on the property he'd inherited from his father's family. Mat wondered if Martin remembered Claribel was nearly ninety and planning Martin's sister's funeral. There was no denying Claribel was devious and used to getting her own way on the island, but Mat didn't think she would stoop to killing animals. The only person who'd been missing from the circus was Harry Harrison—apparently, there'd been no wolf sightings recently. Thank you very much.

Then in the midst of the fray Shay Delacombe showed up, in all his coiffed and well-dressed glory. Mat was wary of Shay's motivation, but he couldn't help but be impressed with how Claribel's great-nephew was able to convince all the parties to step back from their accusations.

The island had a long and complicated history, and all resident children were forced to learn it starting the minute they were born. A livestock murder over two hundred years ago had sparked an international incident the Reynolds, Delacombe, and Elberman clans were *still* pissed about. Mat's ancestors, Mary and Declan Dempsey arrived about fifty years later, eventually buying up and settling on land the leader of the Delacombe clan was forced to sell off during the Great Depression. So, in truth, there was no love lost there either.

Mat was fucking exhausted, and there was no time for rest.

They needed to figure out what the hell was going on and whether the deaths and killings were connected. Not for the first time that day, his thoughts drifted, unwillingly, to Niall Hamarsson. Mat was certain Niall would have some theories about the situation, and Mat didn't think they would have to do with conspiracies.

NINETEEN

HAMARSSON

Niall's first thought when he unlocked the door to his recently rented room at the Orca Motel was, it was not nearly as welcoming as the guest room at the Dempseys'. The room wasn't homey. It was sterile and clean and encouraged visitors to go out and see the sights, not stay in and read novels. The bed didn't entice him to relax on it, there was no kitchen to stumble downstairs to, no coffee. And he had only himself to blame.

Niall hated it.

But his only other choice was to accept Mat and Alyson's hospitality, and he couldn't do that. He couldn't. A little voice in his head whispered, *But you could. What would it hurt?* Niall ignored it. Accepting hospitality meant letting people in, and letting people in was fucking dangerous.

The kid at the front desk informed him a big-name cell phone company had a store on Front Street. Since his room had nothing to offer except for a miniature Mr. Coffee, Niall left again, shutting the door behind him. He needed a phone, and he needed to order a new key for his car. And probably to make some other phone calls as well. But he'd take on one task at a time.

The Orca Motel was, ironically, nowhere near the harbor and had no view of water or any possible orcas. It was a mile or so walk from the motel to the cell phone store. Niall took the walk slowly, checking out all the buildings as he passed, noting what had changed and what he remembered from years ago. There were new businesses, but most places he remembered were still there.

A real estate office had opened on Spring Street, snapshots of homes for sale taped to the inside of its front windows. Niall stopped to look at the photos. He saw a lot of recently built homes and soon-to-be-built housing developments. From the map on display, it seemed a few old-timer families had sold off parcels. Back when Niall had lived on the island, there'd been a population of about six thousand. It seemed there'd been an influx of new residents, or an influx of hopeful investors. Some things had definitely changed. After a few minutes he continued on his way.

Niall slipped his shiny new smartphone into his pocket. He'd had to get a new number, and of course all his contacts were gone. Another irritating detail he would need to deal with. He supposed he could call the station; that number he knew by heart. Unfortunately, the same was true of Trey's cell number, but then, he'd called it enough times from his desk phone, hadn't he?

It would be a mistake to call Trey at this point, as Niall had no intention of resuming their relationship. He sighed. On the other hand, Trey deserved for him to at least end things permanently. Before he could talk himself out of calling, Niall got his phone out and punched in Trey's number, then waited while it rang. His call went to voicemail.

"You've reached Trey Jackson, leave a message."

"It's Niall. Call me back when you get this."

Niall clicked off, hoping Trey would call back sooner rather than later. He wanted to be done with him. His justifications for not breaking things off with him before now were shitty. No one, not even someone as shallow as Trey, deserved to be strung along because it was easier than being honest.

Next, Niall stopped in at the Hook. The diner had been in business since the fifties—and looked exactly the same inside as it had when he was a kid. A gray-haired waitress waved him to an empty table next to a window. Niall ordered a coffee and the daily special omelet with a side of hash browns. Once the waitress took his order, he got his phone out again and began the process of rebuilding his life.

By the time his omelet came, Niall had a new car key on the way. It would be delivered by express mail to the motel the next morning.

Halfway through his omelet, his phone thrummed against the linoleum tabletop. Niall glanced at the screen; it was Trey. Swallowing his bite, Niall pressed answer.

"Hamarsson."

"Niall, where the fuck are you? I've been so fucking worried."

Trey's voice grated, shrill and insistent. Niall wondered if he'd ever found it attractive.

"Look, Trey," Niall said, cutting him off, "I know it's uncool of me to do this over the phone, but I'm out of the city and I don't know when I'll be back. Our relationship doesn't work, and neither of us are happy. It's not fair to you or me to drag it out any longer."

There was silence on the other end, just for a moment. "You motherfucker," Trey ground out. "You're calling me after you disappear for a week with no contact to fucking break up with me?"

"Trey—"

"Don't fucking 'Trey' me!" Trey yelled. Niall winced, certain everyone in the diner could hear each word.

"Look, I know you're upset. And it's my fault for letting things go on as long as they have. I should've put a stop to things sooner."

"Upset? Up-fucking-set? You can't do this to me." His voice was quiet now. "You can't, I've sacrificed everything for you. You've met someone else, haven't you? You've been cheating on me. I knew it."

Niall wondered what Trey thought "sacrificing everything" was, because he was pretty sure their relationship had been extremely selfish, on both sides. Sex was the only subject they communicated about, and it was Niall giving and Trey taking— at least when they slept together. In hindsight, it seemed to Niall, their whole relationship had been about Trey. Trey wanting things, wanting or bitching about not having something he wanted.

And they'd never discussed being exclusive. He wondered what he'd seen in the younger man that had been worth his time. And Trey couldn't have been impressed by Niall's salary as a detective. The only reason Niall had extra money was because he lived simply and had a tiny inheritance from his grand-parents.

"I haven't met anyone else."

Although, as he spoke the words, an image of Mat Dempsey floated into his mind. Mat in street clothes, his t-shirt just a little tight, showing off his muscled chest and abs. Yeah, Niall wasn't going there either. *But you want to,* the same traitorous voice from earlier whispered.

Niall shut his eyes for a moment. "Trey, I know you don't want to hear it—"

The waitress chose that moment to stop by his table, likely punishment for talking on his phone in the restaurant.

"More coffee?" she asked over the clatter of the other patrons.

Niall nodded, watching the hot liquid flow from the carafe into his cup.

"Are you fucking breaking up with me over lunch?" Trey demanded.

"Brunch, actually. I missed breakfast."

"I fucking hate you." Something else was said, but their connection became staticky and Niall couldn't make out the words.

"Goodbye, Trey." Niall clicked off, then blocked Trey's number.

Someone walked by on the street, a quick shadow flitting across his table. He was relieved to have that conversation over with. It had gone about as well as he thought it would. Trey was a selfish, immature man.

Mat Dempsey was not a selfish, immature man. Niall squelched that thought as quickly as it popped into his head. No, no, and no.

Since he was at loose ends until his car key arrived, Niall lingered in the diner and surfed on his phone for an hour or so, catching up on the latest gossip and news around the island. He couldn't remember the last time he'd had this much downtime.

Eventually it was time to pay his tab. He left the Hook and walked across the street toward the Western clothing store. Before he made it there, a different storefront caught his eye: Andersen Lawn and Garden Service. Changing direction, Niall headed for the small office, intending to get to the bottom of why they hadn't been at least checking on his property, but a note taped inside the front door said they were closed until March 15. Great.

TWENTY

DEMPSEY

What an excellent way to top off my already shitty day, Mat thought as he pulled in to park at home and found his usual spot occupied by a flashy silver BMW. His brother must've decided to make an appearance without letting anyone know in advance. That's how Sean was; he expected everyone in his life to attend to his every need, whenever he demanded.

Taking a deep breath and reminding himself not to let Sean get to him, Mat set the parking brake and got out of his car, heading toward the house. He could hear Sean yelling before he opened the front door and stepped inside. Sean had two settings: on/loud and off/quiet. Quiet only happened when he was sleeping.

"You let that piece of trash sleep in our house?" Sean yelled.

Mat didn't have to ask who Sean was talking about. His mother looked furious, and even though she'd married into the Dempsey clan instead of being born into it, Alyson Dempsey had a temper of her own.

"Sean Dempsey, you watch your mouth. As long as I'm alive, this is my house and I choose who is a guest here. Including you."

Mat interrupted them. "Mom, Sean, what's going on?"

Sean turned on Mat. "You actually let Mom invite that piece of shit Hamarsson to stay at the house?"

Mat frowned. "What is your problem? What have you got against Hamarsson? He's a cop. He's not a danger to Mom."

Everything about his brother rubbed Mat the wrong way, from his pressed preppy button-down shirt to his shiny loafers.

"Have you forgotten where he came from? It wasn't bad enough he lived on the streets, exposed to criminals and drugs and god knows what else, he's a fag too. Something happened to him that made him that way. I heard he was passed around as a kid—who knows what he's really like."

Mat froze. He'd known his brother was conservative, but a homophobic asshole on top of it? Whatever he'd been about to say died on his lips. Mat suspected his mother knew he was gay, but living here on the island full time, being sheriff, it seemed better not to say anything.

"Get out of my house." His mother's voice came out a feral growl that had the hairs on the back of Mat's neck standing up.

"What? Mom?" Sean seemed genuinely confused at their mother's reaction. "It's all true."

"Get out. I will not listen to your hateful, rumor-filled innuendo."

"Mom, calm down, we can talk about this," Sean said.

Mat cringed. In his limited experience with women, telling them to calm down was one of the worst things a man could do.

"We have nothing to talk about. Niall Hamarsson's life experiences, anyone's sexuality, are not up for discussion. There is no shame for what Niall went through before Jo and Od found him. There is no shame in loving someone of the same sex. I thought we taught you better than that."

Sean didn't move to leave. Instead he got a petulant, mulish expression on his face. "Really, Mom, you're overreacting. Mat," Sean pleaded, "talk some sense into her. Help her understand how dangerous it is to have someone like Hamarsson in the house. I don't know why you would allow it."

"Mom asked you to leave."

"Hamarsson's mother was a drug addict and a thief. Like mother, like son."

"Sean, I'm not asking you as your brother. I'm telling you as the Piedras County sheriff, Alyson Dempsey asked you to leave her property. If you don't, I will have you arrested for trespassing. How long do you think it would take the entire island to find out you'd been arrested? I'll tell you, it's even faster than you think."

Sean looked from Mat to their mother. He sneered. "Whatever. You'll be sorry."

"Is that a threat, Sean? Should I be taking you down to the sheriff's office now?"

His brother grabbed his leather jacket from where it lay across the back of the couch and pulled it on as he walked toward the front door. Mat moved around him and held the door open.

"Don't let the door hit you in the ass on the way out."

This time Sean didn't respond. He took the porch stairs two at a time before striding to the beemer. Alyson came to the door, and together she and Mat watched as Sean turned around and gunned his car up the drive, dirt and gravel spitting from under his tires.

"I'm sorry about that, honey. I'm so angry with him."

Mat looked at his mom. "What are you sorry about? Sean's the asshole."

"I don't know why he's so full of hate and discontent."

Mat almost blurted out that he was gay, but again, why did it matter? What was it going to change if he came out? He would still be sheriff of a small, sometimes conservative, sometimes just eccentric county off the coast of Washington State.

"It is what it is, Mom."

It had taken Mat a while to realize he was gay. When his friends were experiencing their first crushes, he'd figured he was a late bloomer. The online porn his friends had watched obsessively did nothing for him—until Mat started watching the men.

That had been truly frightening.

In that instant, Mat had gone from a blissfully ignorant teenager who had no idea what desire was to scared out of his mind. He knew he couldn't let his friends know, even the liberal ones whose parents raised llamas. If one knew, the news would spread over the whole island. Mat hadn't been kidding Sean about how quickly people talked.

"'It is what it is' doesn't mean it's right, Mat."

"I know."

"How'd your chat with Niall go this morning?"

"About how I expected. I dropped him off at the Orca."

Alyson let out a deep breath. "He's a stubborn one."

Mat snorted. "Is there a stronger word than stubborn? He's that."

While the two of them were eating dinner, a long text from Birdy came through on Mat's cell phone. The first half was an update on the fact that so far no one had spotted anyone like the person Stu Dennis had described, but they were all keeping their eyes open. Also, WSDOT had sent over the video for the dates Stu had ridden the ferry. It was irritating to think he needed to thank Shay Delacombe for the speedy service. Birdy didn't see anything, but Mat should look in the morning. Last was a nine-digit phone number with the comment, "Niall Hamarsson stopped by and said to give this number to you."

Huh.

"What?" his mother asked.

"Niall gave Birdy his cell number to give to me."

Her eyes widened with surprise. "Maybe he's not as stubborn as you think."

Mat chuckled. "I seriously doubt that."

"It's a step in the right direction, anyway."

"I suppose."

"Let Niall tell you about his life in his own time." His mom moved close and gave him a quick squeeze. "And don't let what your brother thinks he knows get in the way of building a friendship with Niall." Mat hugged her back. She was getting older and it scared him. It was weak of him, he knew, but Mat didn't know what he'd do if she got sick… or worse.

Was it his imagination, or was there a slight hesitation before she'd said "friendship"? Did his mom somehow suspect he had conflicted feelings about Niall Hamarsson? It would be nice if Mat had an idea of what the "right" direction with Hamarsson was. He felt stuck, like any and all directions were wrong. The frustrating man was so prickly, it would be easy to misstep and—what? Ruin what?

After helping his mother with the dishes, Mat went upstairs to his room and watched mindless TV until he fell asleep.

TWENTY-ONE
HAMARSSON

"Thanks, Doc."

Soper looked up from examining Niall's hand. "It is my job, after all. Taking care of people."

Niall shrugged. He was attempting to thank Soper for offering a stranger a safe place to stay; it had been above and beyond.

In a less joking tone, Marshal added, "You're welcome. I have the space, and you were an easy guest. But—"

"Yeah?"

"Could you give Felicity Meyers a call? Somehow—through Richard, I imagine, since for an ME he is a remarkable gossip—the powers that be have my number and have called several times asking about you. I've assured them you're fine, all in one piece thanks to me, but I'd appreciate if you'd take over from here."

That wasn't embarrassing at all. Niall could only handle one difficult phone call a day, so he'd put off calling Chief Meyers.

"Don't worry, I didn't tell them anything that would violate HIPAA, but they were very concerned."

Niall nodded, watching as Soper expertly wrapped his hand

again, not as heavily this time. Niall was able to move a few fingers.

"How much longer on the stitches?"

"Come see me in ten days. You're healing well, but I don't want to risk taking them out early. You can make an appointment, don't need to scare Marissa at the front desk." Soper's eyes glinted with humor.

"Thanks again. I hate not being able to shave or at least, shave well."

"I think Harbor Barber is open today. Kim does a nice shave and haircut. All right." Soper gently tapped Niall's hand and sat back on his stool. "You're good to go."

Niall rolled his eyes at the comment. He had his car key now but still needed to get from Hidden Harbor to where he'd left the vehicle.

"Is there a car service on the island these days? I suppose I could check online." He probably should've thought of that earlier.

Soper's eyebrows drew together. "Yes, but it's pretty limited this time of year. I think the two companies focus on dragging tourists back and forth from the resort to the ferry during the summer."

Niall stood up. "I'll just walk. Thanks, Doc."

Soper stood as well, opening the exam room door. "Where do you need to go?"

"My place—my car, actually, since the cabin is a pile of ash."

"I heard about the fire. I'm sorry."

Niall glanced over at him. "Me too. Me too."

"Are you on a time frame?"

Niall walked down the bright hallway toward the waiting area. "No, unfortunately. I have nothing but time on my hands."

At the entrance to the waiting area, Soper stopped him, gently grasping Niall's shoulder. "How about I give you a ride out there? I have a few more patients, but my clinic is over at one. That'll give you time to see if Kim can do something about your face." Soper grinned, chuckling at his own joke. He was a hard man not to like. "Give me your phone number. I'll text you when I'm finished here."

First, Niall bit the bullet and called Chief Meyers to assure her that, regardless of the rumors flying around, he was fine. And no, he was not planning on returning. No, he didn't know what he was going to do. By the end of the call Niall was still on leave, but he heard the resignation in her tone and knew this was her way of doing him a favor while he sorted his life out.

"We're going to miss you, Hamarsson."

"Maybe you'll miss me, Chief. Everyone else thinks I'm a pain in their ass."

"Not everyone is as thorough as you."

After clicking off, Niall walked from the hospital to Harbor Barber, about a mile and mostly downhill. The shop was open for business and was actually Harbor Barber and Tattoo. Niall contemplated the wall of art displayed behind the front counter.

"See anything you like?"

A lanky man appeared from behind a curtain of beads on the other side of the counter. His t-shirt showed off two intricately tattooed arms, and Niall spotted the hint of a vine or leaf peeking from underneath his neckline.

"Is Kim available? I need a shave and a haircut."

The man stuck his hand out. "I'm Kim, and yeah, I've got the time to clean you up. Are you looking for a clean shave or a trim?"

Kim sat Niall in an old-fashioned barber chair and draped a cover over him before spinning him around so he faced the mirror. Niall avoided looking at himself in general, but it was impossible not to here.

"So, what are we doing?" Kim ran his fingers through Niall's hair.

As he always did, Niall replied, "Short on the sides and longer on top."

Kim rolled his eyes. "Men are *so* predictable. Fine. Let's get this mop washed up before I take the clippers to it."

As they moved from the chair to the wash station and back again, it became obvious that Kim liked to talk—and that he was good at his profession.

"The island is too small to maintain just a tattoo parlor, especially November through April, so I shave the old men and save up the stories they tell me. You're lucky. Fridays, the senior center brings a van down here and the place is packed."

"You don't have anyone else?"

"I do, but only part time. Are you thinking about getting a tattoo?"

"I have several already."

"Yeah?" Kim clearly wanted to know what Niall had inked on his body. "Are you looking for a new one, or adding to?"

Niall shrugged, causing Kim to glare menacingly and shake the razor at him. "I need to think about it."

He'd gotten his first tattoo after his grandfather died. It was a depiction of the Norse legend his grandfather told him most often, the story of Tyr. The tale seemed to Niall to be appropriate for a young police officer. The artwork crawled up his arm, a visual tale of war and justice. Only when it curled around his shoulder could you see Tyr's hand being bitten off by the fearsome wolf Fenrir.

Niall could relate to both Tyr and Fenrir. As a child, he'd hated how Fenrir had been tricked by the gods because they were afraid of him. How Tyr had known Fenrir would take his hand if the gods were lying—and they were always lying, it seemed to be what gods were best at—yet he put it in the wolf's mouth anyway.

Kim spun the chair back around, and Niall almost didn't recognize himself—or, rather, he *did* recognize himself. Gone was the beard that made him look like a mountain man, and while Kim had stuck to Niall's directions, he'd done something with Niall's hair that made it look a little more stylish.

His phone buzzed as Kim was swiping his credit card through the machine. Pulling it from the pocket of his jacket—which was the fleece Dempsey had loaned him and he needed to return—Niall checked the screen. The text was from Soper. Niall quickly replied he was finished.

Another customer came in, and Kim swept them into the back, leaving Niall alone while he waited for Soper. He was glad he didn't have to chat with Kim anymore. The man was nice, but Niall was exhausted from having to make conversation. He had a hard enough time keeping up with the shit in his own head, much less someone else's.

A few minutes later, Soper's Land Cruiser peeled around the corner and pulled to the curb across from the shop. Soper grinned at Niall from the driver's side, gesturing for him to hop in. Niall began to jog across the street as he reached the middle of the road, right when a second car came around the corner fast. Instinct alone had Niall hurtling himself sideways. He landed hard on the concrete and kept rolling until he was underneath Soper's car.

He heard metal grinding on metal as the Land Cruiser shuddered, and debris rained down where he huddled. The sound of screeching tires was followed by absolute silence.

A car door opened, and then Soper was crouching at his side.

"Christ, Niall, are you okay?"

Nodding, Niall rolled back out from under the car. Soper grabbed his good hand to pull him up and Niall started to brush himself off.

Soper looked up the street where, presumably, the other car had disappeared. Niall hadn't seen anything.

"I don't even know what happened."

The door of Harbor Barber was flung open, and Kim came rushing out.

"What happened? Is everyone okay? I called the cops. What the hell was that? I just happened to be looking out the window and saw the whole thing. Whoever that was, they deliberately tried to run you down!" Kim seemed more shaken up than Niall was, his voice reedy and thin.

"I'm okay," Niall assured him. "A little banged up but not hurt."

"I can't believe it... was the driver high?" Kim's hands were shaking. "You could've been killed. You almost *were* killed."

"I wasn't, but if I had been, my hair would've looked great."

A siren sounded, and it occurred to Niall that there was a very good chance Dempsey would respond to the scene. He was a hands-on sheriff who didn't leave all the shit work to his deputies. He sent a little prayer up that it wouldn't be Dempsey behind the wheel.

No prayers regarding sheriffs were being heard that day.

Dempsey parked, blocking the street with the cruiser and leaving its lights flashing.

"What happened?" Dempsey asked, looking directly at Niall.

"Do you mind if I check your hand?" Soper asked.

"Go ahead." Niall shrugged, discovering a twinge in his left shoulder. To Dempsey he replied, "I was crossing the street after leaving the barber shop, and a car came around the corner. I jumped out of the way. Whoever it was scraped along the side of Soper's car and took off."

"Marshal, what are you doing here?"

"I offered Niall a ride out to his car."

"Did anyone note the make and model?"

Niall had only gotten a glimpse of a larger vehicle, SUV size or a crossover of some kind.

Kim piped up, "It was a newer car, like a hipster shade of gray. Maybe a Hyundai or something. Not big, like a Suburban—more sporty."

Dempsey looked at Soper.

He shrugged. "Don't look at me. I like old cars. I never know what the new ones are. But I'd agree with Kim—an SUV of some kind, and now it has a streak of red paint along the side. I'm pretty sure it took more damage than it gave." Soper patted his car, which had some paint missing but no serious damage. "This baby has a steel body."

Dempsey stalked back to his car and leaned inside. They all listened as he relayed the details back to Dispatch. After he finished, he stood next to his car for a minute. Niall watched as the man consciously took a deep breath and released it before returning to where the three of them waited.

"He's pissed," Soper whispered. "Really, really pissed."

What the hell was Dempsey pissed about? Niall was the one who'd nearly been run over by a car.

Kim asked Dempsey, "Um, can I get back to my client? I kind of left them waiting inside."

"Go ahead. Deputy Flynn will be by in a few minutes to take your statement."

Kim bolted across the street and disappeared inside the building.

"Marshal, I'll give Hamarsson a ride to his car. He and I need to have a talk. Would you mind waiting for Birdy? She'll be here in less than ten minutes."

Marshal raised his eyebrows and shot a sympathetic look toward Niall. "Sure thing, Sheriff."

Dempsey ignored his friend and grabbed Niall's arm to steer him toward the cruiser. Niall shrugged Dempsey's hand off but didn't say anything.

When he was seated and buckled in, Niall asked, "What's with the attitude?"

Dempsey didn't answer right away. Instead, he maneuvered a three-point turn and gunned the car up Spring Street past the sheriff's office and out toward the highway bisecting the island.

When they passed by the high school—"Home of the Piedras Gems," according to the weather-beaten sign out front—Dempsey spoke. "I know you're going to take this the wrong way, but since you've been back on the island—what, seven-eight days?"

Niall nodded. "Since last Thursday."

"Okay, a week plus. Since you've been back, we've had more criminal activity than in almost a whole year. In Piedras County we have accidental deaths—you'd be surprised the variety of ways people die by accident, or maybe not, since you're a cop too. We have petty theft—a lot of drug activity, that's the big one. But since you've been back, we've had a homicide, an arson, and now an attempted hit-and-run."

Niall didn't know what to say. It was odd, but there were always odd things in police work, coincidences that led investigators astray.

"So, who have you pissed off lately?"

"No one out of the norm." The phone call with Trey flashed through his mind. "I broke it off with someone I'd been seeing off and on, but that was only yesterday."

"What about cases? Anything open or particularly dicey?"

It was a legitimate question. Niall leaned back against the seat, mentally rolling through his more recent cases. The thing about working homicide was, the families were usually happy to have closure, and the perpetrators usually didn't have a lot of friends to seek revenge on their behalf.

"No. The ones who are pissed are behind bars where they belong, and I don't think they have the power to reach me. I don't work gangs or organized crime, just good old-fashioned homicide."

"They overlap, though: gang killings, drug killings."

"Yeah, they do, but I haven't put any big names away."

Niall considered the Tanya Nichols case. The sixteen-year-old girl had been forced into a car, raped, and murdered, her body discovered weeks later by hikers. Actually, they'd only found a mandible; searchers never recovered her skeleton. Niall knew damn well who'd killed her, and Jeremy Vaughn was a free man because the DA's office didn't believe the jawbone was enough to convict. They couldn't place Vaughn where the partial remains were found. It was likely he'd buried her somewhere else and a hawk or some other bird had picked up the mandible, carrying it several miles before dropping it.

"You honestly have no idea who would want to run you down or set fire to your property?"

"I thought *you* thought it was Martin Reynolds." Niall sure did.

Dempsey stared out the windshield. He flicked on the wipers, as it was starting to sprinkle. "I did. It still could be him, but… first of all, he's fucking lazy. I'm having trouble imagining him rushing out to torch your place. He can't do his own laundry, much less round up gasoline, drive all the way to the cabin, douse it, and then take off. He was pretty outraged when we questioned him and I tend to believe him."

"Okay, then who?"

"That's the problem." Mat pounded the steering wheel with his open palm. "I don't know who. I don't know who is stirring up all this other shit, either. Livestock dying—and it's not by accident unless a sheep can shoot itself. Harry Harrison thinks there's a wolf roaming the island. And nobody, *nobody* except Stu Dennis has come forward with any information about Chastity, and so far we haven't been able to confirm what he thinks he saw."

The access road to the cabin—to his property—came up and Dempsey turned onto it.

"Why are you telling me all this, Dempsey?"

Dempsey brought the car to an abrupt stop, set the parking brake, and turned to face Niall. "Would you *please* call me Mat?"

It was past midafternoon, and the sun was threatening to set. Dempsey's dark eyes glittered in the dim light.

"Mat." Saying his name felt uncomfortable—like Mat was offering something Niall wasn't sure he would be able to return. "You told me to butt out. I think those were your very words."

"Niall—can I call you Niall? I'm tired of Hamarsson."

Niall nodded. What was he supposed to say, that hearing Mat speak his given name was almost more frightening than the familiarity of saying Mat's? The lines they'd drawn so long ago were becoming blurred and indistinct.

"You were right about my department not having any experience with homicide, and I can't give the investigation my full attention with all this shit going on. I apologize for before. I overreacted. Also, I think someone has it out for you, and the best way to protect you is to keep you close."

"Why would you want to protect me?"

His question was met with a silence that lay uncomfortably between them. Niall sensed a shift of some sort, one he couldn't identify.

"It's what I do, Niall. It's what I do."

Now, instead of silence, those words hung between them, echoing as Mat navigated the turn onto Niall's driveway.

The cruiser's headlights lit Niall's car and the pile of rubble that had been the cabin. Mat sighed and cleared his throat. "Promise me you're not staying out here tonight."

"No, I'm at the Orca."

Mat nodded, and Niall got out of the car. As an afterthought, he poked his head back inside and asked, "Is it okay if I go to the Reynolds funeral?"

"You think the killer will be there?"

"No. I mean, I suppose it's not out of the realm of possibility, but I want to see how the mourners interact. Get a better idea of family dynamics."

"How about we go together? I'm taking my mom anyway."

"Okay. Deputy Flynn gave you my number, right? Text the details."

Niall watched Mat back up the driveway and out to the road and wondered what the hell had happened.

Mat had invited him back to his house for dinner. Niall'd declined… for tonight. He wasn't ready for that quite yet. He needed time to reassemble his mental armor. Accepting emotional handouts from Mat Dempsey was a habit he couldn't allow himself to get used to.

As he stood there, finally alone, he had the odd feeling someone, or something, was watching him. He marked it down to paranoia and the aftermath of the adrenaline rush from almost being hit by a car. The driver was probably just a stupid kid, not anyone actually wanting to harm him. *Right*, the voice said, but Niall ignored it too. Still, he looked around and didn't see anything that felt out of place.

He wasn't ready to head back to the Orca. The groceries he'd stashed in the back of his car the other day were still there, and the weather had been cold enough for them to keep. Opening the rear hatch, Niall rummaged around for the bread, cheese, and turkey he'd purchased at Chester's a few days ago. As he did, he realized that his grandfather's hand tools from the shed were in there too. He'd forgotten he'd moved them.

He hadn't lost everything after all.

Niall picked up the planer with its rusty blade and turned it over in his hands, remembering his grandfather working on projects while Niall watched him. It was a good memory. His grandfather always told stories while he worked.

Setting the planer back inside the car, he wandered down to the beach with his sandwich makings and sat down on a log to watch the waves and the weak sunset. His stomach rumbled while he constructed his banquet. Pausing, he sniffed the turkey then set it down next to him; it'd been hours since he'd eaten, but maybe he wasn't willing to risk food poisoning.

A quiet, unidentifiable sound caught his attention. If the water hadn't been so smooth, barely lapping against the shore, Niall might have missed it. Mat's words came back to him, and Niall had the thought that maybe it was stupid of him to sit out in the open when *possibly* someone wanted him injured or dead.

The bread bag he'd placed on the log next to his thigh slipped backward, the movement slow and deliberate. Cautiously, Niall turned his head to the side and calmed his breathing. Surely a killer wouldn't be stealing a loaf of bread?

Perhaps it was his upbringing, but what Niall saw didn't frighten him. Unlike Harry Harrison, he knew it wasn't a wolf. It was a dog—likely a wolfhound, but not a wolf. The animal tracked Niall's movement and froze, staring back at Niall with golden eyes. Ever so slowly, Niall reached for a slice of cheese and held it out toward the beast. The dog was skinny, its fur matted. Some asshole had probably abandoned it, unprepared for how much a dog the size of this one ate.

The dog looked at him, then at the cheese. With a gentleness belying its size and fierce looks, it took the cheese and swallowed it in a single bite.

TWENTY-TWO
DEMPSEY

"What the hell is *that*?"

Mat eyed the gigantic beast standing next to Niall, gray and darker gray, a large walking shadow with teeth. When Niall had texted, asking if he could stop by the house before Chastity's service, he hadn't mentioned bringing a guest.

"Can I have a puppy?"

"Excuse me?"

"I'm reasonably sure this is your wolf," Niall said as he stroked the top of the dog's head with ease. The dog was so tall he didn't need to bend down.

"Explain."

"He came out of the woods after you left last night. I think that's where he was, anyway. I was minding my own business, eating a sandwich on the beach, and suddenly he appeared out of the dark. It didn't take much to make him my friend—a few pieces of cheese and turkey and he wasn't going anywhere."

Mat eyed the... dog. He could see why an old man with poor eyesight had thought he'd seen a wolf. The dog stood two and a half feet tall at the shoulder. Even skinny, he was imposing.

"Wow. Is this why you wanted to meet me outside?"

"Yeah. I, uh, snuck him into the motel room last night. He's clearly house-trained, and the poor guy was cold. I can't imagine where he's been sleeping or what he's been eating. He needs to see a vet. Maybe they'll find a tag of some kind and we can get him back to his owner."

"More likely his owner purposely left him on the island. We've had more than one case of animal dumping."

Niall scratched the top of the beast's head. "I guess. My gain."

"You're going to keep him?"

The dog suited Niall. It was as big a dog as Niall was a man.

"We've come to an agreement: I told him he can stay if his owners don't want him, and he promises not to chew off my arm."

"If we find his owners. What are you talking about now?"

Niall quirked his lips in a half smile and raised an eyebrow before answering, "An old story, my grandfather used to tell it to me, about the Norse god Tyr and the wolf Fenrir, who was also a god—a very powerful one. The other gods were scared of Fenrir and tricked him into being chained up after a whole bunch of trials. Fenrir knew the simple-looking rope was a con and demanded one of the gods stick a hand in his mouth while they 'tested' the rope on him. If Fenrir was right and the rope was actually the strongest chain ever created, he'd bite off the god's hand. Tyr was the only god brave enough—and yes, he lost his hand. So even though Fenrir was chained up, justice was served."

"Huh. Seems kind of a grim story for a kid."

"My life was grim, Mat. That story gave me hope."

Shit.

Niall shrugged. "Don't apologize. It's just what it was. I didn't care about nice stories. I wanted to hear ones with justice, where the bad people went to hell and were punished in the most horrible way a young kid could imagine—and I had a pretty vivid imagination. I knew there was no place like Sesame Street. There's a lot of gruesome shit in Norse mythology. Anyway, I've named him Fenrir."

Niall patted the dog again. It leaned against his leg, nearly reaching his hip.

"He kind of needs a bath. Do you think… maybe your mom would let us use the hose or a bathtub?"

If Mat hadn't been watching Niall, he would've missed the glint of humor in the other man's eyes. Mat gaped at him. Niall refused to stay with Mat and his mom, but he wanted a bath for this—he glanced over (not down, *over*) at the dog—beast? Now it was Fenrir staring back at Mat, his golden eyes wise and certain, knowing he'd hit the jackpot with Niall Hamarsson.

"Let me make sure it's okay with Mom. I try not to bring monsters home on a regular basis."

"You brought me home."

Mat pretended he hadn't heard him. Niall's words meant more to Mat than he wanted to admit. Instead he turned and went back inside to see if his mom was willing to allow the dog in the house or if it would be the hose in this cold and damp February weather.

Alyson agreed to allow Fenrir in the house, laughing at Mat's muttered explanation as she opened the front door for Niall and Fenrir.

"Don't worry about it, Niall," she said. "I raised four children, and if you think that almost every one of them didn't try to bring a stray animal home at one point or another…" She looked at Mat, her eyes narrowing while she thought. "Mat was the worst. He rescued baby raccoons, birds of all sorts—he found an injured fawn once and managed not only to put a makeshift splint on its leg, but he got a passerby to take him and the fawn to the vet. There was a muskrat. And probably more I never found out about. Niall, you got a haircut. You look quite handsome."

Niall self-consciously ran a hand across the top of his head, managing to look sheepish. "Thanks."

"The memorial starts at one," Mat reminded Niall as they shepherded the dog into the bathroom. They only had an hour or so before they needed to leave.

Niall grunted, "Yeah, I know. It won't take long to give him a bath."

Famous last words.

It took both of them and a significant amount of cheese—like, an entire block of perfectly good cheddar disappeared down the dog's gullet by the time he was mostly clean. Cleanish. Mat glared at Fenrir, and Mat swore the dog smirked back at him. The small bathroom was not meant to hold two large men and an equally large dog.

"You are a master con artist."

Fenrir's elegant tail moved back and forth, a dog shrug. Mat looked down at himself. His jeans and the front of his t-shirt were soaked through. It was a damn good thing he hadn't changed into his uniform before Operation Bath. Niall was barely damp, as he'd been on the teeth end, feeding Fenrir cheese and talking to him as if he were human. The animal did act remarkably like a person.

Fenrir had immediately liked Alyson. She cooed and hovered over him, telling him how handsome he was going to be after his bath, as if he were one of her own children or grandchildren. Mat shook his head; the damn dog had wooed his mother.

Strident voices jarred him from his meandering thoughts. It took him a second to recognize Sean's voice. What was he doing at the house again? Their mom had made herself clear the other day, and Mat didn't feel like dealing with him right now. Maybe if he was lucky Sean would leave before they were done drying Fenrir.

Niall glanced up from giving the dog more treats. "Hand me one of those towels and I'll dry him off."

"Just a second," Mat said, stepping away from the side of the tub to grab the doorknob and open the door just a crack, when all hell broke loose.

"That piece of trash is in this house?" Sean continued yelling, his words crystal clear. "You know he's a fag, right?"

"Sean Allen Dempsey! I'm ashamed of you. Your father and I did not raise our children to be hateful!"

Something shoved against his thigh. At first Mat thought it was Niall pushing him aside, and Mat's reaction was to try and grab him, to keep him from giving Sean the beating he deserved. Instead, a gray streak shot out the open bathroom door and the house went silent for an instant.

"Jesus Christ, somebody get this animal off me!" Sean's voice shook.

If he hadn't been worried about bloodshed, Mat would've found it funny when he and Niall were momentarily stuck in the bathroom door as they both tried to exit at the same time, their shoulders colliding and sending a spark down Mat's spine. Mat was able to get out the door ahead of Niall, and he raced into the living room, halting when he saw his brother wasn't being mauled, merely threatened.

Fenrir had backed Sean up against the living room wall. Mat's brother had always been a bully, and Mat felt a stab of satisfaction that Sean was scared of Fenrir. A buzzing sound reached his ears. The dog was emitting a low-frequency growl that was one of the scariest things Mat had ever heard. Not doing anything else, just growling and standing close enough to threaten Sean's balls.

"Do something, get it off me." Sean's voice was thin and reedy with fear.

"Fenrir, come."

Niall's deep voice rolled across the room, pealing thunder. He tapped his thigh. The dog turned its massive head from Sean to Niall but didn't move away. Niall tugged him aside.

"He wouldn't bite you," Niall sneered, leaning in close so Sean was forced to press his head against the plaster wall. "He doesn't like the taste of bullshit."

"Niall, I apologize for Sean's words. They didn't come from me. Would you mind taking Fenrir into the kitchen while Sean leaves?"

Sean stared at their mother and opened his mouth—to spew more hate, Mat was sure. But his mother spoke first. Her voice shook, but her words were firm.

"Sean, you aren't welcome in this house anymore. I don't know how you ended up on this path of hate, but it wasn't me or your father."

"Is it because Mat's a fag too?"

Mat felt like he'd been punched in the stomach. He looked quickly at his mom, but she was scowling at her oldest child. Mat couldn't tell if she was surprised by Sean's words or just angry in general.

"Yeah," Sean said as he looked at Mat, a sneer marring his features, "you think you hid it from us, but I—"

He didn't finish his sentence; Niall had stealthily returned from the kitchen with Fenrir padding behind him. He walked right up to Sean, stopping only inches away from him.

"Do you want to repeat yourself?" Niall asked him quietly, the kind of quiet Mat knew could be very dangerous.

"I'm not scared of you."

"You *should* be scared. *This* faggot is going to punch your lights out if you don't get out right now. I'm bigger than you now, Sean, and I don't fight fair."

Mat saw fear and resentment in his brother's eyes, but he turned and slipped past Niall and the dog toward the front door.

Mat beat him to it, holding the door open as he had when Sean stormed out the other day. They all watched as he hustled down the steps to his car.

"Hey, you didn't try to run Hamarsson down the other day, did you?" Mat called after Sean as an afterthought.

Sean turned, the sneer back on his face. "No, but it's an excellent idea." He climbed into his car and drove off.

"Mom, why was Sean here *again*?" Mat asked.

Alyson sighed. "He's been relentless about me moving off the island. It's been a discussion for a few years, but lately he's been more persistent. He keeps bringing pamphlets and brochures advertising assisted living and other 'senior solutions.' I've told him over and over I am not moving, but he's got it in his head." She looked at him, smiling grimly. "I'm not going anywhere."

"How long has this been going on?" His mom hadn't said anything to Mat about Sean bothering her.

"Mat, can we discuss it later? I didn't want you to worry about it because it's not going to happen. Now, if we're going to be on time to the memorial, we need to leave."

Mat wondered what other things his mom didn't want him to worry about—and if he'd been too busy to pay attention to things going on in his own house.

TWENTY-THREE

HAMARSSON

Niall had been to many, many, funerals. As a detective he'd often made the time to go to victims' funerals. Nothing was different about Chastity's memorial except it was on Piedras, and the last one he'd been to here was his grandmother's. There were mourners there who saw themselves as friends, family, as well as the curious and gawkers. Maybe the crowd was smaller than it would have been on the mainland, but it was still made up of the same population.

The yoga center was packed. Many people Niall knew from the past were in attendance, as well as some he'd only met recently, like Fred from the general store and Kim the hair-stylist–tattoo artist. It shouldn't have surprised him so many people were there; the islanders stuck together, something he'd forgotten.

After a short discussion with Alyson and Mat about "the beast," they'd decided to bring Fenrir along rather than leave him alone in the house. Niall didn't think he would misbehave, but after the incident with Mat's shithole of a brother, he didn't want to risk Fenrir deciding he didn't like the living room furniture. Alyson dug an ancient rope-style leash out of her utility room, and Niall looped it around Fenrir's neck. He'd stopped for dog food that morning, but he was going to need to get a real collar and tag next time he was in Hidden Harbor.

If anyone asked, Niall didn't think he would be able to find the right words to explain how the instant he'd laid eyes on the dog he'd recognized a kindred soul. Once he got over his loaf of bread disappearing and offered the dog his sliced cheese, he'd known Fenrir was his—or, more likely, he was Fenrir's. If Dempsey managed to locate the assholes who *hadn't noticed* their one-hundred-and-fifteen-pound dog was missing, he would offer to buy him—but only if he kept himself from putting his hands around their necks first. People who abused animals belonged in the same circle of hell as murderers.

From his vantage point at the back of the group, set aside from the crowd so Fenrir didn't make anyone nervous, Niall watched the mourners. Mat looked irritatingly splendid in his crisp uniform. Niall forced his thoughts to skitter past Piedras County's sexy sheriff. After the blowup with Dempsey's older brother, Niall's suspicion about Mat's sexuality was confirmed. Didn't matter, though, since Dempsey was in the closet and Niall wasn't going to be the one to drag him out.

Remarkably, it wasn't raining, and Claribel held the remembrance ceremony outside on the sloping green lawn of the yoga center. The head of the center had been chosen to speak about Chastity first. She was followed by several other friends, and then, to Niall's surprise, Kim spoke. He looked nervous but determined.

"A little over two years ago, Chastity came to my shop and asked me to design a tattoo. She wanted wings on her back. I didn't know Chastity very well then, but a large piece like the one she wanted takes hours and several sessions. She probably came to the shop at least six times over a two-month period, until she and I were both happy with the outcome. We talked a lot, of course, because that's kind of what a tattoo artist does, but it wasn't until the very end of our sessions that I asked, *Why angel wings?* If you ever saw them, you'll know one was fully extended and the other partially furled—hard to tell if it was opening or closing."

Kim stopped for a moment, looking up at the gray sky before continuing. "Chastity was a funny person. She always joked around with me and had a smile on her face. I don't know how many of you knew that about her. That day she looked at me and said, 'It's not because I think I'm an angel, it's a reminder that I always have choices. The one wing is a question to myself —am I growing? Am I changing? Am I embracing the future I want for myself? The open wing is my tomorrow.'

"I can tell all of you, I hope Chastity's wings flew her to her tomorrow, where she wanted to be." Tears streamed down Kim's cheeks now. "She didn't deserve this. No one deserves to have their life cut brutally short." He cleared his throat. "We became good friends, and even though Chastity didn't think she was an angel, I'm damn glad she had those wings."

Kim looked down at the index card he held in his hand. "She loved it here, on the island and at the yoga center. She will be missed." Without saying anything else, Kim left the front and sat back down in the audience. No one else stood to speak, and after a moment the yoga instructor returned to the front and announced there was food and drink inside, and if people were interested, the school was setting up a memorial fund they could donate to for students who might want to be a part of the center.

Fenrir shifted beside Niall, finding a different comfortable position against his leg. Niall continued watching as people stood and made their way inside. He wondered how many of the people in the audience knew Chastity as well as Kim had. He wanted to talk to Kim about Chastity now that Mat had given him the go-ahead to ask questions. Someone on the island knew something. Information had a way of percolating to the surface whether the guilty wanted it to or not. The year-round community was just too small.

"Excuse me, is your dog safe?"

The voice came from behind him. Niall turned to find a short weather-beaten older man standing there. Niall thought he recognized him but couldn't place a name to the face.

"He is. He only looks scary."

"Ah, well, that's nice." He stuck out a wiry, scarred hand. "Bill Andersen."

"Niall Hamarsson."

"I was sorry to hear about the fire, such a shame."

One and one added together and became two. "You own Andersen Lawn and Garden Services. If you don't mind my asking, why did you stop the maintenance on my place?"

Bill's eyebrows shot up. "You asked me to. Sent a letter saying you didn't want the monthly service anymore."

Niall felt his eyes widen in surprise. "I'm sorry to say I never sent any such letter."

"I have a copy on file. We always keep customer correspondence."

"Do you mind if I come in and take a look? I never sent you a letter, and since I don't pay attention to my bank account, I guess I never noticed you'd stopped charging me." Mat was right, something was funny about all this—and Niall wanted to get to the bottom of it. Why would someone pretending to be him send a letter to Andersen ending the lawn service?

Bill had the same thought. "Who would do such a thing?"

"I really don't know. When I see the letter, maybe I'll have a better idea." A thought struck Niall. "How did you know Chastity?" he asked.

"Such a shame. Chastity was a good person." Bill looked honestly upset. "She worked for us off and on during the busy season."

"Where did she work when it wasn't busy?" Living full time

on the island wasn't easy for young people or those with limited funds.

"Well, I can't say I know for sure. She did the yoga, but as far as I know she was still a student when…" Bill's voice trailed off. No one liked using the word murder.

"She never mentioned anywhere else, work friends or names of associates?"

"It's possible she had a part-time job in Anacortes. I know I saw her getting on the ferry a few times, pretty regular."

Another older man approached them. He'd once been tall and was now wiry and slightly stooped. Mat chose that moment to walk out of the yoga center building toward where they were standing. Fenrir wagged his tail; Niall wanted to do something similar. He squashed the feeling, reminding himself of Sean Dempsey's words and Mat's reaction. Mat wasn't out. Niall didn't mess with men in the closet.

Yeah, a little voice said, *and you ended up with a shit like Trey, so maybe try something different.* He told the voice to fuck off.

"What's up, Sheriff?" Niall asked.

Mat straightened his shoulders as he came closer, looking every bit the lawman he was. Niall looked over Mat's shoulder toward the choppy gray water.

"Sheriff stuff."

Niall rolled his eyes and suppressed the smile threatening to emerge.

Mat greeted the other man. "Stu, how are you doing? Do you know Niall Hamarsson?"

Stu nodded. "I remember Niall, but he may not remember me."

Niall shook his head. "My apologies, I don't."

"Stu's the island historian," Mat said by way of introduction.

Stu nodded. "It's a hobby, keeps me out of trouble for the most part." He glanced at Fenrir standing quietly next to Niall. "That's quite an animal."

"He showed up last night while I was out at—well, what's left of my grandparents' cabin. Dempsey tells me he was likely abandoned."

"That's too bad." Stu looked at Mat. "I'll bet you found your wolf."

"Niall said the same thing. I'm damn glad you and the rest of those hotheads didn't go running into the woods."

"What are you talking about?" Bill asked.

Dempsey rolled his eyes. "Harry Harrison claimed he saw a wolf around the same time another resident found one of his goats dead. Looks like it ate something bad, not an animal attack. On the other side of the island, the Wainwright farm has reported two sheep dead—shot. They're worth a lot of money, and Wainwright is pissed off. Piedras is usually quiet this time of year, but instead of catching up on paperwork, we're running around putting fires out everywhere *and* investigating Chastity's killer."

Niall said, "Bill was telling me a little about Chastity, that she worked for him. He also told me I sent a letter ending my yard service—which I didn't. I'd like to go into Hidden Harbor and take a look at it."

Bill offered, "I can go to the office now, if you like?"

Dempsey nodded. "I should go to the station. Ride with me?" Niall had left his car at Mat's and ridden with Alyson, knowing parking at the memorial would be difficult. Mat looked at Fenrir, who was still leaning comfortably against Niall's leg. "Yes, the invitation was extended to you as well."

"Huh." Niall read the letter again. Dated a few years earlier, it was short and to the point and definitely not written by him. His signature had been forged, but how would Bill Andersen know that? They had no way to know what his real signature looked like and why would they think it wasn't from him, anyway?

To Whom It May Concern:

From this day forward I no longer require your services.
Niall Hamarsson

"Whoever wrote this was a real asshole," Niall remarked.

Dempsey coughed into his hand.

"Have a cold, do you?" Niall asked.

The three of them and Fenrir were packed into Andersen's tiny office facing onto Spring Street. After flipping through several folders in a huge gray filing cabinet, Bill had pulled out a file and apologetically handed the letter to Niall.

"As I said, we keep everything our customers send us."

There was nothing Niall could say. Bill wasn't at fault. Niall hadn't been on the island for years. How would Bill know Niall hadn't given up on the island but that it was just too hard to come back? It had been easier for him to live in Seattle and quasi imagine his grandparents were still alive than it was to return and face their absence. Piedras was magic, and Niall knew in his heart he didn't deserve such a thing. The peace Piedras tempted him with was not something he could accept. If he let his guard down, something would go wrong. Niall didn't know what would go wrong, he just knew it would.

So he'd distanced himself from the island for reasons that, *maybe*, were reactionary. Much of his childhood had been hell, and that hell followed him to the island after his mother died. Stupid kids saying hurtful things—having no idea what Niall'd been through, only knowing he was different, odd, not what they were used to. And yet, Piedras had saved him and he didn't feel he'd deserved it. So he'd left and resisted returning.

A car drove past on the street outside, jolting him from his thoughts. Niall caught it out of the corner of his eye, and the odd color grabbed his attention. It was the same funky gray as the car that tried to run him down outside Harbor Barber. Shoving the letter at Dempsey, he dashed to the door and out onto the sidewalk. The car was just turning the corner toward the high school.

"Goddammit." Niall stood looking in the direction the car had disappeared, hands on his hips.

"What was that about?" Dempsey asked. He held onto the end of Fenrir's leash, although Niall didn't think the dog would go anywhere. Bill peered over Dempsey's shoulder, the office door ajar behind them.

"I thought I saw the car that tried to run me over. I'm pretty certain it was the same one, but if there was damage, I didn't see it."

"Did you get a look at the driver?"

Niall shook his head. "Not really. I had the impression of a dark head, maybe wearing a hat?"

"Dammit. Let's go on a ride and see if we see anything."

Of course they didn't find a thing, no handily parked gray cars with left-side damage, no neon sign pointing them in the right direction. Niall's thoughts kept returning to the silhouette of the driver. There was something about the man—he was sure it was a man—but his brain refused to cooperate, and he was left with the sinking feeling that he was missing something vital.

Mat invited Niall back to the station with him, knowing Niall was as frustrated as he was; it was possible the perpetrator had been close and had slipped through their grasp.

"You want coffee?" Mat offered. Fenrir slumped onto the floor with a whump next to where Niall sat in the spare chair by Mat's desk.

"I guess. Is it going to give me an ulcer?"

"Probably."

The office was empty except for them, as it was Mat's weekend to be on call. He left Niall at his desk and went into the break room. In an upper cabinet was his private coffee stash. With luck, none of the unappreciative had found it. Success— the still-sealed bag of Fidalgo Bay coffee waited for him. Quickly, Mat set the coffee brewing and headed back out to where Niall was waiting.

Niall was bent down, murmuring and running his strong hands along the top of the dog's head. Something Mat recognized as jealousy tore through his chest and made him stop in his tracks. Did he want Niall like that? As more than just a quick screw? Did he hope to have Niall's secret tenderness directed at him? God, he was a fool.

There was no one for him on Piedras, so what was the point. This was the justification Mat used for not coming out. As sheriff he certainly couldn't bed-hop around the island—and that wasn't his style, anyway. The few serious relationships before he'd moved back, he'd been all in, mentally planning a future together, but his boyfriends had been planning something very different. He obviously didn't have a clue how to choose a partner, and his parents' example of meet, fall in love, and get married in the space of eight weeks was zero help.

He and Mom were going to have to *talk*. Mat mentally groaned; here he was, in his mid-late-ish thirties and not wanting to talk to his mother about his sexuality. From her reaction to Sean's words, Mat knew she supported him—and maybe she'd guessed—but he *still* didn't want to talk about it.

"Are you coming back, or are you just going to stand there?" Niall's voice brought Mat back down to earth.

"Shit, sorry. Just thinking."

"Oh yeah? What were you thinking about?"

The heat of embarrassment bloomed across his cheeks; Mat hoped Niall didn't notice.

"If you're thinking I'm going to tell the entire population of the island what your brother said about me—and about you— don't worry about it. I'm gay. I've come to terms with it. People like your brother, they can't hurt me."

Mat found himself answering honestly. "I'm not worried you'd say anything—that's ridiculous, why would you do that? I am gay, my brother isn't wrong. I was out when I lived in San Fran." Mat started moving toward his desk again. "When I came back, it seemed easier to pretend."

"Was it?"

"Was it what?"

"Easier."

Had it been? Sure. Mat hadn't had to answer hard questions from his constituents about his sex life. But he had been lonely—still *was* lonely. And any passing fantasy he had regarding Niall needed to be banished, because the man had made it clear he was not planning on staying.

"No, I guess not. You're out in Seattle?" Mat wondered how that had been for Niall.

Niall shrugged. "I was never not out. I think I look at women wrong or something. But the department was good about it. Maybe not every cop was decent, but things were fine in general. Most of the guys knew me well enough not to fuck with me, and"—he shrugged—"I'm bigger than most of them."

Mat nodded right as the coffee maker beeped from the break room. He left Niall again, calling over his shoulder, "You take milk?"

When they were settled with coffee, Mat pulled the Reynolds file out of his desk drawer and handed it to Niall. "Have a look."

While Niall flipped through the file, Mat read emails and checked his calendar for the upcoming week.

"That fabric around her neck…"

"What about it?"

"I bought a scarf similar to this one for Trey, my ex-boyfriend. I don't normally do that sort of thing, but he kept hinting about it and how buying it supported some microbusiness in the Philippines or Ecuador, that each one was unique. He must have sent the link ten times. Finally, I went online and bought one for him."

"So this could be coincidence?"

"I suppose." He sat up and tossed the file back on Mat's desk. "I mean, obviously, someone else could have a scarf similar to this one—and as happy as I am to have finally parted ways with Trey, I don't want to believe he is a murderer. And how would he have known Chastity anyway? But you and I both know coincidences like this don't just happen. What are the chances my ex-boyfriend *and* someone on the islands both had a handmade scarf from the same place?"

"Probably a lot higher than you think. I've had weird stuff happen to me."

"Dempsey—Mat—I don't want it to be Trey, okay? But…"

"Fine, lay it out for me. How would your ex-boyfriend know Chastity, and if he did, why would his scarf be around her neck?"

"I don't know. We've been on-again off-again for a couple years. Now it's permanently off, and he didn't take it very well."

Mat raised his eyebrows, waiting for Niall to continue.

"I talked to him yesterday and ended it, had been dragging it out. I should've done it earlier, but…" He shrugged.

"How did the two of you meet?"

Niall scrunched his nose. "At a bar in Belltown. I used to stop in on my way home, and we got to talking. One thing led to another."

Mat thought about the seemingly random events of the past few days. He couldn't put a finger on what was bothering him. How—*why*—would Niall's ex-boyfriend have been involved in Chastity's murder—it didn't make any sense. If Trey Jackson had come to Piedras, it seemed like he would be focused on Niall. And hadn't they broken up *after* Chastity had been murdered?

"Is it possible he was the one who tried to run you over?"

"Anything's possible. He's always been high maintenance, but murder seems a poor way to get my attention. I don't know, maybe it's nothing. Coincidence, like you said." He slumped back in the chair with a loud sigh.

"Right, but what about the letter?"

"What about it?"

"Why would someone cancel your yard service?"

"I don't know." He ran a hand through his hair, obviously

frustrated. "It's stupid. I mean, the only thing I can think of is someone wanted to be out there without being caught—but it was pretty clear when I was there that no one had been there in ages. The cabin was a mess, but that was my fault. I never asked anyone to keep it up, and I sure as hell didn't check on it myself."

"Okay, so this is a dead end for now... but it deserves returning to. Humor me, what's the ex's name again?"

"Trey Jackson."

"Okay, date of birth, address, et cetera."

"He's thirty-ish, I don't remember exactly. He's an event planner—you know, office parties and stuff, networking." Niall shuddered. "Something I would never want to do. He lives in Belltown. I can give you directions, but I don't know the address."

"Family? Anything else you can tell me?"

"Dempsey."

Mat looked up from taking notes.

"I'm not a nice guy. I didn't care about those kinds of things. I'm not the kind of person people take home to their parents. I never met his family, I don't know the name of the company he worked for, we didn't go on vacation together—" Niall stopped.

"What? You thought of something. What is it?"

"Trey did nag me to take him on vacation. I guess I might have said something about how I had a ton of time I wouldn't be able to use. He bugged me about it, but I shrugged him off. I wasn't going to take a vacation with him. Ever. If I went on vacation, I wouldn't want to have to make meaningless conversation. But he did mention Piedras. I don't remember talking about it with him, but I must have at some point—still, I would never have brought him here."

"That's pretty harsh."

"Look, I told you, I'm not a very nice person—but I felt like I was the same for him, a convenience when his less-permanent hookups weren't around or he wanted something."

Mat glanced from Niall to the dog. He disagreed: Niall was, in fact, a nice person. "Give me a good description of him, and I'll have my deputies keep an eye out. It's a long shot for sure, but if he is on the island, I'd like to have a chat with him."

"There are a lot of places to hide on the island."

Mat grinned. "And I know where most of them are."

Mat's desk and cell phones rang almost simultaneously. Leaning across paperwork, he picked up the receiver and held it to his ear.

"Mat?" His mom's voice was low and husky. He knew immediately something was terribly wrong. God, he hoped nothing had happened to one of his sisters, or his niece.

"Mom? What's wrong?"

"It's Sean."

"Did he come back? Don't talk to him, I'll be there—"

"Mat. He's dead, I think. Shot. I don't know what to do."

She drew in a jagged breath.

"Don't touch anything. We'll be right there."

Mat had the errant thought that at least he was certain Niall hadn't been responsible because he'd been with Mat since they'd left the house that morning.

TWENTY-FIVE
HAMARSSON

"He'll be fine in my car. We don't need him tromping around.
I'll leave the windows down for him."

As the cruiser came to a stop, Mat jumped out. Niall
followed, releasing Fenrir from the back seat. Crossing to where
his car was parked, he opened the hatch and thumped the floor.
Fenrir daintily stepped into the Subaru; he didn't have to jump.
Slamming the hatch shut, Niall hurried after Mat, who was just
pulling his sobbing mother into his arms.

Niall'd driven Mat's cruiser from Hidden Harbor to the
house—probably a county violation, but Mat wanted to stay on
the phone with his mom who, understandably, was close to
breaking down. From what Niall was able to put together from
eavesdropping, Alyson had stayed at Chastity's memorial for an
hour or so after he and Mat had left before heading to Killegen's
Point to pick up a few groceries and then heading home.

She'd pulled into the drive and found Sean's car parked in
front of the house. She had been infuriated that he'd come back
but determined to confront him, but once she got to the front
porch, she'd discovered only horror.

"It's okay, Mom, we're almost there. No, I'm not driving, Niall is," Mat had reassured her. "Yes, he's coming too. This is us now, we're just turning in."

They'd arrived before the ambulance. Niall had accepted the keys from Mat and driven as fast as he dared on the rural road, blue and red lights flashing and siren sounding, alerting anyone in their way. Mat called Marshal Soper as he got out of the car; from what Alyson described, there was no coming back from where Sean Dempsey had gone. As he walked toward the house, Niall pulled his sleeve over his hand and tested the doors of Sean's car. It was locked.

Alyson waited for them outside at the base of the front steps, her arms wrapped around herself. She was pale, shivering with cold and shock. When Mat reached her, he pulled her into an embrace, gesturing with a nod for Niall to check the porch as he attempted to comfort his mother.

Niall didn't have to go much past the top step. Sean lay splayed out in the middle of the decking, a good portion of the back of his head missing. A handgun lay next to his body. Body fluids had seeped into the flooring and welcome mat, but not much blood from what Niall could see—not unusual, regardless of how Hollywood portrayed crime scenes. The question was, why would Sean do this to himself? Niall didn't know Sean Dempsey at all, but something was off.

Avoiding the porch swing and without touching anything, apart from his feet on the floor, Niall circled the body. He didn't immediately see anything to indicate Sean's death *wasn't* a suicide, but it felt damn wrong. There was no note he could see, although the ME would have to confirm there wasn't one somewhere on the body or underneath it. The gun was nothing special: a Glock, popular and easily obtainable. Niall tested the front door, which was locked.

Would Sean have taken his own life? Instinct told Niall he wouldn't. When Sean had been at the house earlier that day, he certainly hadn't seemed the type of person to do such a thing. He was egotistic, brash, and very willing to hurt other people, not himself. Niall didn't know Sean as an adult, but as a boy he'd been a bully, and nothing in their recent interaction had changed Niall's opinion.

The crunch of gravel alerted Niall to the arrival of other agencies, likely Marshal Soper or the ambulance—or both. He stood from where he was kneeling, several feet from the body, and watched Mat mount the steps, followed by two EMTs and Soper. They crowded onto the porch, making it seem smaller than it was.

Deputy Flynn arrived seconds later, along with another deputy Niall hadn't met yet. Flynn covered her mouth in horror but to her credit didn't get sick. The other deputy paled, and Niall watched his Adam's apple bob up and back down, but he kept his composure. Niall supposed Piedras County did get its share of accident victims. They'd all seen dead bodies before this.

"Mat, we'll need to search the house. The door is still locked from this morning, but just in case."

Mat reached in his pants pocket and pulled out a key ring. He tossed it to Niall.

"Flynn, Holstrom, help Hamarsson search inside the house."

Together the three of them searched the premises, making sure no one was hiding inside. It didn't take long; there was no one and no obvious evidence of robbery or vandalism. Niall didn't think anyone had been inside since they'd left for Chastity's funeral.

Mat spoke quietly to Niall when they returned to the porch. "Claribel Delacombe is here with my mom now. She's the nearest person I could think to call. And, dammit, the woman drove herself over with a suspended license." The last seemed to be more to himself than Niall. Niall looked over to where cars were parked. An older Cadillac sedan sat with the engine running, exhaust pluming in the cold air. Claribel was in the driver's seat, Alyson beside her.

"That was nice of her." Niall figured Alyson appreciated the gesture, even if the two women didn't always agree.

He and Dempsey stood out of the way on the lawn while the EMTs confirmed this was a scene for Soper and not them. As the younger people checked Sean's body, Soper watched with the solemn air of a man who knows his work has only just begun.

"Would you like us to wait and transport the body, Dr. Soper?" one of the EMTs asked as he peeled off his blue medical gloves.

Soper nodded. "Unless you get another call, Foster, I'd appreciate it."

Soper carried a camera in his kit. Quickly and efficiently, he snapped pictures of the body and its surroundings. After handing the camera to Mat, he knelt at the head and examined the wound and Sean's hands. Rolling the body slightly, Soper checked through the pockets of Sean's clothing. He found a wallet and a key ring with several keys on it but nothing that looked like a note.

The responders were quiet while Soper worked. Niall'd worked many crime scenes; depending on the responders, they could be chatty or quiet or a mix. Sometimes a scene was so gruesome the only way to get through the initial response was with terrible humor. Niall had resorted to that himself some-times. Today the only sounds were the rustling of leaves as a slight wind started up.

"Sean was left-handed," Mat said into the silence.

Niall looked again. The gun lay to the right side of the body and close to Sean's right hand, as if he'd had it in his hand when he fell to the floor. It wasn't conclusive evidence, but most left-handed people did not use their right hand if they were determined to take their own life. Niall could shoot using either hand, but he was an exception—and he'd worked hard to be able to do it.

"Would one of you follow my mother and Claribel over to the Delacombe place?" Mat asked the deputies. "And Flynn? Remind Claribel her driver's license is suspended."

Niall rolled his eyes. Mat was going to get huffy about Claribel's driver's license? The Delacombe place was only two driveways or so away, making them neighbors. She hadn't driven far. Also, dammit, Niall was thinking of the sheriff as Mat. He needed to force the man back into the Dempsey box and keep him there.

Deputy Holstrom ended up on taxi duty. He didn't look upset at leaving the scene to Flynn and Dempsey. Deputy Flynn and Mat bagged the weapon. Niall stayed on the sidelines and watched Mat—*Dempsey*—work.

They searched the car as well, Soper raising the plastic evidence bag with Sean's keys in it and pressing the fob to unlock the doors. Niall could tell Mat was balancing his personal grief, regardless of how he had felt about his brother, and the need to approach the investigation with as little prejudice as possible. There was nothing in the car anyway; it was impeccably clean, not even a dirty coffee cup or fast-food wrapper.

A few minutes later they watched Soper depart, followed by the ambulance carrying Sean Dempsey's body.

"Talking to your mother needs to be a priority," Niall reminded Dempsey as gently as he knew how.

Mat looked back at him, his eyes full of emotion, grief, remorse, anger—all the things Niall expected to see. He was momentarily tempted to reassure Mat things would be all right, but that would be a false promise.

"This morning Alyson said Sean's been bugging her about selling the property."

"Yeah, I remember," Mat replied.

"Why would he do that? It's clear she's happy and healthy here, and there seems to be enough money for her to live on."

Mat shrugged. "Yeah, there's money, and the property's paid off. She put my name on the deed a few years ago in case something happened to her. I pay the property taxes and utilities now." Mat sounded defensive.

"Crap, Dempsey, I wasn't thinking you're a freeloader. I was thinking—well, now I'm thinking Sean must not have known that if he was trying to get your mom to sell."

"No, she didn't tell him. It would've caused a family fight. The house and land are my inheritance. The rest of my siblings will inherit the cash and some special things Mom wanted to make sure they got. Shit." Mat tugged at his hair and grimaced.

"What?"

"I need to call my sisters. Fuck me."

"Do you want me to do it?" Deputy Flynn asked, surprising Niall; he'd forgotten she was still at the house. She rolled her blue plastic gloves off and wadded them into a ball before sticking them in her back pocket.

Mat sighed. "No. Shit—yes, Flynn, I owe something around one hundred dollars to the swear jar—I need to be the one who tells them. What I'd like you to do, while I call them, is walk the perimeter with Hamarsson. If Sean didn't do this, who was with him and where did they go? We need to find out where he's been on the island. We'll need his phone and bank records. I didn't think to look for tire tracks when we drove in but if this is a crime scene, we drove over any evidence out there. Call Patrick and Theo and tell them they're on duty for the foreseeable future—and yes, it will be overtime. We'll assign Patrick to overnight guard duty here."

Niall tried to reassure him. "Dempsey, we were focused on getting here, plus the mud and other tracks would probably make it impossible to find anything helpful anyway."

Mat glanced at him again, conflicting emotions marring his features. "I wish... I need to treat this scene as if it was any one of my constituents. I can't let the fact that my brother was a homophobic, selfish asshole cloud my judgment."

"We will, sir," Flynn interjected. "We'll find out what happened here." Mat grimaced, probably realizing she'd heard his harsh assessment of his recently deceased brother.

Niall and Deputy Flynn left Mat alone to call his sisters. Together they descended the porch steps and made their way around the side of the house.

"What should I be looking for, sir?" Flynn asked.

"Call me Hamarsson, or Niall," Niall replied.

"Yes, sir."

Niall glanced over at her; she was smirking. Deputy Flynn had a long career ahead of her.

At the edge of the grass, he stopped walking and Flynn waited next to him while he considered how best to search. They didn't know what they were looking for—likely footprints or a dropped item—but when and if they found it, they'd know it.

The Dempsey house, built in the early 1900s, stood toward the back of the cleared property. Niall wondered how far into the woods the Dempsey land extended. He imagined the property was at least a few acres. Over the generations a somewhat grassy lawn had been encouraged to grow, along with hardy rose bushes and other types of plants—hard to tell what they were when they were dormant.

Niall spun around, looking toward the road where the driveway cut in and cars were parked. Any remaining daylight was gone now, and a raindrop glanced against Niall's cheek. The weather was not cooperating.

"We'll start at the top of the drive and walk parallel to each other about ten feet apart. I'm sure you've done something like this before," he said. "We'll stay in sync, and if either of us sees something we call it out so the other can come look. Be sure to take pictures of anything you think is out of place."

"Okay."

They walked in tandem. There was no reason to talk; they needed to concentrate on the ground in front of them. Niall sincerely doubted they'd find anything along the drive. Mat was right; if there had been evidence there, it was gone, obliterated by the arrival of other cars and the ambulance.

They'd made a preliminary sweep from the beginning of the driveway almost to the house when Niall heard the front door open and Mat came back outside. Mat looked at him expectantly. Niall shook his head. "Nothing yet."

"My sisters will be here sometime tomorrow or the next day. I asked if they'd talked to Sean recently, and neither of them had. No smoking gun, huh?"

Niall shook his head, but just then Flynn, who'd kept searching, let out a quiet gasp and knelt in the grass near one of the clumps of rose bushes close to the side of the house.

"Footprints, sirs, unless Mrs. Dempsey has been gardening in February."

There were footprints in the damp soil, larger than Alyson Dempsey's feet could possibly be. Niall listened to Mat griping about department budgets and crappy evidence kits while he dug through his trunk trying to find something to save the prints with and Flynn took pictures using a flash while Niall held a flashlight. News of Sean Dempsey's death would've spread across the island already. The deputy who got guard duty at the house would make sure no one came back—and, if someone did, they would be detained and questioned.

Mat found what he was looking for, a small white tub with casting material inside. Taking a bottle of water from the trunk, he poured it into the mix until it reached the correct consistency. Back at the garden bed, Mat very carefully poured the sludgy liquid into the footprints.

"This stuff doesn't take too long to dry," Mat commented.

"Nope." Niall had used it many times.

"Birdy, stay here please, and make sure absolutely nothing happens to this casting. Try to protect it from this fucking rain. Excuse me for a moment while I call my mom and make sure she's settled in at Claribel's."

Birdy nodded and took the plastic sheeting Mat handed her to hold over the casting while it dried.

"Niall, would you do me the favor of stringing up the tape? We don't need any visitors."

"Sure."

Mat stepped under the eaves to stand out of the thin rain and pulled out his cell phone.

At the cruiser, Niall grabbed the roll of police tape from Mat's still-open trunk. He draped it across the driveway using shrubs as anchors, then walked back to the porch and blocked it off too.

His car wobbled as he moved past it. Crap, he'd forgotten about Fenrir, who was probably hungry and needing to relieve himself. The dog stretched and shook out his big body while Niall held the leash with his good hand and wondered what he should do. The last thing anyone needed was a dog tromping through the scene. Niall was aware, even with a deputy on guard duty, that Dempsey would be determined to stay the night and guard his home from the possible return of a killer—but he wasn't staying alone. They'd just have to deal with Fenrir.

As he walked Fenrir out in the grass farthest from the house, Niall decided his gut was right: Sean's death was murder. Even apart from Mat's comment about Sean being left-handed, the scene felt *off*. The mere fact that Sean was on the porch and not inside the house, in a bedroom or another more private area, struck Niall as odd. People who took their own lives tended to do it privately. Not always, but more often than not.

The footprints could possibly be innocent but, as Deputy Flynn had pointed out, they were oriented as if the person had been standing or crouching there, waiting for someone to arrive. The question was, had Sean been planning on meeting someone here while almost everyone on the island was at Chastity's funeral, or had he stopped here by chance? He had to have known his mother would be at the funeral. Was Sean's murder premeditated, or had the lurker been waiting for Dempsey—or possibly Alyson?

Something sharp, cold, and *discomfiting* sliced through Niall's belly at the thought of either of them being hurt. He tried to push it aside—he was known for his ability to keep his emotions separate from crime scenes. Mat fucking Dempsey was complicating his life. He'd returned to Piedras solely to… what? He had no fucking idea. Lick his wounds? Pout? Get his life together? After turning in his badge to Chief Meyers, he'd run away to the only place he'd ever called home, but that home didn't exist any longer and hadn't for some time, even before some asshole had burnt it to the ground. He was such an idiot.

Niall found himself thinking about Trey. The man crept into his thoughts, reminding Niall of the conversation with Mat earlier. There were all these weird pieces floating around with the wrong shapes and no straight sides for the edges to make them easily fit together, and Trey was one of the pieces—or maybe he fit across more than one. Niall could, in all honesty, imagine Trey angry enough to try to run him down. Trey's temper was volatile, and he seemed to think the world owed him something. But that didn't explain Chas Reynolds or the scarf around her neck that looked an awful lot like the one Niall had bought Trey. Niall still couldn't see Trey as a cold-blooded killer. And anyway, *why*? Why would he kill Chastity?

The only connection *Niall* had with Chastity was that she'd worked for Bill Andersen's lawn service. But he'd quit maintaining Niall's property because of the letter he'd received several years ago. Niall had never met Chastity; to be honest, he hadn't known she existed. He did the math in his head, and Chastity was probably a newborn when he'd been a senior in high school.

Fenrir tugged at the leash, giving Niall an admonishing look to quit thinking and start walking—there was still dinner to be taken care of. Niall headed back to his car, focusing his thoughts on the case at hand.

Except.

What would have happened if he'd never come back to the island? If no one had ever found out Niall actually did care about the property left to him by his grandparents? The letter had been dated about four years earlier. If whoever had sent the letter had been trying to take the land from him through adverse possession? Well, he supposed it would've been entirely possible. He hadn't visited or shown any interest in it for over a decade. Someone *could* have been using or living on the land, and Niall would never have known about it.

"This is fucked up," Niall growled into the dark. "Completely fucked up."

Money would be at the center of all this; Niall would bet his own savings on it. Sean Dempsey had cared a lot about money. It showed in the clothing he wore and the car he drove. He'd needed or just plain wanted more of it. The pressure on his mother to sell seemed to indicate that, although Niall wasn't sure how Sean would've profited from the sale of the land as long as Alyson was around, even if he didn't know the property was destined to go to Mat. Back at his car, Niall opened the gate again and lifted the large bag of dog food up onto his shoulder. His hand twinged at the effort, but he ignored it. With Fenrir at his side, he went around to the back of the house and let himself in through the kitchen door.

TWENTY-SIX

DEMPSEY

"Sir," Birdy's voice pulled Mat from his grim thoughts, "Dispatch took another call about the abandoned house out on Preacher. It was Mrs. Herrmann who called it in, said there were weird lights moving around." Birdy set the box with the casting carefully placed inside it down on the kitchen table.

Mat sighed and scrubbed his hands against his face. The universe was testing him tonight—this entire week was way past his pay grade, and that was *before* his asshole brother got himself killed. He glanced at the clock on the stove, which claimed it was seven fifteen. It felt like midnight. He was beyond tired and wanted nothing more than to fall into bed, but he doubted he'd sleep tonight, even if there wasn't a call. Mrs. Herrmann generally did not call the sheriff's office, so one of them would need to drive out and check the house.

Since Deputy Holstrom was with Claribel and his mom, and Mat didn't trust Patrick Radden to investigate much of anything yet—he'd had him park a cruiser at the top of the drive to keep people out, but that was it—it would need to be Mat who drove across the island to investigate while Flynn stayed inside the house. Somebody had to stay with the evidence, and he couldn't call one of his deputies from Orcas to do it.

"You stay here. I'll go check it out," he said.

"I'll go with you."

Niall's gruff voice surprised Mat. He hadn't heard the back door open—some cop he was. Niall set a large bag of dog food on the counter and rummaged around for the bowl Mat's mom had provided... yesterday? This morning? Had that been just this morning?

Kibble clinked into the metal bowl, and Niall set it down on the floor and stepped aside. Fenrir took his place and began to eat. The dog was too skinny, even for an elk- or wolfhound, but he ate delicately. Niall found another bowl, filled it with water, and set it next to the food.

"Thanks," Mat said, knowing he wasn't going to protest Niall coming along. Upstairs in his bedroom, he unlocked his gun safe and removed one of his spare weapons. It was a Glock much like the one they'd found with Sean. He brought it downstairs to Niall.

"Here, just in case you need it."

The three of them—because Fenrir assumed the invitation had been extended to him as well—tromped back outside to Mat's cruiser. Niall swung open the back-passenger door and Fenrir climbed inside, settling comfortably against the seat. Mat didn't know what to say but figured he'd probably lose the argument anyway.

Neither of them spoke while Mat turned the car around and rumbled down the driveway toward the road. They passed Deputy Radden, and Mat sketched a wave and turned right. He liked driving at night when only his headlights illuminated the road ahead. There was something soothing about the thrum of tires on the road and the darkness. It gave him space to think.

Having Niall in the car with him was less distracting than Mat expected. He was inherently quiet. Maybe it was something he'd learned as a child, a survival tactic, but Mat suspected it was the way the man was built.

"What's the story about this place?" Niall finally asked.

"It's on the north side. The property's been a thorn in my side for years. The owner passed away, and none of the heirs wanted to live on the island. They fought about it for a while, and meanwhile the house fell into worse and worse disrepair until it became unlivable. If they'd just rebuilt the house at the time it would've been fine—the original home was grandfathered into the county code—but any new structure has to meet a lot of complicated environmental regulations because of its location close to protected shore. Most recently it's been a meth cooker. We do our best to keep people out of there, but... actually, we found Chastity's wallet there."

"Huh."

"We couldn't find a connection. Chastity didn't run with that crowd, unless it was when she was in high school. My guess is one of those creeps found it somewhere and that's how it ended up there. If she had credit or debit cards, they were gone."

The cruiser rounded a corner, its headlights sweeping along the evergreens and bare shrubs and lighting the access road he was looking for. During the spring and summer, the house wouldn't be visible from the road, but this time of year, before the deciduous trees leafed out, there was a clear line of sight from the road to the house. He couldn't see any lights or activity, but he turned in anyway, leaving his headlights on.

They got out. Mat wanted to tell Niall he should leave Fenrir in the car, but once again he was silently overruled. Niall didn't bother with a leash, and the dog stayed next to them as they moved silently toward the crumbling house. Mat switched his flashlight on and shone it out toward the shrubs and bushes encroaching on the house. A glint of red caught his eye. Niall must've seen it too. In sync they moved in that direction, and as they got closer the shape resolved itself into a car. Whoever the driver was had driven it into the bushes in an attempt to hide it, but its brake lights gave it away.

Niall spoke quietly. "I think it's the car that tried to run me over."

Mat moved closer, peering at the vehicle. It was a newer slate-gray Subaru, and the left side was scraped all to hell. In the battle between vehicles, Marshal's Land Cruiser had definitely won.

"I'd say you're right."

Niall squeezed in between the car and the bushes to try the doors; they were locked.

He shrugged. "It was worth a try."

"You don't recognize it?"

"Nope."

Back at his car, Mat typed the license plate number into his laptop. The search immediately came back with the make and model—which matched what they saw, a late-model sporty Subaru. Mat also noted the car had hundreds of dollars in outstanding parking tickets and was registered to one Trey Alfred Jackson. "Well, now."

"What?" Niall asked from where he and Fenrir were waiting beside the cruiser.

"It's registered to Trey Jackson."

Niall sighed. "Why am I not surprised? I guess I really can pick 'em. I didn't even like him that much."

Mat didn't imagine Niall liked many people, so it wasn't hard to get on that list. "Did he have access to anything personal of yours? I don't know, like bank stuff or your mail?"

Niall shrugged. "I didn't give it to him, if that's what you're asking, but if he wanted to steal information, it wouldn't have been difficult. Maybe when he stayed overnight he went through my wallet or something."

"You don't have anything at your place in Seattle that points here to Piedras?" It was hard for Mat to imagine cutting Piedras completely out of his life.

"I'm kind of a minimalist, but I have a few framed snapshots of me and my grandparents when I was still on the island. We talked about it at some point. That's about it."

Mat tucked the information away to think about later. He was sure the connection would become clearer the more they investigated.

"We'll search the house. I'm going to boot the vehicle first, but the island tow service won't come out to impound it until morning."

"You have one of those things?"

Mat snorted. "All the cruisers have them. The county paid for them after a rise in complaints over illegal parking. Don't talk to me about our ridiculous budget."

It didn't take long to fit the boot on. If Trey was close by, he wasn't getting away by car.

"It had to be him—nothing else makes any sense at all," Niall said. "Trey and your brother somehow knew each other. And somehow Chastity Reynolds fits into this, because there is no way this shit isn't connected. There's two DBs in ten days, the fire at my place, and the scrapes on the car indicate Trey was the driver who tried to mow me down."

Mat was thinking the same thing. They didn't have a connection between the two men, or either of them to Chastity, but Mat was certain Niall was right.

"If it was him, he's dangerous."

Niall looked past the cruiser toward the house. Mat wondered what he was thinking about now.

"Trey's a coward." Niall spoke a little too loudly, loudly enough to be heard over the rustle of leaves and distant waves. "Just a fuck toy to use and throw away. I'll bet he couldn't look your brother in the eye when he killed him—he skulked in the flower bed waiting for his chance. And then what, Trey? When

Sean got there, did you quiver? Did your palms get sweaty? What about Chastity? What did she do to you?"

Niall shot Mat a look, nodding toward the house. Mat took the hint and slowly, quietly moved toward the house, pulling out his weapon as he went.

Niall kept talking into the dark. "Did Chastity figure out what you and Sean were up to? Did she want a piece of the action, or did she threaten to turn you in? Give it up, Trey. You and I both know you're only good for your looks. I bet Chastity was too smart for you, didn't fall for your pretty-boy act. Did she figure it out? And then, like the coward you are, you killed her."

Mat winced. If Trey was out there listening, Niall's words had to hurt. But would Trey react to the taunts? They had no proof of a connection between Sean and Trey. Not yet. Niall was right, but they needed more.

Out of the dark came a response. "We paid the bitch good money, but then she was going to ruin everything. When things got a little dicey, she wanted out. She figured out we were trying to buy up land to develop. We had the blueprints for a planned community. Sean must've told her something, and all of a sudden she was yelling about conservation and preserving the island and fucking green space. We'd already had one setback. She deserved what she got." Not exactly a confession, but at least it was a reaction. Mat tried to calculate where Trey was. His voice wasn't coming from inside, that much was clear. He needed him to speak again.

Niall continued, "Trey, you know you're going to prison for a very long time. If you give yourself up now and tell us everything, maybe the DA will go easy on you. They take care of people like you in prison." Not that Niall could make any promises.

"No, I don't think so, *Niall*." Trey's words dripped with venom. "That's what cops always say, and then boom, the deal's off. Kind of like your phone call the other day. Boom, 'We're done, Trey.'"

His voice was getting quieter. He was moving farther away. Mat tried to map out the property in his mind, but when they'd been here a week ago he'd been focused on the inside, not the outside. He did know the parcel extended to the water on the other side of the house. Unlike Niall's property, there was a bluff, so Trey would find no escape that direction—and where did he think he would escape to, anyway?

Niall laughed. It was a terrible low, menacing sound, a suffocating fog filled with the promise of retribution. "Trey, Trey, Trey, that was just a courtesy call. We'd been done a long time—you were only ever good for a quick fuck." He paused, then said, "Is that why you tried to run me over? Because I finally broke it off? You couldn't even do that right."

Mat thought maybe Niall should stop antagonizing Jackson; he had, after all, most likely killed two people—that they knew of.

"What is this all about, Trey? What was in it for you—I know you don't do things for free, so to speak. Where's the money for you?"

Mat was freezing. He hadn't remembered to put on his heavier coat. Whatever cat-and-mouse game Trey was up to, Mat wanted to put an end to it. His fingers were going to be too cold to pull the trigger if he needed to.

It was Trey's turn to laugh, and it sounded like he'd stopped moving. "Dempsey had a plan to make a lot of money. It was such a random thing—we met in a real estate class. He'd already invested megabucks in some property on Orcas Island and wanted to do the same thing here, so I bought in. The time is ripe for housing developments outside of the cities, but then the Orcas one fell through because some overly concerned citizens wanted to keep their fucking green space. We needed to get one going here, to show other investors the money."

"But you had no money."

Mat heard the shrug in Trey's voice, which he was now even closer to. "We'd get it."

"What, by terrorizing the citizens of Piedras into selling? That's called coercion, Trey, and it's illegal, just like murder." Niall was right again, Mat realized. Jackson and Sean had conspired to try to get residents to sell their land using whatever tactics they could. Things must have been getting hot for them to resort to killing livestock and attempting and nearly succeeding to set the residents against each other. It hadn't been difficult; most of them had been feuding on and off for years—generations.

Mat finally managed to pinpoint Trey in the darkness. He was trying to make his way to the road, but the tangled undergrowth made it nearly impossible. Mat doubted he was prepared for hiking through the woods. They would have to wait him out. Again he wished he'd put on a warmer jacket.

"Why'd you burn down my cabin, Trey?"

The question startled Mat. He'd put the incident at the back of his mind for the time being, but it made sense that it was Trey's doing.

"That was Sean's deal, but I guess maybe he got the idea from me."

Mat wanted to shut his eyes against the truth of Trey's words but didn't want to lose track of where Trey was standing, only about forty feet away now. Mat hadn't been an Eagle Scout for nothing. As quietly as he could, while Niall kept Trey talking —the man had a gigantic ego—Mat circled around from behind, keeping his weapon directed at Trey's outline. Finally, when he was close enough that he could've whispered the words in Trey's ear, he instead said them loud enough for Niall to hear.

"Trey Jackson, put your hands up. You're under arrest."

Trey bolted forward but tripped, landing face-first in a prickly Oregon grape bush. Mat didn't feel inclined to let him escape, so he kept him there with a foot in the small of his back while he handcuffed him. When he was satisfied Jackson was subdued, he grabbed the smaller man by the back of his pants and lifted him from the ground.

"Move it."

Ahead of Mat, Trey stumbled out of the bushes toward where the cruiser was parked. Niall and Fenrir waited there for them, darker shadows in the dark night. Fenrir's eyes glinted, and Trey sucked in a breath.

"What the fuck is that?" he shrieked.

All in all, after the day they'd had, the arrest was anticlimactic. The best part, if there could be a best part, was Fenrir riding in the back seat with Trey on the way to the sheriff's office. Trey was not a fan of the dog.

Back at the station, Mat stowed their guest away in the tiny lockup. He and Theo relieved Trey of his wallet, cell phone, belt, and footwear—those were stashed in a separate paper bag. They made him empty his pockets but found nothing of interest in them.

"I want to make a phone call!" Trey demanded as Deputy Jones led him down the hall to the holding cell.

"Sure, Jackson, you can make one as soon as it's practical. Nobody's going to answer your phone call tonight. Deputy Jones, keep your eye on him. I'll be back to question him." It would do Trey good to sit and stew for a while, and Mat was exhausted. Quickly he called Birdy and gave her the news. "No need to stay at the house. Bring the box in to the station and lock it up. I'll see you in the morning."

His mother was safe, staying with Claribel Delacombe— something Mat never thought he'd experience in his lifetime. Deputy Holstrom was with them as well, although with Jackson under arrest Mat didn't think anyone was in real danger any longer. All he wanted to do was shut his eyes for a few hours before he had to return and take care of sheriff business.

"Thanks," Mat said to Niall as they headed to his car. Last time he'd checked it had been just after midnight, and he was feeling twitchy and exhausted. Fenrir was curled up into a ball on the back seat of the cruiser. He sat up as they approached.

"I don't know what you're thanking me for," Niall replied.

Mat was too tired for this. "I don't want to argue. I want to go home and lay in bed for a few hours before I have to be back here."

The ride to his house was silent. Mat assumed Niall was as tired as he was. When he turned into the driveway, passing by Deputy Radden—who, to Mat's surprise, was not asleep—to park between Sean's and Niall's cars, Niall finally spoke.

"Would it bother you if Fenrir and I stay here the rest of the night?"

"Why would I mind? I tried to get you to stay before."

Niall shrugged but didn't reply. Instead he heaved himself out of the car and then let the dog out.

Mat led the way around the side of the house and unlocked the back door. Inside, he flicked the overhead light on. The yellow kitchen walls glowed cheerfully. Everything was so *normal*. The events of the day had had no influence in this room; the bowl with three red-and-green apples in it still sat on the kitchen table, two coffee cups waited in the sink to be washed, a dishrag lay forgotten on the counter. Mat looked at Niall. The bright kitchen light illuminated his face, and what he saw there made him wary.

"Why would I mind if you stayed?" Mat asked again.

Niall stopped walking and turned his head to look directly at Mat, his pale green eyes expressionless. "I brought him here. This—your brother's death, Chastity Reynolds," he muttered, waving a hand, "all of it is my fault."

"It's not your fault. We don't even know who killed Chastity yet." But somehow Mat knew Niall wasn't listening. "Please stay. The room upstairs is still ready for you, and Mom won't mind Fenrir. I think she kind of likes him." And you, Mat wanted to add, but something warned him not to.

Niall nodded. Quietly he left the kitchen and headed toward the stairs. Fenrir gave Mat a knowing glance before following. Damn dog had done in two days what Mat had wanted for years—but admitted to himself only recently. He'd been drawn to Niall since high school, when something about him had Mat on edge and made him want to protect the quiet boy from the bullies who made his life miserable. Niall was right, though; in high school, Mat had been smaller than Niall. The Dempsey name and his older brother had protected him somewhat, but that wouldn't have lasted long if he'd tried to stand up for a kid Sean and his buddies had targeted.

Niall hadn't had anyone to protect him. He hadn't let anyone get close—except Od and Josephine—but, Mat supposed, after Niall's childhood, that would be very difficult for him. Maybe impossible.

After the events of the day, suddenly Mat wasn't tired. Instead of going upstairs, he filled the kettle and put it on the stove to heat. Then he picked out his favorite of his mom's custom teas and sat down at the kitchen table, waiting for the water to boil.

He'd quietly kept up with Niall's career over the years. The man hadn't gone far, after all, only to Seattle, where he attended college and then went into the police academy. That had surprised Mat. He'd always wanted to be a cop, to do what his dad did, only in a bigger city—so he'd moved to California. He'd always wondered why Niall chose law enforcement.

He and Niall were different people these days, grown men now, but Mat's attraction remained, and it had grown stronger with Niall's return. If Niall felt something similar, Mat had no way of telling, and now with Trey Jackson at the bottom of everything, any movement between them had been erased or pushed backward.

Fucking hell, he was a mess.

He sat at the kitchen table sipping his tea and thinking about the case, Niall Hamarsson, his brother, and Trey Jackson for hours before he finally went upstairs to his bedroom. Unlike the last time he passed by the spare room with Niall inside, he did not give in to the urge to check on him.

It was nearly five in the morning. He'd been up almost twenty-four hours. Still, he lay in bed unable to fall asleep, waiting for the sound of the other bedroom door to open, waiting for Niall to leave without saying anything.

TWENTY-SEVEN
HAMARSSON

It was stupid for Niall to stay at the Dempsey house. It was ludicrous of him not to get back in his car and make the drive to Hidden Harbor. Twenty minutes and he and Fenrir would be safe in the hotel room, away from the lure of Mat Dempsey.

But... he couldn't force himself to leave. The need to stay and make sure the Piedras County Sheriff was safe and slept through the night could not be overcome. Niall's reaction was over the top for sure; neither one of them had been in any particular danger during Trey's arrest. It had been kind of pitiful how easy it had been to call Trey out, to get him to react to Niall's harsh words. Aside from taunting Trey by telling him what he really thought of him, there'd been no violence, no acrid smell of gunpowder.

For a minute, though, when Mat was sliding silently into the dark, overgrown woods, Niall had felt a stab of panic. He should've been the one going after Trey, not Mat. Trey was Niall's fault. He'd cursed his bad hand and instead continued to mock Trey and everything about him.

Now it had been hours since Mat had handcuffed Trey, and the feeling of panic hadn't dissipated. He hadn't meant to ask if he could stay; the words had spilled out unbidden, surprising him.

Fenrir circled three times before plopping down on the floor and curling into a ball, his bony spine facing Niall. Niall stripped off his coat and boots, then lay down on the bed fully dressed. He didn't feel like he was going to be able to sleep; his body was still on high alert. Had they missed something? Something was off. Everything had been easy, too easy. Sean Dempsey's death followed so quickly by Trey's arrest...

Niall turned onto his side, trying to find a comfortable position, and wished it only took him three magic turns and flopping down to fall asleep. He did fall asleep, or at least he dreamed. It was the same dream he usually had, the far-too-vivid memory of the last time he saw his mother as she told him it wouldn't be long, then quickly shut the closet door, leaving him in darkness.

He started awake and saw by the digital clock he'd slept for a few hours, long enough for the sky outside to change from pitch-black to a shade slightly less dark. Something creaked in the old house. Mat, Niall realized, was just coming upstairs. His footsteps hesitated by Niall's door before continuing on down the hallway. He wondered what had kept Mat up, what Mat would do if Niall went to his room and lay down with him. Mat Dempsey was a nice man, a nice person; he probably wouldn't turn Niall away. Niall turned onto his back again. Mat would never have to decide if he wanted Niall in his bed, because Niall wasn't built for a man like Mat. A good man.

Niall was not a good man. Sometimes he wished he was, but he'd been tainted from the beginning. There was no hope for something more between Mat and him.

But you wish there was.

The next time he woke it was to find a pair of golden eyes patiently staring at him.

"Are you hungry?" Niall asked.

Fenrir wagged his tail in response, and Niall heaved himself off the bed. His back popped as he stretched; getting older was just great.

"Fine. Let's go see what there is to eat."

In the kitchen, Niall poured kibble into Fenrir's borrowed bowl. While the dog happily munched, Niall opened the fridge. It was like trying to read a book in a foreign language. Niall didn't cook. He hadn't had time for it in his old life, and now... he hadn't figured out what he was doing next, had he? Maybe he'd learn to cook. It wasn't entirely outside the realm of possibility.

He stared into the refrigerator, at its meticulously organized interior: eggs, bacon, sandwich meats, tidily contained leftovers. Niall reached in and opened one of the clear containers. Inside was rice and sausage. A sound alerted him that Mat was coming down the stairs, and he hastily stuffed the container back on the shelf, feeling he'd been caught with his hand in the cookie jar.

"Hungry?" Mat asked from the doorway, his voice rough from sleep.

Niall looked at him. He wasn't wearing his uniform. Instead, he'd chosen a worn pair of jeans with a long-sleeved t-shirt stretched taut across his shoulders. It was effortless for Niall to imagine Mat in another world, walking the rocky shores where the waves of the Irish Sea crashed ashore—or on the Aran Islands, Mat's form silhouetted against the stark stone walls of his ancient keep. Niall blamed his grandfather for his imagination. Then he noticed Mat's feet were bare, something Niall, in this spare moment, found incredibly sexy. He was so fucked.

Yes, he was fucking hungry. So hungry he had to look away.

Fenrir, done with breakfast and blissfully unaware of Niall's internal struggle, padded over to the back door and stared at it.

Grateful to put more distance between them, Niall moved to the door and opened it, letting Fenrir out into the backyard.

"You aren't putting a leash on him?" Mat asked, crossing the kitchen and crowding Niall's space. Niall gritted his teeth, his body responding to Mat's heat.

"He's not going anywhere. He's figured out where the gravy train is."

Sure enough, Fenrir discreetly took care of his business at the edge of the property. He did that stupid dog thing where he kicked random grass and dirt into the air, then bounded back across the lawn to Niall.

"Smart dog."

Something in Mat's tone had Niall quickly glancing at him again, but whatever he thought he'd heard, he didn't see written on Mat's face.

"So, are you hungry?" Mat asked again.

Niall stared at the ceiling. A few cobwebs had formed in one corner—he could only see them due to the angle of the light coming in through the kitchen window. He was certain Alyson wouldn't allow them to stay.

"I could eat," he finally said.

Mat grinned, his face lighting up with pure joy. "That's great! I don't get to cook anymore, living with my mom—and my work schedule, of course—but I love to cook, even if it's scrambled eggs."

He headed over to the stove and started banging pots and pans. Then he grabbed eggs and some cheese from the refrigerator.

"Don't you need to go in to the office?" Niall asked. If the man was going to feed him, well… he'd eat. But he knew there was a lot of work for Mat to do, including questioning Trey. Wrapping up an investigation was a lot of paperwork.

Mat straightened but didn't turn around. Instead he futzed

with a pan on the stove, turning the handle one way and then the other.

Finally, he answered, "My brother, who I didn't like very much, was killed last night, and I'm feeling guilty for not mourning him more—I wasn't able to sleep at all. My mom… god, I don't even know what she's feeling. We talked a little last night, but she's struggling. I can hear it in her voice. So, anyway, what I'd like to do right now is make some eggs and bacon, toast on the side, with several cups of coffee strong enough to stand a fork in, okay? I don't want to think about the shit that's coming down the pipeline."

Niall could respect that. Most days he'd rather have coffee than talk about shit.

"Okay. I like mine over easy."

"What?" Mat turned from the stove to face him. "Over easy is… a travesty," he sputtered. "I make some of the best scrambled eggs you will ever put in your mouth—quite possibly the best *thing* you will ever put in your mouth. They melt on your tongue like honey. Golden, delicious, buttery and… purely sublime."

Niall couldn't help rolling his eyes. "Fine, scrambled." He was pretty sure that the *best* thing he might ever put in his mouth was Mat Dempsey's cock—but that was off-limits. Off-limits like the moon.

The eggs were damn good.

Halfway through breakfast, Alyson came home. She had to walk around to the back, since the porch was still blocked off. She looked terrible, the heavy weight of guilt writ across her face. Niall sympathized; he really did. He had firsthand knowledge of what it was to grieve for someone you despised, who made your life hell. Maybe Alyson hadn't despised her oldest son, but even being close to that emotion when it was someone you were supposed to love unconditionally… it fucked you up.

She attempted a weak smile for them as she passed

through on her way to the living room. They both watched her, neither saying a word as she went through the familiar motions of setting her purse on the hutch in the living room, then taking her coat off and hanging it up in the closet. Fenrir ambled out to greet her and was rewarded with a scratch on the head.

Niall caught Mat's eye. Mat stood from the table and went to his mother.

"Mom, come back in the kitchen, there's coffee. How did you get home?"

"Shay Delacombe drove me. Your deputy is still at the house enjoying Claribel's hospitality, but I needed to get home."

Mat pulled a chair out, but Alyson wouldn't sit down. Instead she stepped past him to the counter where the coffeepot was and poured herself a cup, then turned back to face them.

"I need to be busy doing things, not sitting and wondering what's happening, wondering if you're okay." She swiped at her eyes, which were already puffy from tears and lack of sleep. "Mat, I'm so angry with Sean. I'm angry he got himself involved in something that led to this—and on our front porch." She turned to face him. "Why? What was he thinking? I don't understand any of this."

"I don't know all the answers, Mom, but I'll do my best to find out everything I can. We have someone in custody. Niall and I will finish up here and go into town and question him." Mat glanced over at Niall.

All the reasons why Niall couldn't stay rushed forward, an incoming tidal wave from where they'd been gathered, waiting, at the back of his mind. The main one being, he was the reason Trey had come to the island. Sean Dempsey, no matter how despicable he was, was dead because of Niall.

"I should leave," Niall said, getting up from the table.

The temperature in the kitchen dropped as if all the warmth was sucked out of the room by a bellows.

"Don't you dare." Mat glared at him. Twin glares, actually, because he got one from Alyson too.

Mat growled, "Don't you fucking dare run away now."

"I just—" He needed to make Mat understand...

"Don't. Don't make me beg. I need your help on this. You are the only other experienced investigator—" Mat broke off, shaking his head in frustration.

Niall didn't know what to say. Instinct pushed him to leave.

"Stay for now," Alyson interjected. "Please?"

How could he refuse the woman who'd let him cry in her kitchen—was that only a few days ago? And now it was Alyson grieving and asking the impossible of him.

"Fine." He ground the word out, knowing he sounded like a petulant child and not a grown man.

"Fine," Mat repeated with a snarl. "Sit down and finish your goddamned breakfast."

Alyson turned her attention back to the coffeepot. Niall obeyed, sitting back down and picking up his fork. The remaining eggs were cold, but he ate them anyway, along with the four pieces of bacon piled on the side of his plate. He'd stay for now. When this was over, he and Fenrir would leave, and that would be that.

Before he and Niall left for the sheriff's office, the two of them spent an hour sweeping the porch and lawn for the spent cartridge they'd been unable to locate the night before.

"If Jackson—okay, the perp—waited here and was able to surprise Sean as he walked up the steps, it seems like the bullet would be in the ceiling of the porch," Mat commented from where he was standing by the rose bushes. The bullet was very much not in the porch ceiling, but bullets didn't always act like investigators thought they should.

"The cartridge would be somewhere around there, but he must've picked it up."

"We didn't find it in his car or his pockets." And Trey hadn't confessed to killing Sean—or Chastity, for that matter. He'd only said she'd "gotten what she deserved." Mat needed to call in the tow service and have his car searched. That Trey was the driver who'd tried to run Niall down wasn't in question, but they were going to need more to connect him to Sean and Chastity.

"He probably threw it out the car window while he drove. It'll be a needle in a haystack trying to find it."

"Okay, then what about the bullet? Why aren't we finding it?

What are we missing?" They'd looked everywhere in and around the confines of the porch. Thinking it could possibly have penetrated the floor, Mat had even crawled underneath the house, braving cobwebs and giant spiders, but found nothing. He hated spiders and hoped Niall recognized the extent of his sacrifice.

"We'll need Soper to take measurements of the powder burn on the body anyway. It'll help determine how far away the gun was—and how far the bullet could have traveled after leaving the body."

Mat knew all that. He just didn't want to think about the victim being his brother. "Marshal will call me as soon as he has any information. He's an experienced ME, not just some randomly appointed one."

Niall straightened from where he'd been bent over with a flashlight looking for the bullet. "How'd he end up here, anyway?"

Mat shook his head and snorted. "We met in San Francisco when I was on the force there. Just about the time I decided to move back, Marshal came into an inheritance. He'd been estranged from his family for years, but when an aunt died, she left everything to him. He decided he didn't want to live in the city anymore and came up here."

"Huh." Niall was quiet for a minute, shining the flashlight back and forth against the bottom of the outside wall of the house where it met the porch, then asked, "Were you guys together?"

Mat snorted. "Marshal and me? Where did you get that idea?"

"I don't know, Dempsey. You're gay, Soper's gay, he moved up here to be near you... did he follow you up here hoping for more?" Niall had his back turned while he spoke, and it bugged Mat. Niall was hard enough to read as it was.

"Yeah, well, me and Marshal are friends, and that's how it's always been. I'll admit it's been nice having him on the island with me, but there's never been anything else there."

"Huh." Then, "Aha! Got you, you little bastard."

Fishing in his jeans pocket with his left hand, Niall pulled out a red penknife while awkwardly trying to hold the flashlight with his injured hand. Mat moved closer to where he was standing.

"Goddamned motherfucking stitches. Here." Niall handed Mat the penknife and dropped to his knees, shining the flashlight into a dark corner of the porch. Following his lead, Mat kneeled and contorted himself so he could see what Niall had found. There it was: a gold glimmer wedged in a crack between the siding and the porch floor, back far enough not to be easily found. Hunching farther down, Mat jabbed the tip of the knife as far under the shingle as it would go, barely managing to pry the spent bullet from its resting place.

When he sat back up, Niall held out a baggie for him to drop it into, and he couldn't help but grin at him. "Nicely done!"

For this trip into town, Niall agreed to leave Fenrir at the house. The sheriff's office wasn't really equipped to accommodate a large dog, no matter how easygoing it was, and Mat thought his mom appreciated the company anyway. The drive into Hidden Harbor was quiet. Niall stared out the passenger window, his full attention seemingly on the trees and shrubs flashing by.

Mat was learning to listen to Niall's silences. This silence, he thought, was Niall thinking. Not brooding so much as *pondering* the case and everything they still needed to sort out. By no means were they close to figuring out all the nuances.

Niall finally spoke. "I still can't put together the pieces as to how they were going to get their hands on enough cash if they did get residents to sell. If they thought I'd agree to sell after the cabin burned… I just don't know. If they hoped I'd abandoned the property, that still doesn't follow, because the moment I set foot back on it the adverse possession law resets—they'd have to wait another ten years. And there was no evidence of anyone else using the land anyway. We're missing something."

"Something had them panicking," Mat agreed. "When we get access to their bank records, I bet more will become clear. I'll have Deputy Flynn work on that when she comes in later."

"Wasn't Sean a software guy? What was he like?"

Mat nodded. "He was in tech, and we weren't close—as you know. All of my life he was an asshole, and now I have to clean up the mess he made. My mom's upset, but she's also angry—seems like she didn't know him either."

"Okay, hear me out. When Sean was at your house the other day, he said some shitty things."

Mat nodded; he hadn't forgotten.

"Dempsey, there's no way Sean didn't know Trey was gay. Maybe if they'd only met once or twice, but if they've been plotting this for a while, certainly more than a year, Sean knew Trey was gay."

"Okay? So Sean knew Jackson was gay. Why does that matter?"

"I don't know, but it bothers me. It doesn't fit. He was spouting such homophobic shit, I can't believe he would willingly work with a man he knew was gay."

It *really* bothered Mat when Shay Delacombe waltzed into the office half an hour after they arrived, demanding to see his client, Trey Jackson.

"Motherfucker," Niall muttered loudly enough Shay was sure to hear. "It's Shady D. How the hell did you get here so fast?"

Mat suppressed a smile as Shay's jaw visibly tightened. Shay Delacombe's nickname had been forged in high school and unfortunately had stuck. He doubted many people dared to call the lawyer Shady to his face, but Niall was not "many people."

"Hamarsson," Shay ground out, "lovely to see you."

He stuck his hand out for Niall to shake. Niall looked at the proffered hand and wrinkled his nose. "I'll pass."

Shay's cheeks reddened with anger. He didn't reply to Niall's snub but instead moved his hand over so Mat could shake it. Internally shrugging, Mat shook Shay's hand, rolling his eyes when the man tried to crush his hand in some sort of masculinity test.

"I'd like to see my client."

Mat led Shay back to the holding cell, then returned to his desk, where Niall lurked in the spare chair.

"What was that about?" Mat asked.

"Aside from the fact I've always disliked Delacombe? He's the lawyer for Jeremy Vaughn. Vaughn is the prime suspect in a cold case of mine. The DA refuses to try it, but we know Vaughn is the perp. Unfortunately, there isn't enough hard evidence for the DA—she wants everything tied up with a red ribbon. Vaughn murdered Tanya Nichols and dumped her remains somewhere in rural King County. Part of her jaw was recovered, but we've never found the rest. So Vaughn is a free man working for City Light up in Newhalem, while the Nichols family waits for closure. It just pisses me the fuck off."

Mat understood the pain Niall felt. Sometimes the scales of justice took far too long to weigh out. Even now, ten years since he'd left San Francisco, there were cases of his still unsolved.

"He's probably going to get Jackson out on bail. He didn't actually confess to anything when we talked to him last night."

"I've known Trey for several years, and I find it hard to imagine him being able to choke someone face-to-face. He tried to run me over with his car. Can he shoot a gun? I have no idea. Did we get a print of his shoes?"

"Yeah, we got a print of his shoes and we're comparing it to the mold we made, but you know we're going to need to send it out to get official confirmation of a match."

"If Trey wasn't the shooter, who was?" Niall asked.

"And how does he know Shay Delacombe?" Mat added.

"That's the question of the hour, isn't it? There's a reason he's still called Shady, and it has nothing to do with trying to rig a student council election in high school."

Trey got out later that day, smirking as he left the courtroom accompanied by his lawyer. Mat shook his head as the arrogant young man sauntered out believing he'd won. Niall was on to something when he said there was more to this case then met the eye. The judge was reasonable but sided with Shady Delacombe when it came to keeping Trey in custody—as long as he met the bail terms.

In the hours before the hearing, Mat and all available deputies had scoured the roads leading to and from his house for any evidence of a second gun—one Trey might have tried to get rid of as he fled—because they hadn't found anything in his car or at the Preacher house. The spent bullet was all they had at this point, that and the fact that Sean was left-handed.

He didn't know what Trey's role had been, yet.

"The little shit thinks he's off the hook. This is the time when he'll do something reckless because he's not as smart as he thinks he is."

"The judge ordered him to stay on the island, so we'll have eyes and ears on him."

"Only if they don't drop the case."

"If they do, we'll bring him in for trespassing at the Preacher place."

"Sirs!" Birdy called from her desk.

"Sirs?" Niall asked Mat.

"Don't ask," he told Niall. Turning to Birdy, he asked, "What do you have?"

"We got access to your brother's accounts. At least the legit ones. It's going to take a while to analyze all the transactions, he moved a lot of money around." She frowned at the screen, her focus complete.

"You see anything?" Mat stepped around Niall to look over Birdy's shoulder.

"Well, nothing obvious, but"—she pointed at the computer screen—"this is a regular transfer on the fifth of every month, and I haven't been able to trace the receiving account. There are other regular ones, water and sewage, car payment, that kind of thing."

"Hello?" A voice called from the reception area. "Hellooo? Sheriff Dempsey?"

Mat recognized Stu Dennis's voice.

Birdy started to get up, but Mat stopped her. "You keep looking at this. I'll talk to Stu."

Out in the lobby, Mat greeted Stu and shook his hand. "What can we do for you?"

"I think it's more of a matter of what I can do for you," Stu answered.

"Come on back and tell me."

Stu followed Mat. Niall stood and offered the older man the spare chair. He was obviously excited.

With an air of enthusiasm, he announced, "I've identified the young man I saw on the ferry with Chastity."

"What?" Mat and Niall leaned closer. "Who was it?" Mat asked.

"Well, that's the thing. I spotted him at one of the little espresso shops in Anacortes by the ferry a few days ago. After he left, I pretended I knew him but couldn't remember his name, and the nice girl looked at the receipts and told me his name was Jeffrey Reynolds. I have to say it certainly is handy no one pays cash these days."

Mat leaned back in his chair, disappointed.

Birdy groaned. "Back to square one." Her voice dripped with disappointment.

"I got a picture of him," Stu said smugly.

"What?" Mat leaned forward again. Stu waved a smartphone around. It was everything Mat could do not to snatch it from his hand.

The three of them crowded around the old man while he pulled the picture up on the phone. It was slightly out of focus and crooked from the way Stu had been holding his phone, but the man in the picture was Trey Jackson.

"I'm sorry for not bringing this to you sooner, but I left my phone at my sweetie's and went this morning to retrieve it. I felt it was more important to be at Chastity Reynolds's memorial yesterday."

"The hell?" Niall sputtered, grabbing the phone and holding it so he could see it better.

"Sir!"

Niall glanced at Birdy, then back at the screen.

"The swear jar." She pointed to the large glass canning jar sitting on the corner of her desk.

Niall handed the phone to Mat, dragged his wallet out of his back pocket, removed two crisp twenties from it, and shoved them inside the jar. "I'm paying in advance."

Birdy sighed and shook her head at him.

"Anyway, which one is his legal identity?" she asked.

Mat watched Stu perk up. They did not need him listening in. "Thank you, Stu, this has been incredibly helpful information. Birdy, would you escort Stu to the front?"

Once Stu reluctantly left the building *and* Birdy made him promise to keep the information secret for the moment, they got back to work. Mat did a search for Jeffrey Reynolds, an unfortunately common name. He clicked into Facebook, searching for the right face. After a while, he found the profile they wanted. In the chair he'd rolled up next to him, Niall grunted his agreement.

"That's the one."

"Yes, I see, just a second."

Unless Trey had a doppelganger, he and Jeffrey Reynolds were one and the same. He didn't share information with people he hadn't friended, but there was still plenty there for them to see. There were pictures of Jeffrey working out, at parties, and with men. None of the men were Niall—he'd been careful to keep his two lives separate. Mat kept scrolling down, wondering how they'd get access, when Niall stopped him, pointing at the screen. Mat had almost missed it, but it was a recently posted picture of Trey/Jeffrey with another man. The other man was only partially in the picture, looking at something out of the frame, but it was most definitely his brother, Sean.

"Sirs," Birdy interrupted, "the regular payments from Sean Dempsey's checking account go to a PayPal account."

"Keep working on that end, Birdy. We're going to try and figure out who Jeffrey Reynolds is. It cannot be coincidence that he shared the same last name with Chastity and Frank."

The truth, as it is wont to do, made itself known once they were on the right track, just like untangling string. Trey Jackson was an assumed identity. A stolen Social Security number and Jeffrey Reynolds had set up a whole new life, and he'd been living it for at least four years. Mat and Niall sat shoulder to shoulder, scrolling through the information that kept loading and loading. Every time they clicked a link, there was more for them to find.

"Click there," Niall said impatiently, pointing at the screen.

It must have been driving him up a wall to have Mat in control of the mouse. He clicked on the link Niall wanted. It was an LGBTQA business owners' networking site, and Trey was featured in several of their photos.

"He has to be related to the Reynoldses," Mat said. "But why would he hide his identity? Claribel has never turned anyone away that I know of. She and Chastity didn't always get along that well, but she would've never refused to help her if she really needed it."

"Okay. You know her better than I do."

"I think we need to talk to her."

"Jeffrey Reynolds?" Claribel repeated, "I don't know a Jeffrey Reynolds."

"We have a picture. Would you mind taking a look at it?"

Claribel sighed and opened her front door so the two of them could come inside.

"Fine. Let me see the damn thing."

In her living room, Mat pulled his phone out and loaded the image Stu had forwarded to him. He held the phone up so Claribel could see the screen.

She stared at it for a moment and then said, "Huh. This boy is named Jeffrey Reynolds?"

Mat nodded. "Do you recognize him?"

"Not exactly, but he looks like my ex-husband. This young man looks to be in his twenties, meaning he was born before I kicked Frank Senior to the curb, as they say, but long after I was done having children. Not that I wanted any more—the two I had were trouble enough, took after their useless father. Biggest mistake I ever made was marrying that man. It doesn't surprise me he might have been out running around with other women."

Mat nodded his agreement. "I think it's time we brought Mr. Reynolds in again, and this time he's not getting out," he said to Niall as Claribel showed them out.

Back in the cruiser, Mat radioed Birdy. Then he called Shay Delacombe. "We need to see your client again."

Shay argued, but once Mat informed him his client was not who he claimed to be, Shay agreed to the meeting.

"This is serious, Delacombe. I don't know how you're involved in this—if it's merely coincidence—but if I find out you are a part of it, I will take you down too."

"Are you threatening a member of the bar?"

"No, Delacombe, I'm stating a fact. If we discover you are involved in what is happening on the island, you are done."

"I don't expect you to believe me, Mat, but I'm not involved."

"How did you become Trey Jackson's lawyer?"

Their connection was silent for a moment before Shay answered, "A friend of a friend kind of thing. We'll meet you at the sheriff's office in an hour."

This time Trey Jackson, aka Jeffrey Reynolds, did not look cocky or arrogant as Shay accompanied him into the station. Mat met them and brought both men to their small interview room—also the staff break room.

"Coffee?" Mat asked.

They'd decided Niall would watch the live video feed instead of participating—after all, he wasn't a deputy, and his appearance might do more harm than good. If he saw anything, they had a signal: Birdy would come into the room and tell Mat he had a phone call.

"Why am I here?" Trey demanded as he sat down at the small table.

Mat saw no reason to beat around the bush. "Do you recognize the name Jeffrey Reynolds?"

Trey—Jeffrey opened his mouth to say something and then snapped it shut.

"Right. See, *Jeffrey*, we have a witness, a solid one, who can identify you as the person of interest Chastity Reynolds was last seen talking with before she was found floating in the marina. We also have someone who can identify the fabric found around her neck. The scarf that belonged to you, Jeffrey."

They didn't actually know the scarf was Trey's, but Mat was happy to let him think they did.

"Furthermore, *Jeffrey*, we can place you at the scene where Sean Dempsey was killed. Those are very distinctive boots you were wearing last night while you waited for Sean in the mud. The casting came out quite nice. It helps, of course, that Sean kept meticulous records—and the PayPal account you had him sending money to? We traced it back to you."

"As your lawyer I have to advise you say nothing," Shay said to Trey, "but since I just quit, feel free to incriminate yourself." He stood up from the table, pushed his chair in, and left the room.

Jeffrey Reynolds sat there unmoving. Mat thought he looked slightly stunned at the turn of events. This was usually the case when a perp finally realized they weren't as smart as they thought they were. And it was a damn good thing Birdy Flynn *was* smart; she'd spent last night and all day today tracking that money down. They still didn't know what Sean had been paying Jeffrey for, but that would come later.

"Well?"

"I want a lawyer."

Mat stood up. "We'll call the public defender's office in Anacortes for you, if that's what you want. Jeffrey Reynolds, you are under arrest for the murder of Sean Dempsey." Justice for Chastity would come soon enough. Mat could sense it on the horizon.

Much of the truth did come out. By midafternoon Tuesday, with Jeffrey in custody, the lies began to untangle. The biggest, most harmful lie was what had started it all. Frank Reynolds had a son late in life with a much younger woman. Frank had refused to recognize Jeffrey, but his mother had named him on Jeffrey's birth certificate and Jeffrey grew up resentful and jealous of the "real" Reynolds family.

Jeffrey knew everything about the Reynoldses, the Delacombes, and the island. His mother had made sure of it, and he'd wanted his piece, what he knew he deserved. He was getting it now, wasn't he? It must have seemed like kismet when he met Mat's brother at the fast-money seminar. Jeffrey insisted the meeting was chance, but Mat suspected somehow he'd known everything about his brother beforehand and used it to his advantage when they met. Just as he'd used Niall Hamarsson. They still hadn't found the weapon that killed Wainwright's sheep, a fact that nagged at Mat, and Jeffrey claimed he had nothing to do with the killings. Before the case went to trial, they would know more.

Niall left the office once it was clear Jeffrey Reynolds would be staying in jail where he belonged. Mat hadn't liked the bleakness in Niall's eyes but was too busy to stop him from leaving. He'd find him later.

TWENTY-NINE
DEMPSEY

Tuesday evening, Mat found Niall where he expected—skulking on a mangled beach log in front of where the cabin had once stood. Fenrir sat next to him, his silhouette shaggy yet imperial. Niall didn't turn around, but he had to have heard Mat's footsteps. It had been one of those February days in the Pacific Northwest that promised spring was coming... eventually. Temperatures had been in the low sixties, but now that the sun was starting to set Mat felt the chill in the air.

"I'm leaving." Niall's voice was barely louder than the gentle surf.

Mat frowned at the words, even though he'd expected them. "What the fuck are you talking about?"

He stomped around the pile of logs and beach debris until he was standing in front of Niall, who didn't respond to his question but instead stared out into the distance much like he had the night of the fire. Had that been only a week ago?

"Why would you leave? You belong here, Niall. Most of the time it seems like you belong here more than I do. We talked about this." He threw his hands up toward the sky in pure frustration. "You have got to be one of the most infuriating people I know. No—you *are* the most infuriating person I know.”

Niall's lips quirked upward, but Mat would never have called it a smile.

“And I brought death with me. My ex-boyfriend killed your brother, Mat.”

“Yes, I am well aware of that.” Mat's hands rested on his hips for a moment before he let himself do what he'd come here for: sit next to Niall and try to convince him to stay. He sat on the side of Niall Fenrir wasn't guarding, close enough that their shoulders bumped and Mat's thigh felt the chill of Niall's. He'd been sitting out here for a while.

“Jeffrey killed Sean because they'd hatched a scheme to make money and were so busy double-crossing each other they lost track of what was happening with their deals. You are not responsible for his, or Sean's, actions.”

“If it wasn't for me, Trey would never have come here.”

Mat gritted his teeth. Niall was determined to play martyr, and it was fucking irritating.

“Niall, they met at one of those sketchy 'make a million dollars without lifting a finger' seminars. The fact that you owned property up here you seemed to not care about was… coincidence. Sean would've known about it too; we'll never know whose idea this all was. And remember, initially their plan was to develop property on Orcas, but the community there banded together and stopped it. I'd guess Sean was already leveraged to the hilt by that time. Probably he'd borrowed more money based on speculation, making him desperate when the first development was stopped. The truth will come out.”

“The fact remains, Trey—Jeffrey, whatever—came to the island because of me and my connection here.”

Mat's patience snapped. What was it about this man that made him vacillate between wanting to strangle him and wanting to rip all his clothes off and get him out of his system?

"So, what, you're going to give up?" he spat, "Let Jeffrey and Sean win, even though Sean's dead and your ex is probably going to prison for a very long time?" Mat stood up, anger fueling his movement. "You're going to leave Piedras, sell this incredible piece of property to some... some *techie* who'll dig everything up and build a shitty monstrosity in the cabin's place? They won't care about Viking legends or your grandmother's fucking flower baskets. Are you trying to tell me you don't care? Because I don't believe you."

Suddenly they were toe to toe. Niall stood in front of him, his pale eyes flashing. "Don't you fucking tell me what I care about."

"Jesus Christ, Hamarsson, convince me you care, then. Show me something—"

Niall's lips crashed against his. Niall's hands—as large as Mat's own—clutched his jaw, his fingers cold and taut against Mat's cheeks. It wasn't a nice kiss, it was an angry, scared, *fuck you, what do I do in this mad world* kiss.

Mat had refused to admit just how much he wanted this, an acknowledgment of the attraction between them. Instead he'd convinced himself he was worried about Niall and that's why he'd come looking for him out here on the beach. But Mat hadn't had to search at all; he'd known where the man would be. He would always know where Niall was.

Shutting his eyes, he ground into the harsh kiss, letting Niall devour him, Mat's response equally aggressive, nothing about what they were doing soft or pliant or giving. When Niall demanded entrance with his tongue, Mat opened and let his empty hands fall to rest on Niall's jean-clad hips. As soon as his hands landed, Niall jerked his mouth away from Mat's, his eyes wide—feral.

Niall rubbed his mouth with the back of his hand. "I'm nothing," he rasped. "I shouldn't have done that."

Mat clenched his jaw and looked away. he was going to

spend his savings at the dentist's office having his cracked molars repaired at this rate. Trey Jackson, aka Jeffrey Reynolds, scumbag, thief and murderer, had had a chance with Niall, but Niall was going to push Mat aside? Great for a person's ego. Mat wanted to say something, to have a reply ready that would change Niall's mind, but something warned him words exchanged now would carry too heavy a weight.

Niall didn't walk away from Mat like he expected him to, and he didn't tell Mat to leave, so Mat stayed where he was. Niall went back to staring out over the dark water. Mat wondered what he saw there. His own imagination conjured images of wild Viking marauders rattling their long swords as they rode their mighty wooden serpent into the waiting shore, ready to take the island as their own.

"I don't know what happened," Niall finally said.

Mat squinted, trying to change lanes in his head. "What do you mean?"

"We never knew what happened to my mother. As far as I know, she may have gotten tired of the life, tired of being a single mom with a difficult son, so she left."

Oh.

"What *do* you remember?" Mat had never been brave enough to ask Niall about his past. It hadn't occurred to him that maybe Niall *wanted* to talk about his past, that maybe he needed to. Mat waited.

Niall shrugged. Several rounds of waves rolled ashore and back out before he answered.

"I remember her leaning over me, just a shadow with long hair swinging down toward me—she pushed it out of the way, behind her ear. Then she told me not to worry, it wouldn't be a long wait this time, and she shut the closet door."

Mat didn't move, didn't want Niall to stop talking.

"It was the longest wait of my life. Sometimes I feel like I'm still waiting."

"Have you ever tried to find her?" As a cop, Mat meant.

"No. I'm not sure which would be worse, finding out she just left me there to start a new life or finding out she's been dead all this time and I've been angry with a ghost."

"I'll help you."

Niall looked at him, frowning. "With what?"

"I'll help you look for her. Or I can look for her and you don't have to. If I find out anything, I'll let you know, and when you're ready to hear what happened you can ask me."

"I don't know if I'll ever be ready."

Mat figured that was tacit agreement from Niall, so Mat would bear the burden. When, or if, Niall was ever ready to learn the truth about Ana Hamarsson, Mat would be there for him.

"So you'll stay?"

"Fuck, you are persistent."

Mat grinned. Niall hadn't said no.

"What can I say, I'm a man who knows what he wants."

"I don't know if I can give you what you want."

"I guess we'll figure that out as we go along."

"I'm going to stay at the Orca," Niall said in a tone about as flexible as granite.

"What about Fenrir?" Mat still hadn't done any looking for the dog's prior owners, but there were no Lost Dog posters up around the island with pictures of Fenrir gracing them. Mat thought his initial assessment was right and the dog had been abandoned on purpose—possibly like his new owner had been.

"Just until I can get the cabin up again. Then I'll move out here."

"That's going to take months. Have you called your insurance company yet? You know, like I said before, there are people on the island who want to help you."

"I'm not very good at accepting help."

Mat gestured at Niall's bandaged hand. "I think you're going to need it whether you want it or not."

"Fine."

Mat grinned, hoping Niall couldn't see it in the gloom. Fenrir chose that moment to start barking and chasing the waves rolling to shore.

"What a weirdo," Mat commented.

"You, me, or the dog?"

"All of us, I guess."

Niall chuckled. "I can live with that."

Shoving his cold hands into his pockets, Mat commented, "I figure you owe me at least fifty bucks before you leave."

Niall looked at him as if he was one card short of a full deck. "What are you talking about? How the hell do I owe you any money? Until a couple weeks ago, we hadn't seen each other in years."

Mat sighed. "Deputy Flynn is trying to clean up the office. If we cuss, we have to put a dollar in that damn jar. Since you've been back, I've managed to rack up quite a bill."

Niall huffed out a chuckle. "If you can't control your mouth, that's your own damn fault. Besides, I paid ahead."

"Hmm. You're really going to stay at the Orca? The tiny shower stalls, the thin mattresses, no coffee service? No yard for Fenrir to romp in. It's quiet now, but wait until spring really gets here."

"I'm staying there," Niall reaffirmed.

Mat didn't leave. He stood shoulder to shoulder with Niall, a companionable silence between them. The waves continued to roll in and slide backward, leaving rocks and shells behind over and over. "My mom's going to try to change your mind."

Niall turned his head to stare at Mat. "Really? What does it take to keep you quiet?"

"Is that a rhetorical question?" Mat asked.

With an exasperated huff, Niall spun to face Mat, his back to the waves and the dog's antics. This time the kiss wasn't angry or aggressive, and it definitely kept Mat from saying anything. Niall's spiky whiskers scratched against his cheek, his tongue hot against his lips and then, finally, inside his mouth. Mat opened his mouth wide, taking everything Niall offered, wanting it not to end.

He rocked his hips against Niall's, needing some sort of contact. His rapidly awakening cock was uncomfortably hard. It had been so long—and much longer since he'd been with someone like Niall, who infuriated him and aroused him at the same time. Having him close and yet untouchable was a form of torture.

Niall groaned into his mouth, pressing his hips back against Mat's. Shit. Mat sucked on Niall's tongue and ran his own tongue along the roof of Niall's mouth, wanting everything Niall would give him.

"Open your pants."

Mindlessly, Mat obeyed, unsnapping the top button and sliding the zipper down while Niall kept licking and rubbing against him. They were on private property, the sun had set, no one would interrupt them. Even if it was the worst bad idea.

Niall slid his left hand underneath the waistband of Mat's jeans and boxers, gripping his ass, pulling him closer. Mat pushed his hand back between them, unbuttoning Niall's jeans. If they were going to do this foolish, *foolish* thing, at the very least he was going to get to hold Niall's cock in his hand. Closing his fingers around Niall's hot, hard flesh was almost more than Mat could withstand. Sparks began rolling up his spine merely from touching the other man.

A groan sounded in Mat's ear. Niall's forehead rested on his shoulder now, and something told Mat they were at the tipping point. He pumped Niall with his fist, unable to stop himself—he didn't want to stop, he wanted to come. He wanted Niall to make him come.

The man in question let go of Mat's ass cheek, instead shoving his good hand down the front of Mat's pants and stroking his tip with a rough thumb. Mat groaned and shuddered, trying to keep from coming like a fourteen-year-old boy.

"Fuck, Dempsey, you're almost there," Niall whispered just before he gently bit the lobe of Mat's ear.

That was all it took for Mat to come—a nibble on his earlobe and he flew past the edge of everything and out into the stars. From far away he heard Niall's deep shuddering groan and was aware he'd come too. Mat's chest heaved as he tried to pull air into his lungs, to bring himself back down to earth. Niall was breathing hard along with him, his forehead tucked against Mat's neck.

"I'm still staying at the motel," Niall growled into his ear.

Mat rolled his eyes. "Fine, stay at the motel."

"That's what I said."

"You are fucking stubborn."

Niall shrugged, and Mat chuckled. He would wait. Maybe not patiently, but he would wait.

They began the uncomfortable business of cleaning up, tucking things back into place and trying to wipe themselves down. Mat walked to the tideline and waited for a wave to sweep across his hands, and after wiping his wet hands on his jeans, he turned to watch Niall, something that could easily become a habit.

Niall stood with his back to the water now, his hands in his jacket pockets, the cabin—or where it had once stood—the object of his attention.

"Are we going to talk about what just happened?" Mat asked, knowing the answer.

"No."

Mat laughed. "Okay, are you going to let me help you rebuild the cabin? What was that TV show from the '70s?" he asked, continuing before Niall had a chance to reply. "'Gentlemen, we can rebuild him. We have the technology. We have the capability… He'll be better than he was before. Better, stronger, faster.' Something like that."

Niall frowned fiercely at him. "What in all the hells ever conceived are you talking about?"

Mat had forgotten Niall probably hadn't watched much TV as a child, much less horrible reruns. "I'm talking about *you* letting *me*"—he gestured with his thumb toward himself—"help you rebuild the cabin. You know, bigger and better than it was before."

"In exchange for us *not* talking about what we just did, you want to help rebuild out here? I think there is something seriously wrong with you. Were you dropped on your head as a child?" But Mat could see the corners of Niall's eyes crinkling as he smiled, and he hadn't said no, which to Mat's mind was as good as a yes.

Leaving the shore, Mat crossed the rocky beach to stand next to Niall so they were shoulder to shoulder. "I know you said we weren't going to talk about it," Mat began, "but I feel l should let you know—"

"Jesus, Mat."

Niall turned toward Mat, grabbed him by the front of his fleece jacket, and dragged him close enough to take Mat's mouth again. Mat smiled into the kiss. He'd gotten what he wanted: another mind-blowing kiss and a sort of promise of a future. There was a lot of work to do between them. But, anything that kept Niall close—anything that kept Niall from running away from both Mat *and* Piedras—felt one step closer to Mat keeping Niall for himself.

Fenrir bounded up to them in a way only a ridiculously large dog could. His tongue hung out, and he was wet from chasing waves, his coat stringy and shaggy. Well, shaggier.

"Woof," Fenrir commented.

"Yeah, 'woof,' that's exactly what I was thinking," Mat replied.

Together the two of them, and Fenrir, trudged back up toward their parked cars. Fenrir brushed against Mat as he hunted around for his keys, leaving an impressive streak of salt water and sand on his jeans and boots.

"You're at least going to bring Fenrir over for a bath, right? You can't take him back to the motel like that."

Niall shook his head—likely in disgust, but at the dog or Mat, Mat wasn't sure. He stared at Mat for a second over the roof of the cruiser.

"I'm just not going to win here, am I?" A tinge of silent amusement lurked in Niall's tone. Mat was learning to read him, a little.

Not if I can help it, he thought smugly, *and if I need to recruit Fenrir to help me, I am not above that either.* The rest of the week was going to be difficult enough. He and his mom had Sean's funeral to plan. Mat's sisters were arriving in the morning, and the house would be full of people. Mat desperately wanted these stolen hours with Niall before the realities of life came crashing down on him and what remained of his family.

He shrugged, not even trying to hide the hopeful expression he knew was spreading across his face. "Nope. See you at the house."

With that, Mat slipped behind the wheel of his car, turned on the engine, and backed up and out of the driveway, heading toward home. A minute or so later, headlights caught in his rearview mirror and followed him all the way there.

1/3 Not The End

Jump right into book two: Long Shadow where Mat begins to realize just how stubborn Niall really is. And maybe Niall learns a thing or two as well.

Click over and join my newsletter, and grab your copy of Get Real. Kim is the owner of the Island's only tattoo parlor. Ten years have passed since they've seen each other. Winston hopes Kim doesn't already have a partner because he's coming to the island to claim his man.

Be sure to check out *The Last Grift, Elle's latest book and first in in the Subtle Deceptions series.*

Somewhere between right and wrong, the truth lies.

Gabriel Karne made a dangerous mistake, one that will prove fatal if the wrong people catch up with him. Now he's on the run and has only one place to hide.

The Last Grift is first in the Subtle Deceptions Series. Written in third person, Subtle Deceptions follows the unplanned adventures in the life and love of the disreputable Gabriel Karne.

AFTERWORD

This is a work of fiction, created without use of AI technology. Any names, characters, places or incidents are products of the author's imagination and used in a fictitious manner. Any resemblance to actual people, places, or events is purely coincidental or fictional.

Elle Keaton's creative body of work cannot be used in any manner for the purpose of training AI.

The author, Elle Keaton, supports the right of humans to control their artistic works. No part of this book has been created using AI-generated images or narrative, as known by the author. The primary style sources used in the writing of this book are the online versions of the Merriam-Webster Dictionary and The Chicago Manual of Style. Due to their inherent limitations for fiction-writing and the author's personal style choices, there are instances where other style guide rules have been consistently applied. Region-based idioms, age- or era-appropriate slang, UK spelling and style rules, and other deviations based on specific dialects may inform some of these choices. Should you have questions, please contact the author at: dirtydogpress@gmail.com

ABOUT ELLE

Do you love inclusive, swoony, and often suspenseful small-town romances featuring complex characters and a unique sense of place? I do too!

My characters start out damaged and, maybe, they're still a tad banged up by the end (let's be honest, healing is hard!), but they find the other half of their hearts and ALWAYS get their happily ever after.

I've been publishing since 2017—making this the longest period of time I've stuck with a job *in my entire life*. Currently, there are over forty Elle Keaton books available for you to read or listen to. I love cats and dogs. Star Wars and Star Trek. Pineapple on pizza, and have a cribbage habit my husband encourages.

Romantic Suspense Series by Elle Keaton
    Shielded Hearts
    Veiled Intentions
    West Coast Forensics
    Reclaimed Hearts

For more information, and to purchase special editions or audiobooks, please visit my direct sales website

ElleKeatonAuthor.com

Thank you for supporting this indie author!

Copyright © 2019 by Elle Keaton and Dirty Dog Press LLC

All rights reserved.

No part of this book may be reproduced in any form or by any electronic or mechanical means, including information storage and retrieval systems, without written permission from the author, except for the use of brief quotations in a book review.

Cover art by Kanaxa

Originally Edited by Alicia Z. Ramos

Lightly reedited by the ElusiveSB

Translated by